BENEATH
THE
PHOENIX
DOOR

BY LEE WITTING

Beneath the Phoenix Door

Copyright © 2020 by Leland Witting

ISBN 978-1-09834-273-9
Printed in USA by BookBaby (www.bookbaby.com)

Dedication

My love and gratitude to two marvelous sisters, Charlene Kent, my wife and friend, who fortunately enjoys debating theological quandaries, and her sister, Laurie Rich, who demonstrated amazing patience with me as she prepared this book for publication. My thanks and admiration, as well, to Janice Goff, who constructed the Phoenix Door – an actual door at Orphic House, in Rimrock, Arizona. It inspired the title, and graces the cover.

Preface

When I told a friend I was writing a novel about finding the Garden of Eden, he said to me, "I never read novels. I only have time to deal with the truth." His statement provoked me to ask him Pilate's question to Jesus – namely, "What is truth?"

"What do you mean?" my friend responded with feigned annoyance. "Stuff that's real – news, facts, books by historians and scientists. You know what I mean." Then, to lessen the putdown, he thought to add, "Well, what's your novel based on, anyway?"

I appreciated the belated consideration. "It's a story involving multiple sources that claim to be true – near-death experiences, sacred texts, ancient mythologies, seminaries as truth-tellers, lessons from the dying environment, parallel realities with wormhole connections, struggles between power and love, the created duality of evil and good – that sort of thing. It's meant to raise the theological questions you encounter in seminaries, but at a fraction of the cost."

I winced at the memory of seminary tuitions. Then, to break the subsequent silence, I added, "And to keep the story moving, it relies on fiction. That's why it's called a novel. But think about it – calling it a novel is a form of truth-telling you usually don't find in books that proclaim to be true. Too often their assumptions come out of unacknowledged fictions."

"Granted," he said. "But then I read other fact-based books and make up my own mind."

"Fiction can broaden that perspective," I replied. "You know the allegory of Plato's cave. He said we are like people chained in a cave, only able to see shadows projected on the wall by others moving things in front of a fire. Today those shadows are generated on computers, phones and TVs, and they are just as ephemeral. For Plato, truth was discovered by the occasional heroes who found a way to break their chains and escape out of the cave into the bright light of reality."

"Well, if you're going there," said my friend, "let me pose another question – namely, what is reality? Sci-fi movies often suggest we are living in an artificial reality, one imposed on us, or at least one we've agreed to believe is true."

"You could say the two terms are one and the same – reality and truth. We can be fooled for a while about what is real, but the truth will out in the end. That's because truth is eternal – that which can't be destroyed. We forget reality when we reincarnate here, according to Plato, by drinking from Lethe, the river of forgetfulness. Back in physical bodies, we think the shadows are reality. Meanwhile, eternal truth carries on in the light beyond our view. Mystics and near-death experiencers may catch a glimpse of it, if they're so blessed. When they are, they recognize its basis as the eternal oneness of love."

"So, humans *can* tell the difference between truth and shadow," my friend replied. "Doesn't that suggest that truth can be discovered in the physical world, as well? For instance, the cave itself could be real. It just limits our view. Reasoned analysis in that cave would show the source of those shadows, and might even explain why they were being made in the first place. That's what science does. And what about the power of words for revealing truth? Just hearing Plato's cave allegory conveys some truth about reality."

"You have a point," I said, "but maybe you're making mine, as well. After all, NDErs who have seen the other side often say there aren't words to describe the truth. And yet they go on to write books and make movies about their experience. The narratives go on and on. Our brains take revelation and rationalize it as best we can."

We went on talking for a while about where truth might be found. After all, Pilate's question to Jesus – what is truth? – resonates loudly today as cries of fake news, trolling and bot-spread lies pervade our social media, while the self-serving baloney of authoritarian politicians accelerates the confusion. Mix that with manipulative advertising, and our perceptions get exhausted by contradiction and division. Even our ability to make sense of the shadows gets more and more disrupted.

"It seems we've emerged from a post-modern world," I said, "where truth was considered relative, to a post-truth world of tribal 'truthiness'. That means if a statement rings your emotional chimes, then it's true for you despite all proof to the contrary. Unfortunately, that makes for factions that play right into the hands of authoritarian religious and political leaders. They've figured out their loyal followers hear and remember selectively, in tune with the dear leader's pronouncements."

"So where do we look for the truth?" my friend asked.

"Pick your poison," I replied. "No human source is perfect, even where the effort is sincere. Reporters offer stories based on researched sources. Historians and economists promise objectively verified facts. Scientists base their 'laws' on repeatable evidence – which, by the way, leaves unique events such as honest-to-God miracles beyond the range of study. Meanwhile, people clinging to power simply claim their lies *are* truth, and often get away with it."

The United States Constitution protects freedom of the press, but news sources like radio, TV and newspapers survive by not totally alienating the government and the advertisers. So they often hedge the story to benefit their sponsors. Against that, freedom of speech can be misleading enough to allow anything – short of crying fire in a crowded theater.

Under the law, money is now considered free speech, as well, so whoever can afford to buy the media coverage gets to have the loudest voice. And too often, the loudest voice establishes in people's minds what is thought to be true. A quote attributed to Jim Carrey sums it nicely: "America is morally upside down because the wealthiest one percent tricked the dumbest twenty percent into believing the rest of us are so evil that lying to us and cheating us is not only okay, it's godly." The influence of broadcasting can be bought to repeat lies until they become the public's truth.

How bad can it get? Novelists have pointed to this threat for years – famously George Orwell's dystopian novel *1984*, and Aldous Huxley's *Brave New World.* Repulsed by Henry Ford's assembly-line visions for a stable society, Huxley foresaw that happiness drugs, casual sex and mindless entertainment would easily distract a socially engineered population from reading books or otherwise studying disruptive truths. On the other hand, Orwell, writing in post-Nazi 1948, described how totalitarian power can invent lies and then cruelly enforce them. When Orwell's novel came out, most readers thought it was a high-tech communist state he was describing.

Today it's clear that totalitarian governments of any political stripe, given enough social media control, can work on citizens to change their perceptions. In *1984*, War is Peace, Freedom is Slavery, and Ignorance is Strength foretold some of today's advertising of logical con-tradictions. *1984* calls these the newspeak teachings of big brother, enforced by the thought police.

You can ask who got it right, Orwell or Huxley, but it seems ultimately that both did. Huxley, recognizing "man's almost infinite appetite for distractions," described the tools of moral and intellectual decay that make Orwell's lying tyrants possible.

As main-stream newspapers give way to social media, tweets, blogs, and countless questionable news sources, as history is taught less and less in schools, and virtual reality games become kids' favorite alternative worlds, the public's grasp of what is real grows weaker. After a while, any entertaining notion of reality – including the seduction of violence – can win out over truth. Like-wise, as paranoia creates us-against-them attitudes in a society being re-engineered by divide and conquer techniques, the notion that "all men and women are created equal" gives way to racism, sexism, religious bigotry, and the cruelty that results from such prejudices.

"Well, hasn't humankind always behaved this way?" my friend asked. "If I recall correctly, it was Dostoevsky's Grand Inquisitor who told Jesus something like, 'Most people would rather live and die happily in ignorance than take on the burden of freedom.'"

"Yes," I agreed, "but today's technology, from facial recognition cameras to DNA manipulation, has taken the bliss out of ignorance. And in the meantime, we're being hauled up short by Mother Nature. We've encountered one warning, our COVID-19 pandemic, and now we're about to be run over by our on-going destruction of the environment. We're engaged in self-inflicted climate change, with droughts and fires, melting icecaps, methane releases, oceans polluted with plastic waste and radiation, the mass extinction of plants, insects and wildlife, the corruption of food-crop DNA with pesticides, and on and on. And all the while we're being distracted with media propaganda designed and paid for by the political/corporate polluters themselves. The environment is dying and humans will, too, unless we deal with the reality that everything is connected."

My friend and I talked on for a while about the nature of truth itself. In exploring that question, we returned to Jesus and Pilate. Jesus told Pilate:

"My kingdom is not of this world.... For this purpose I was born and for this purpose I have come into the world – to bear witness to the truth. Everyone who is of the truth listens to my voice." Pilate said to him, "What is truth?" After he had said this, he went back outside to the Jews and told them, "I find no fault in him." (John 18:26-38)

I allowed as how some believe the Jesus story is a novel based on truth. That's because it is the monomyth in spades, since his story fits the hero's journey model almost perfectly. Joseph Campbell defines the hero's journey, in *The Hero with a Thousand Faces,* thusly:

A hero ventures forth from the world of common day into a region of supernatural wonder: fabulous forces are there encountered and a decisive victory is won: the hero comes back from this mysterious adventure with the power to bestow boons on his fellow man.

The claim could be made that to live a more authentic life, we should consider the hero's journey and follow the recipe, adding definition from our own better nature. Even in a world of illusion, it seems, it's important what we do. Part of that 'better nature' comes with the recognition that the freedom we are given is not the right to do what we please, but the opportunity to do what is right.

By living the life we came here to live, the magic called coincidence will also be our guide.

One big question voiced in this book, though, is whether the *villain* with a thousand faces is required in a world constructed on duality. Evil claims its role in the creation – that the tree of good and evil is necessary for the tree of life. In this book, Jacob, on impulse, destroys the fake Ark of the Covenant, the copy built by Solomon that has become the seat of Satan. His act is to test whether the true ark of Moses, the ark naked David danced in front of – the mercy seat – can sustain creation on its own.

Getting back to Jesus' conversation with Pilate: some say Jesus stands before Pilate as the embodiment of truth. Jesus describes himself as witness to the truth – that is, as a mirror reflecting the light to us, so that we might glimpse a vision of the truth. Near-death experiencers often describe this vision as the white light that perfectly blends all colors, or a golden light best described as love. Thus, love, light, and truth are attempts at naming aspects of the same thing. We don't know if Pilate glimpsed it for a moment, but there is a clue: he did turn and tell the people, "I find no fault in him."

It can be argued that out of the ten commandments, "thou shalt not lie" is key. Satan is called the father of lies because lies divide us from the light. But the greatest commandment in this world of duality is to have compassion for one another, and to do for others as you'd want done for yourself. The manifestation of love or compassion depends, I believe, on where you're located. Love is the meaning of truth in the oneness of heaven. Compassion is the meaning of truth in the duality of our earth.

Let me share a picture puzzle I've pieced together from the near-death experience. God does not get much love from us on earth because we aren't designed to give it. We are constructed of ego in a world of duality, so mostly we worship God in an effort to get something. Yet despite our selfishness, God does expect us to practice compassion for one another. It's an exercise to help teach us the meaning of the oneness in two, so that, ultimately, we will recognize the oneness in all. The separation and sorrow

7

imposed by COVID-19 has been a last-minute, painful reminder of that fact.

But the kicker, the hardest part for us to understand, ego-wise, is that God ultimately expects us to merge into the light, into the oneness of the highest heaven. Giving up ego for love is the hardest lesson for us to learn; it's a lesson stretching through lives and heavens. I mean, what an expectation – to abandon our ego, our 'selves' entirely, and to become one with the sea of love! It confirms the notion that each of us is God, but only when 'I' am no longer 'me'. We are sparks meant to be reuniting in the fire, water droplets merging with the sea. No you, no me, just the all of love. That's why there are many lifetimes and several levels of heavens to pass through – because learning to lose ourselves entirely in love is the hardest, yet most blessed truth. Understand, we are not martyrs in this act. To become undifferentiated love is the greatest gift of all.

I must admit my friend might have scored on one point: "If every story of heroes' journeys is the same story," he asked, "then why read another novel?" But then, for that matter, why ever look in a mirror again? Haven't we seen it all before? Perhaps it's just to remind ourselves, potential heroes all, that with every day still left in *this* lifetime, our stories here have not ended. And that, also, is the truth.

Lee Witting
Penobscot, Maine

Chapter 1　　Bangor, Maine

Professor Jacob Alexandre suddenly realized he was falling backward. He'd been arguing the case that the Bible's account of Exodus was not historical, and he was feeling authoritative, theatrical. So in mid-sentence, to the amusement of his students, he leaped onto the wooden desk chair to pull a map of the Middle East down from its roller mounting above the blackboard. The landing held but the chair did not, and as a leg gave way, he felt time slow to a crawl as he fell backward and down.

Everything happening to him at that moment seemed both dreamlike and crystal clear. He saw the map he clutched unroll before his eyes, as his slow-motion tumble accelerated backward. It seemed to unroll like some ancient scroll, a geographic Torah, as the map revealed itself from south to north – a yellow Egypt to the left, a green Saudi Arabia to the right, with their narrow, pale blue separation by the Red Sea. Above that came Jordan, then from left to right, the Mediterranean, Cyprus, tiny Israel, Lebanon, Syria and Iraq. Somewhere above Turkey the map tore from its housing, but Dr. Alexandre was too far back to see. Just before his head struck the edge of the oak lectern behind him, however, he did notice the ceiling fan made a strobe of the fluorescent lighting. "Does it always do that?" he wondered, as the sharp blow to his head twisted him around, and he landed unconscious on his right hip.

He heard one of the students, Ginger, perhaps, gasp, "Oh, no!" before everything went black, but the voices after that were different. Jacob thought he heard something comforting in the darkness, but he couldn't make out the words. He couldn't see anything, and yet these voices seemed to be crowding around him, moving all around him, up and down, up and down. "Where am I?" he asked, but he was shut out by his watchers. "Or shut in," he remembered thinking, "like a message in a bottle. They see me lying here, but they won't pick me up."

It was at that moment Jacob realized he was seeing the aftermath of his fall from a startling point of view: from the west corner of the high ceiling above. The students were out of their chairs now, turning on their cellphones, while others knelt by his crumpled body on the floor.

"I'm out of my body!" he realized. "Am I dead? Am I a ghost?" Overriding the commotion below, Jacob felt an absence of tightness, of pain. In the calm, he suddenly recalled the time as a child at the lake, when he had drowned into a similar out-of-body experience.

And with that memory, he was gone.

A huge forest, tall and serene, replaced the chaos of the classroom. "Muir Woods?" Jacob thought, but no – radiance poured from every trunk and leaf. Just beyond, Jacob could see a field and a river, everything iridescent with the essence of color, of music, a vibration that encompassed both and more. It was the symphony of creation.

And then Jacob's long-deceased father stood before him, blocking his way, and Jacob felt like a little boy again, terrified by memories of the piercing blue eyes, the stern, judgmental frown. But moved to look more closely, Jacob recognized a love he'd never seen before. "It's not your time," his father said. "You have things to do before we meet again. Just know that I love you." The words came like a golden honey pouring over the child, thick and sweet, in no way constricting, the message of a shared divinity. All doubts about forgiving and forgiveness disappeared.

And then Jacob felt the pain of his physical body again.

When he finally opened his eyes, he thought for a minute he'd gone blind. Then it reversed, the dark became light, and he realized he was on his back on the floor, still looking up at the strobe of the ceiling fan. His students were all around him, talking to him, getting him water, calling 911. "It's all right," he said weakly. "I'm all right. Help me up."

Two boys pulled him into a sitting position, then hauled him up into a chair. "Are you sure you're okay, Dr. Alexandre?" one asked. It was Jeff, a conscientious student in the divinity program.

"I guess that's the end of class for today," Jacob said, after a pause. "I'm not seeing right. I'd better go home."

Chapter 2

He didn't go straight home, however. What he needed right now was not his rat-trap apartment, with every surface piled high with books and printouts, and not one comfortable chair in the place. He needed sympathy, someone to talk to, and that would be Maggie. She was not always a sympathetic listener, of course. In fact, she was as hard on him as he was on his students.

As she told him often enough, it was because of them she thought he deserved it. Dr. Alexandre had made a career of crushing students' faith in the sacredness of scripture. His approach to teaching both Old and New Testaments was to point out textual contradictions, with special emphasis on literary and historical evidence indicating the Bible was largely a work of fiction. That he was being paid by a seminary to debunk scripture seemed peculiar even to him, at first. Yet his approach was hardly different from most faculty at the school. "We have to be professionals," this core of teachers told each other, "and this is boot camp for ministers-in-training." After all, the reasoning went, how can modern ministers do their job if they don't know how scholarship has debunked the historicity of the Bible?

Maggie was one of the few professors who didn't feel that way. "If we have no faith in the sacred roots of scripture," she'd ask in faculty meetings, "then what are we doing here? If these are nothing more than old stories written to mislead the people, then why bother teaching them? Our students, full of faith, are paying a small fortune each semester to have us destroy their belief in Old Testament prophesy and the divinity of Jesus. Are we doing them any favors for the money they're investing?"

Jacob and Maggie were both in their late thirties, and both shared the mixed blessing of naturally red hair. Nevertheless, the contrast between their teaching styles could not have been greater. They'd both arrived on the Bangor campus for the fall semester, just six months before COVID-19 came to town, sending teachers and students home to finish their classes online.

Of course, at the time of their arrival, everything seemed blissfully normal at King Theological Seminary. Each of them had been asked, as was tradition with new faculty members, to deliver a get-to-know-you sermon at the Wednesday chapel services.

Maggie took the first Wednesday. Feeling a little silly in her borrowed black robes, she had none the less delivered a message that caused consternation among some faculty – and gladdened the hearts of students mired in deconstructing scripture. Her talk was titled "Exegeting Exegesis," and after the sermon, despite himself, Jacob had asked her for a copy. Since then, he'd read it through several times.*

Maggie's message was not well received by some faculty members, who expressed their concerns to the seminary president. Concerns or no, they were told, Maggie was a top scholar of ancient languages who was willing to work for what the school could afford to pay. It was agreed she would be responsible for teaching languages and a chaplaincy course, but nothing more controversial.

Jacob, on the other hand, was welcomed with open arms, as was his sermon the Wednesday following. It was titled "The Torah as Fiction," and except for a denouncing article in the Bangor city paper, followed by a brief flurry of letters to the editor from some distressed Baptists, his observations were absorbed without question into the collective mindset of the school.

But Maggie was by no means shunned by all the others. On the contrary, in an attitude Maggie dubbed 'communal well-meaningness,' teachers invited her to join them for lunch in the cafeteria, a spacious, pleasant room with large, arched windows and a balcony above. The menu changed from day to day, but the homily for dessert remained the same: "If our students leave here empowered to do good works, then it doesn't really matter if they don't believe what they learned in Sunday School – that Moses literally spoke with God, or that Jesus was physically resurrected, or that the disciples were touched with real tongues of flame.

*The text of "Exegeting Exegesis" appears in Appendix A.

"These are our cultural myths and they help empower moral behavior. These are the underlying stories we tell one another to preserve our higher nature. That is reason enough to support what we're doing here. Look at the good works that result from seminary training!"

Maggie didn't buy it, and she often told students, "If you came here to become a social worker, you'll be better paid and more useful to society if you switch to the University of Maine for a master's degree in social work." To the faculty she remained polite – except to Jacob.

Both were excited to be back on campus as the pandemic eased in Maine, even under the remaining rules of social distancing, and delighted to see each other again. And because of that, because she disliked what he taught and told him so, Jacob felt an increasing fondness for her. He was in awe that she could go on teaching the sacred implications of key words in Greek and Hebrew scripture, while in classrooms next door, the same writings were being debunked as myth.

He envied her ability to comfort students when she found them in tears over assigned readings from deconstructing authors like Crossan or Friedman – or Jacob Alexandre himself. And despite the fact that Jacob was among the worst offenders, Maggie still seemed to believe in him – to hold out faith for a change of heart.

He knocked again, but Maggie wasn't home. Awash in self-pity, Jacob made his way back to his one-bedroom hole in the old brick building on the eastern edge of campus.

He climbed the stairs in pain, and without undressing, collapsed on the bed and into a troubled sleep. In his dreams, he was back in the midst of voices, spirits he could barely hear and couldn't see, voices rising and falling around him, and the sense of claustrophobic confusion that he'd felt. And he yearned to see his father again and the Eden where they'd been, but now only the voices prevailed. This time, however, he wasn't completely ignored. One moving voice unstopped his bottle and slipped some kind of rolled-up document inside. He couldn't seem to peel back more than an edge, as if the parchment were glued together. But of what he saw, he thought it might be a map.

Chapter 3

A week later, Dr. Alexandre sat hunched over the worn metal desk in his tiny, fourth floor office. Downstairs someone was burning popcorn again, and it crossed his mind that one day, for certain, the smoke would set off the sprinklers. Jacob hated the desk but loved his office, with its window views of the city – if you could call Bangor a city. He even loved the fact that his office was a walk-up. Students had to really want to see him before they'd make the climb.

He knew from the reflected light on the buildings down the hill that he was missing a fine fall day. This year had brought an early autumn, with the deep reds of maples mingled with bronzed oaks, golden birches, and the evergreen pine and fir trees that stretched north from Bangor all the way to Canada. The seminary campus was small but pretty, with old brick buildings, beds of hardy fall flowers, and some majestic trees with benches where you could sit and read – or place mental bets on who would win, as pigeons battled the squirrels for the remnants of more burned popcorn from that erratic hotplate.

Early in his first semester he had spent time doing just that, but as the word spread that his survey course, "Understanding Scripture as Myth," was controversial, he was increasingly barraged by unsophisticated students asking the wrong questions, and by faculty curious over rumors of his iconoclastic point of view. In truth, Jacob was no more unorthodox than they – he was just more outspoken about it. This was a liberal seminary, after all, where pride of scholarship had dislodged traditional faith years ago.

The winter semester changed everything, of course, with the arrival of the coronavirus. Social distancing gave way to closing the school, and ended with virtual meetings from home, courtesy of Zoom. He had hated the sterility as much as students did, and was excited to resume classes in person. Much had changed, however. In their time at home, many students had witnessed death for the first time in their lives. Now they wanted to believe their faith was not in vain. Now they wanted to believe the promise that life continued after death.

He'd been sitting at this same wretched desk for hours, and his incipient concussion was sending an alarm beyond the containment of his nonprescription painkillers. But Jacob wasn't ready to give in. He was being barraged by end-times questions now, questions about the Book of Daniel and Revelations that, in years past, he'd only have heard in more fundamental-minded seminaries. Suddenly global warming had taken center stage, as well. It seems it took a plague to make these kids mindful of the mess the world had become.

And then there was his brief NDE, and his glimpse of the third heaven. It had him fooling with something called Bible code software again, something he hadn't thought about since high school. Over the summer he'd ordered an updated program that could skip-search through un-spaced blocks of Hebrew text, looking for hidden messages in the body of the Torah. Skip-searching was an exercise going back to Isaac Newton's belief there was hidden code lurking in the Bible text. The point was to look for words and phrases spelled out with every other letter, or every third letter, or every fourth, and so on. Newton failed because it took the speed of a computer to make such searches practical. As long as the spacing remained the same, the computer would look forwards, backwards, up and down – even on the diagonal – to find hidden words. Today, Jacob was going back and forth through the first chapters of Genesis, doing a skip-search for imbedded references to the Garden of Eden.

This exercise was something he would not have considered sinking to before his dramatic fall, his out-of-body experience, and his recent, unusually vivid dreams. For the past three nights he'd dreamt about St. Paul – about Paul's travels, and especially where Paul had gone after his conversion. Jacob woke every morning with the nagging thought that he ought to be able to answer that question, a question that had piqued Bible historians since the year 144, when Christian dualist Marcion of Sinope pushed Paul's epistles to scriptural status.

Jacob closed the laptop and picked up the nearest Bible,

a copy of the Revised Standard Version. Jacob possessed a near-photographic memory when it came to text, but still enjoyed reading the words. He flipped through to Acts, Chapter 9:

Now as Paul journeyed he approached Damascus, and suddenly a light from heaven flashed about him. And he fell to the ground and heard a voice saying to him, "Saul, Saul, why do you persecute me?" And he said, "Who are you, Lord?" And he said, "I am Jesus, whom you are persecuting; but rise and enter the city, and you will be told what you are to do."

"Really," Jacob thought, suddenly self-reflective. "You fall on your head, and suddenly you think *you* are the next St. Paul? Give me a break." This pretense of self-scorn did not stop him from turning to Paul's second letter to the Corinthians, Chapter 12:

I must boast. There is nothing to be gained by it, but I will go on to visions and revelations of the Lord. I know a man in Christ who fourteen years ago was caught up to the third heaven – whether in the body or out of the body I do not know, God knows. And I know that this man was caught up into Paradise – whether in the body or out of the body I do not know, God knows – and he heard things that cannot be told, which man may not utter.

"So possibly his fall came first – he hit his head, had an near-death experience, and saw the light. Well, at least he got a visit with Jesus from his jolt," Jacob said out loud, too loud. "Now I'm talking to myself," he thought, embarrassed that someone might hear. But again, it didn't stop him from turning to the third part of the puzzle – the puzzle he'd been lying awake over for the last three days. Paul himself, in his letter to the Galatians, Chapter 1, left a mysterious clue to his whereabouts following his conversion:

For I would have you know, brethren, that the gospel which was preached by me is not man's gospel. For I did not receive it from man, nor was I taught it, but it came through a revelation of Jesus Christ.... I did not confer with flesh and blood, nor did I go up to Jerusalem to those who were apostles before me, but I went away into Arabia....

"Where did he go in Arabia – and more importantly, why?" Jacob asked himself. "He was there for as much as three years! He'd just undergone a complete conversion experience – a revelation from Jesus complete with all the theology," Jacob thought, as if to convince himself. "In a moment, Paul suddenly embraced the Way of Jesus that he'd done his best to destroy. So, why didn't he go to the Christians and beg forgiveness for his incredible cruelties to them? That would have been the logical thing to do. Instead, he changed direction to find something else.... What was he looking for in that arid patch of Arabia?"

Even as he asked the question, Jacob had a hunch. Many students of Paul's life agreed Paul travelled away from Damascus after his near-death experience with the blinding light, and his encounter with Jesus. And yes, it seems he went there for years, but what was he doing all that time? Well, travel east and you come to the land of the Tigris and Euphrates, the traditional location of Eden. Paul said his NDE took him to "the third heaven," *Gan Eden*. It's where many near-death experiencers describe traveling to, and some claim to have met Jesus there, as well. Could it be Paul was searching for the paradise he'd glimpsed in his fall – the paradise he named in his Corinthians' letter? The *paradeisos* Paul had described, the third heaven, literally meant a splendid park, an enclosure, a *Gan Eden*. God had granted Paul a glimpse of a wondrous place, and perhaps Paul wanted to see more. Did Paul believe Jesus had held out a promise to him that Paul would see the garden again before he died? Jacob couldn't shake the unorthodox notion that Paul had gone on a quest, perhaps for years, to find the Garden of Eden.

Chapter 4

Jacob closed the Bible and reached for his laptop again. He'd ordered this so-called Bible code software from a site he'd found on the internet. His plan had been to debunk it, of course, to parade it before his students as yet another example of the faithful, grasping at straws. He had loved sticking it to them – especially material from the Hebrew bible, the OT, which he could criticize with a freer hand. He liked to dramatize it in terms of a growing enlightenment, where scholarship and truth had at last triumphed over the dark ages of traditional belief. But that was before the pandemic, which, like the plague of the Middle Ages, had refocused students' interest in death and the hereafter.

In his first semester at the school, Jacob had mocked the notion that Moses wrote the Torah. The Hebrew belief was based on tradition, and two statements from Exodus and Deuteronomy:

Moses came and told the people all the words of the Lord and all the ordinances; and all the people answered with one voice, and said, "All the words which the Lord has spoken we will do." And Moses wrote all the words of the Lord. (Exodus 24:3-4)

And Moses wrote this law, and gave it to the priests the sons of Levi, who carried the ark of the covenant of the Lord, and to all the elders of Israel.... When Moses had finished writing the words of this law in a book to the very end, Moses commanded the Levites who carried the ark of the covenant of the Lord, "Take this book of the law, and put it by the side of the ark of the covenant of the Lord your God, that it may be there for a witness against you...." (Deut. 31:9, 24-26)

"In fact," Dr. Alexandre had told his students, "there might have been some oral tradition to go on, but after you look at the way these stories were pieced together from the different writers' styles, you can see that there was no uniform text here, nothing that predates the time of David – that is, if the David stories themselves aren't works of fiction, political tracts to bolster the kingdom, build the Temple, and please the king."

Today, Jacob was having second thoughts, and one reason for it was something in this Bible code skip-search he had heard about before: Over the un-spaced block of Hebrew words on his computer screen – the block of Torah text that told the story of Eden – overlaid on that block, running up and down, diagonally and backwards, were emerging the names of plants, fruits and trees that might very well have grown in the Garden of Eden.

"I don't *get* this," Jacob thought. At first, he'd simply looked for the name Eden in the text, and had been surprised to find (along with three mentions in the surface text), twenty incidents of "Eden" spelled out at various equidistant intervals. Jacob was no mathematician, but he thought that twenty occurrences in only 657 letters of text had to be greater than simple chance would explain. But it was in the Genesis passage beginning:

And God said, "Behold, I have given you every plant yielding seed which is upon the face of all the earth, and every tree with seed in its fruit; you shall have them for food,"

and ending with:
And the Lord God commanded the man, saying, you may freely eat of every tree of the garden; but of the tree of the knowledge of good and evil you shall not eat, for in the day that you eat of it you shall die,"

that Jacob was having trouble accepting. For hidden in that small piece of text appeared the Hebrew words for barley, wheat, vine, grape, chestnut, thicket, date palm, acacia, boxthorn, cedar, pistachio, fig, willow, pomegranate, aloe, tamarisk, oak, poplar, cassia, almond, terebinth, thornbush, hazel, olive, citron, and gopherwood. Jacob had read Genesis in the Hebrew perhaps a hundred times before, but this was something altogether different. Today he felt he was looking at it for the very first time.

Chapter 5

Jacob hadn't always criticized scriptural faith. In fact, he'd related himself to God as far back as the age of seven, when he nearly drowned in a small lake in northwestern New Jersey. He remembered his body sinking into the dark lake, the pain of water sucked into his lungs, and then the look up a long tubular passage that led to light; was it perhaps back to the surface world he knew? He recalled the sudden realization he was out of his body and up in a birch tree! From there he saw his mother, already dressed for Sunday church, rushing from the cottage, shallow-diving into the water and pulling him to shore, where she worked a kind of desperate, maternal CPR on his skinny, lifeless body. After he revived, he was touched by his mother's unbridled gratitude to God. He wanted to feel that same kind of gratefulness, but didn't know quite how.

It wasn't until years later that he related his view of the tunnel-toward-the-light memory, while sinking down, to descriptions he read of near-death experiences. It hit home again what it meant that he *saw* his mother running to the shore, and diving in to rescue him. He could not have witnessed all that from his drowned body; he really had been perched in a tree above the scene. In that moment, he had to acknowledge there really is an afterlife.

From that early age, Jacob had wanted to study religion. He wanted to know why his soul left his body and returned – why his life had been spared. But the more he read, the more confusing the questions became. The earliest dates possible for the writing of the gospels, he was taught, proved that the writers could not have known Christ except through a source like "Q", a document invented by scholars to explain where Matthew and Luke got their material. Jacob went down this road knowing, in his heart, he wanted to provoke another sign from heaven like his NDE at seven. When it didn't come, he began looking in earnest for ways to help deconstruct religious tradition. He did his graduate work at Andover Newton and Yale seminaries.

Jacob had always been a good student, trained in the western classics and eastern religion courses at Columbia

University, so getting his doctorate had seemed a logical move. After graduation they'd invited him to stay on for a while, to teach and do research, and he didn't say no. The idea of actually preaching the gospel at some white-clapboard, bean supper church had given him pause. On campus, the ivory tower dreams could last forever.

Except for the unresolved bitterness he felt. He'd called a friend from high school days, Peter Emery, to ask what Peter thought of Jacob's impending career move to Maine. Peter was not religious, and after getting a doctorate in artificial intelligence from Ann Arbor, had started teaching at a well-heeled New England prep school. He'd learned years ago how thin that ivory veneer really was, and didn't hesitate in telling Jacob – whom he'd nicknamed "Ja" during their high school German studies together.

"Why would you think a liberal seminary in Maine is going to be any different?" Peter had asked. "Smaller, yes, poorer, yes, and forget any prestige. But come on, Ja! You already spent years at a liberal seminary, and you know the attitudes! Doesn't it remind you that no one can serve God and mammon? With scholars on a career track, faith – or any other form of romanticism – yields to publish-or-perish expediency every time. What you're doing is exchanging the university culture for Maine winters. In all other ways, I'm sure you'll feel right at home."

Jacob suspected Peter was right. From the first week of orientation, Jacob had spotted the pros – the teachers who maintained an aura of faith like doctors putting on their bedside manner. He even happened to be present when one of them broke at a particularly bad time. During an evening meal for prospective students, members of the faculty had joined each table in the dining hall to answer candidates' questions. Suddenly, between the pot roast and the Jell-O, a long-time teacher told the new recruits she felt despair in the thought that Christ was called the only son of God. "I went to church services last month and nearly choked on the communion wafer," she said. "I just keep thinking, 'maybe I should be a Buddhist.'" She taught a course titled, "Christian faith and the pastoral calling." Two prospective students excused themselves from the table, and the next day withdrew their applications.

Chapter 6

Jacob lifted his eyes from the computer long enough to remember something. Years ago, he had walked the shore of a cove on Penobscot Bay. It was a brilliant sunlit day, and light shimmered off every ripple of the water. Fifty yards away, a cormorant back from fishing spread its wings to dry in the sun, and in the black, black silhouette, Jacob suddenly saw a door to another dimension. For just an instant he felt if he could walk on water to get to that bird, he'd be invited to step *through* the bird to a world more real, more intensely beautiful – truer, in fact, than the beautiful world of shore and sky and bird he then beheld.

Jacob slowly realized that a peculiar shape, overlaying the code text of Genesis on his computer screen, had jogged that memory. His little block of undifferentiated text was now overlaid with little squares and lines and highlighted words, making it appear more and more like some abstract picture puzzle. Was this, like that silhouetted cormorant, a gateway to a different place?

A year ago, Genesis was a book Jacob thought he knew as well as the back of his hand. So well had he known it, that he was building his career hopes on a current blip, a theological fad, that had led several other scholars and poets in recent years to do just what the world probably didn't need – yet another translation and explication of the text.

Jacob suspected the renewed interest in the creation story and the garden grew from the desperate state of earth's environment, and the devastation being caused by human pollution and the results of global-warming. The world's human population had nearly quadrupled over the past eighty years, while some fifty percent of many other species had gone extinct.

When Jacob told him what he planned to do, Peter just laughed. "You and every other New Age wanna-be," he'd chuckled. "What is it with you seminary types? You're always reinventing the same wheel because you can't find anything more productive to do. Talk about beating a dead horse."

Jacob had listened, as he always, did when Peter was giving him two-edged advice. He trusted Peter – even when he was trivializing what Jacob found interesting. He knew Peter was being honest with him.

"Why not use your Hebrew on some of the supplementary stuff that no good Christian ever reads – Midrash commentaries on the details of keeping a kosher kitchen, say? That alone should make Christians rejoice that Christ took care of the law. Or how about doing something to make Paul's letters popular reading for feminists."

Jacob faked a wan smile at the jokes. Peter was no churchman, but he knew his Bible as one root of English literature. And he knew what was in and what was out – in a word, what was politically correct. There was no doubt Genesis had been nitpicked, practically to death, from several directions.

Of course, there was anti-science creationism with notions of an earth only a few thousand years old. That was hard to understand, given the overwhelming geologic evidence. Then there was the poetry of Genesis' mythology. This was easy to understand, since the old stories were poetic to start with, and popular rewrites hardly ruffled the beliefs of anyone but the most hidebound fundamentalists.

Even in a culture that didn't allow Bible-as-literature courses in the public schools, the stories still held a powerful mythic charm. As Genesis' stock was rising, poets, feminists, and talk show hosts became instant experts on these tales from their childhood. Years ago, Bill Moyers had hosted a Genesis TV series, with fiction writers delivering their profoundly off-the-top-of-their-head interpretations. Then came the inevitable B-movie trivia, and the fad was passing again.

If truth be told, the fifteen minutes of fame for Genesis was actually a recurring cycle, and the book that's supposed to be back on the shelf never is for long. But time moves slowly in the provinces, and Jacob was riding some rivulet behind the crest of the wave, rather than the next tsunami. Peter had tried to break the news gently, but Jacob wasn't taking it to heart.

Chapter 7

Jacob stood and stretched, and at once felt the pain in his hip – the other injury from his fall. But that was hardly a concern to him today, when the words seemed to be leaping off the page. He'd always loved Hebrew, he reminded himself, from the opening day of his first class as a student at the seminary. Since his fall, and meeting his father on the other side, he'd been thinking more about the things he loved.

Hebrew is a language of puns, in part because of spare vocabulary and the multiple meanings of words. Understandings of specific meanings are gleaned in part from context and tradition. His approach to his new translation of Genesis had been a literal one – that is, to set down the essential, bare-bones English equivalent much as Hendrickson had done in the 1970's. These so-called transliterations were awkward but insightful, since they conveyed a gut-level meaning that reminded Jacob of his days at Columbia, reading Beowulf and Anglo-Saxon poetry in the original.

The great challenge to modern Bible translation was the beauty of the King James version, a work of poetry, of genius, but dated by language and the more recent discoveries of other ancient manuscripts. Nevertheless, the power of the King James version was hard to equal. Consider the opening, "In the beginning, God created the heavens and the earth." A more recent, more literal translation by Everett Fox had made use of the original's lack of punctuation to say, "At the beginning of God's creating of the heavens and the earth..." Jacob's unpolished transliteration of that same line read, "First, Gods created the lofties and the firm."

Whether the word 'Elohim' should be translated 'god' or 'gods' has to be re-explored, Jacob thought, though he knew the argument that the plural form had been used only to add prestige, like the royal 'we'. Most commentators didn't want to pursue the implication there might have been multiple entities involved in the creation.

Chapter 8

Jacob found himself once again in front of Maggie's door. It was late, he knew, but he had to talk to someone, and Maggie was the one.

Maggie Colburn had joined the faculty shortly after Jacob accepted the seminary's offer to make him a fully tenured professor. She was younger than Jacob, and more optimistic by nature. Still, they'd hit it off almost at once, perhaps because they were both amused by the strident issues (such as the 'he/she' pronoun for God) infecting this campus a few decades after they had been quietly buried everywhere else. They were in seminary outback, and that recognition was a common bond.

Maggie lived in a three-room apartment on the top floor of a converted mansion, just a block from the seminary. The apartment was a climb, but worthwhile for the small, private balcony that overlooked Bangor, with even a glimpse of the Penobscot River. That first semester, before the arrival of what they dubbed the plague, Jacob and Maggie had spent several happy evenings on that balcony, drinking wine and debating the sources and reasons for Hebrew Bible prophesy.

Maggie opened the door. She was in her bathrobe, and had clearly been asleep. She looked tired, but not really displeased by the visit. "There better be a good reason," she said in mock annoyance. "I've got a nine o'clock class to teach in the morning."

"Sorry to bother you so late," Jacob said, and hesitated at the doorway until she gestured him in. "She looks cozy," he thought, as he brushed past her. Her long, curly hair smelled freshly shampooed. "I need to talk about the birds and the bees."

"Earlier, maybe. But midnight?" Her annoyance was not so mock anymore.

"In Genesis, I mean." He told her about his Bible code discoveries – especially the incredible list of plants.

She didn't seem surprised. "After all," she said, pouring each of them a glass of merlot, "numbers were built right into the surface text itself. Like the number seven, the number of perfection in the Genesis description of creation. The section is divided into *seven* paragraphs, one for each of the seven days. Each of the three key nouns in the first verse – namely God, heavens, and earth – are all repeated in multiples of seven."

Maggie paused to pull a notebook off the shelf. "Here it is," she said after turning a few pages. "Cassuto pointed this out. The words for *light* and *day* appear seven times in the first paragraph, and *light* again occurs seven times in the fourth paragraph. In paragraphs two and three, the word for *water* is mentioned seven times. In the fifth and sixth paragraphs, forms of the word *hayya* – 'living' or 'beasts' – appear seven times. The first verse has *seven* words. The second verse has *fourteen* words. The seventh paragraph, dealing with the seventh day, contains three consecutive sentences – each of which consists of *seven* words with the phrase *the seventh day* right in the middle. Anyone's crazy who thinks this kind of thing just happens by coincidence."

"Well sure, okay," Jacob answered, "But *that* kind of numerology could be constructed by wordsmiths with lots of time on their hands. This hidden code business is something else. Even if the priests had Macs, they'd have been hard put to build this kind of skip-letter crossword puzzle into scripture, and have any of it come out right."

Maggie looked at him. "You mentioned all the trees and plants that were hidden. Does the Bible code mention the tree of life, or the tree of the knowledge of good and evil?" And then she asked, "Jacob – the tree of the knowledge of good and evil. What do you think it stands for?"

"Stands for?" Jacob asked, surprised. "Just what it says, I imagine. The one tree in Eden that was forbidden to Adam and Eve. Some people think it was about sex, but except for being a great phallic symbol, I never thought of it as anything but a tree – and probably pomegranate, rather than apple."

Maggie refilled their glasses, sat down and took a breath. She suspected Jacob was going through some kind of spiritual awakening, and didn't want to overwhelm him. Also, she knew he could throw very cold water with considerable accuracy. Still, it had been on her mind a lot lately, and she had to test it on someone.

"What if I were to tell you that tree was a center of sorcery, perhaps even a city in a different dimension. What if I called it a spiritual/physical vortex that wasn't simply a metaphor for sin and disobedience, but its embodiment."

He sat for a moment, not saying anything. "Have you been drinking – I mean, before I got here?" he asked.

"No."

"Well, what in the hell are you talking about?"

"You know the quote from Paul," Maggie responded, shifting to the edge of her seat. "For our fight is not against human foes, but against cosmic powers, against the authorities and potentates of this dark world, against the superhuman forces of evil in the heavens."

"Sure, but..."

"This morning I looked up every reference to trees that appears in the Bible. Overwhelmingly, it's a metaphor for leaders, rulers, centers of influence, and so forth."

The late hour was beginning to get to him. "So, what's your point?" he asked.

"The point is, that for as long as anyone can remember, Genesis has been treated as either literal truth or poetic myth – with nothing in between. The fundamentalists believe that Adam and Eve were the first man and woman created by God – Adam from the red earth, and Eve from Adam's side. They were placed in Eden, to be their home forever. All they had to do was not eat the apple..."

"Pomegranate," Jacob interjected, but she ignored him.

"Then, as Reason became our religion, the literal interpretation went into decline, and by the time Darwin's theories of evolution were incorporated into the public school texts, it was only the religious fringe, hanging on by their teeth, that kept the story of creation from going right down the toilet. There's not one religious person in this whole seminary – teacher or student – who believes Adam and Eve are historical figures in any way."

"Don't tell me – let me guess," Jacob said mockingly. "You had a cosmic vision in the library and now you're a born-again fundamentalist. Wow, are your students in for a shock tomorrow morning."

Maggie caught the sarcasm, but didn't bite. She and he had undergone long conversations on her balcony through

27

the bright August evenings before the start of their first semester, conversations about what religious twists and turns had led each to the seminary. She knew he knew fundamentalism was an unlikely path for her to follow. The blind adherence of the true believer, be it Christian, Islam, Nazi or Communist based, would be anathema to her. It mitigated against God's gifts of intellect and free will, and made a mockery of faith.

"Yeah, sure," she smiled, getting off track for a minute. "No, look. Why should the answer be one or the other, absolute fact or absolute myth? Why not a third path altogether, like the theories of Intelligent Design? Studies like that often come from ancient beliefs, like panspermia. Ancient writings have often led to new discoveries. Think of Heinrich Schliemann, and how his faith in the text led to the discovery of Troy."

Jacob smiled. Schliemann had been that rare reader to declare Homer's *Iliad* more historic than mythic, and then act on his conviction. By studying the text, he'd been able to locate the actual site of the ancient city of Troy, and his single-minded digging, while unfortunately destroying much irreplaceable archeological evidence, uncovered priceless works in gold. Schliemann's faith in ancient writings, however, was far from unique. Decades before the dig at Troy, Frenchman Paul-Emile Botta excavated at Khorsabad, on the Tigris, and uncovered evidence of Sargon, the king of Assyria, who was mentioned in Isaiah. And in 1845, the Englishman A. H. Layard uncovered the biblical city of Nimrod. The irony of it was that this appreciation for the basic truths contained in ancient texts had been in decline all through the 20th century. The prejudice against the existence of historic truth in the Bible, the Apocrypha, the Book of Enoch, the Epic of Gilgamesh, etc., was an obstacle to be overcome again and again.

Maggie's eyes were closing despite herself, and Jacob had a sudden twinge of pity. "Look, get some sleep," he said, "and I'll meet you over coffee in the morning. He touched her cheek, and she smiled in gratitude. She thought she heard the door click shut as her head hit the pillow, but she really didn't know and didn't care.

Chapter 9

Jacob had no such pity on Peter, however. A night owl by nature, Peter always welcomed a call from Jacob, no matter what the hour. As soon as Jacob reached his own apartment, he was on the phone to Stamford, Connecticut.

"If truth be told," Jacob thought as he was dialing, "Peter has lots of time on his hands – probably because he never really pursued his career." Though he'd been top in his class at Ann Arbor, Peter had opted to teach in secondary schools rather than reach for the post he might have had at Harvard, Yale, or Princeton. He'd settled into a comfortable marriage, raised two kids, and spent a lot of time reading obscure texts, professional journals, and pursuing several hobbies. As a result, he could write a computer program to translate Urdu into Linear B, but couldn't rise high enough in the school's pecking order to avoid study-hall duty. Still, he had found the time and money to travel all over the world in pursuit of his hobbies – a fact that intrigued Jacob. He wondered how Peter always got the time off, but he never probed too deeply.

Without formality or apology, Jacob launched into the conversation before Peter could get out a hello. "I think I'm onto something here, Peter. Just listen for a minute and tell me what you think.

"It looks to me like there's a message encoded in the Genesis creation story that needs to be translated into modern language – or rather, into scientific thought. My first clue came from the incredible improbabilities in this Bible code stuff..." and here Jacob elaborated on the revelations in the hidden text. "And then I got to talking with Maggie about the tree of knowledge metaphor – but let me start at the beginning. You know how the book begins with two creation stories, and how scholars explain by saying that two old myths got lumped together? Well, suddenly I don't think that explains it. I mean, the writer here is no dummy. This is additional material, and not a contradiction or a more detailed redundancy."

"Whoa, slow down, Ja," Peter said. ""What do you think it means?"

"Peter, you know the Mahabharata – how that old Indian text embodies in poetic form some of the great scientific discoveries of our age. The thing is, the oral traditions of the Mahabharata, thousands of years old, were written down in Sanskrit about the time of the prophets. Now why should the ancient Hebrews have any less knowledge than India? After all, Abraham came from Ur, where they knew the Flood story, Moses came out of Egypt, and later the tribes returned from Babylon with knowledge from both cultures. These places were the intellectual centers of their day, and these people were every bit as smart as we are – probably smarter.

"No, I think Genesis contains more than meets the eye. What it's saying is something we're only beginning to recognize today with the invention of the computer. It's telling us, 'We're going to talk about how we actually came to be here, and we'll say it in mythic language, in parables everyone can understand. But the deeper you look, the more you'll find.'"

"So, what's your point?" Peter asked.

"Funny, that's exactly what I said to Maggie not more than an hour ago," Jacob mused, "and that's about the time I decided to go home. The point is, the Bible is telling us more than a myth, and more than a scientific research paper, too. It's talking to us in metaphor, in code, in terms we may even be ready to understand scientifically, once we understand what we're dealing with. I believe we *can* understand it, if we just put our minds to it. Genesis is delivering a message that can be understood by combining story-truth with scientific thought."

"You realize you're going up against everything you've ever taught, don't you," Peter said, with some irony. "Your students – better yet, your employer – will think you've lost your mind."

"Yes, I guess," said Jacob, whose Catholic boyhood had contributed little to his own respect for consistency. "But that's really beside the point, isn't it? If we could prove an underlying basis of fact in scripture, then seminaries like mine would have to rewrite the syllabus."

Peter didn't answer, so Jacob went on. "And there's something else, Peter. Something I think I saw, but I may have dreamed about. It's in that array of hidden Eden references that I saw in the text."

"Yes?" Peter said at last.

"I could swear I saw a map, a drawing of some sort, right there in the text. If I just had a good aerial photo scaled to size, I'd bet my pension I could lay that text on top of it and pinpoint the Garden of Eden."

There was silence at the other end of the phone. At last Peter cleared his throat and said in a surprisingly low voice, "Ja, can you come down to New York tomorrow?"

The question and the tone startled Jacob, who hadn't thought to go any farther tomorrow than the classroom and his ugly office desk. "Why?" he asked.

"I can't really tell you now," Peter said. "Let it be a leap of faith. I guarantee it will be worth your while. Leave in the morning. I have to go." And with that, Peter hung up the phone.

Chapter 10   New York

By 6:30 the next morning, Jacob was on a commuter flight from Bangor to Boston. He'd only had time to call Maggie and ask her to cover his classes for him, and to cram his research notes into a bag with a toothbrush and change of clothes. As he settled into the high-backed seat, he had a moment's regret he hadn't had that cup of coffee with her. He wanted to tell her what he'd told Peter, and felt he hadn't explained why he had to leave. Explain? He didn't know himself, so how on earth could he have explained it to Maggie?   Still, he missed not having that cup of coffee, seeing her smile and smiling back. He suddenly realized he was growing too fond of her.

As the small plane bumped down the Maine coast, Jacob stretched and looked up the aisle. There was only a handful of passengers on board, and they were ignoring the foliage below to read their cellphones. Despite several empty seats up front, a large man sat next to him. Clearly the coronavirus hadn't taught him a thing about social distancing on planes, Jacob thought, but the guy was wearing a mask, so Jacob decided it wasn't worth moving. He closed his eyes and went back to wondering what it was he'd said to make such a change in Peter's behavior. When he'd phoned him again, just before getting on the plane, Peter still wouldn't tell him why he wanted him to make this trip on such short notice. All he would say was, "You won't be sorry."

In Boston, Jacob descended the narrow steps and crossed the pavement to a waiting bus. Air service from Bangor could still expose you to the weather. Awhile later, he boarded the flight to Kennedy. He'd offered to meet Peter at his house in Stamford, but Peter gave him an address on West 54th St. and told him he'd meet him there. "I don't want my family getting caught up in this," Peter said, which only added to the mystery.

To tell the truth, Jacob loved going into the city. Ever since his undergraduate days at Columbia, he'd detected an ambient energy in New York that existed nowhere else in the world. He got off on it like some potent drug, and during his time at Andover Newton he'd taken Amtrak into the city two or three times a month. It was one of the reasons he'd moved to Maine, he thought – to get that NYC monkey off his back. Still, it had been a shock to see TV coverage of an empty Times Square at the onset of the virus. He hoped they wouldn't have to go through a repeat of that disaster anytime soon.

It was afternoon by the time his taxi reached midtown, but Jacob decided to walk the last few blocks to 54th St. A fall afternoon in New York was one of life's great pleasures, not to be missed. Perhaps he'd take a detour and walk up to Central Park. The soft black bag had a shoulder strap for easy carrying. Jacob felt suddenly energized, setting off on an adventure in the greatest city in the world.

Chapter 11

Peter stood facing the window wall of the 30th floor apartment, watching as the lights of the city replaced the afternoon sun. It was a commanding scene at any time, but Peter did not feel empowered by the view. In fact, he felt sick. After all, he was about to tell his best friend that he'd been lying to him for most of their adult lives.

He had always known this day would come, but never planned on it to be so soon. When he thought about it, he'd envisioned his confession happening in some backwoods cabin on a lake in Maine, where he and Mary and Ja and whoever (Maggie, perhaps?) would be on a fishing trip together. The fact he'd never in his life been fishing had not made the plan seem foolish. It was simply the setting that mattered, after all.

The intercom beeped, and the doorman's voice crackled an announcement of Jacob's arrival. Peter cleared his throat, looked around the immaculate apartment, and then decided to meet Ja by the elevator. "Might as well get on with this," he muttered to himself.

Meanwhile, Jacob was feeling both suspicious and impressed. He'd lived in New York as a lowly student, where a rundown, rent-controlled railroad flat on West 106th St. had been his home. Peter and Mary had a nice home in a suburb of Stamford, and Jacob had visited there a dozen times over the years. But this was the first he knew that Peter had access to a midtown apartment that must rent for more than his and Peter's teaching salaries combined.

Peter was standing there facing him when the elevator door slid open. "It's good to see you," Peter said with a forced smile, and shook his hand – a move too formal by half for Jacob's liking.

"So, are you ready to tell me what this is all about?" Jacob blurted out, as much at the handshake as anything.

"Not here," Peter said softly, taking Jacob's bag and leading him down the long, plush-carpeted hall, passed carefully lit, reproduction Monets in way too ornate gilded frames.

"Really puttin' on the dog," Jacob remarked, a familiar reference to an old Firesign Theater routine they had committed to memory when they were teens. Peter didn't come back with the requisite, "These are the kennels, Nick" bit, and Jacob realized with a sinking heart this was not going to be a fun trip to the Big Apple.

Chapter 12

"Now, what the hell is going on," Jacob nearly exploded, as soon as the door was closed.

"First, let me get you a drink, Ja. Jack on the rocks?" Peter was going to lubricate this confession just as much as possible. Jacob could see from the half empty glass on the mantle that Peter had already started, so he didn't say no.

While Peter was in the kitchen, Jacob took a careful look around. It had an incredible view for sure, but the apartment seemed implausibly neutral, far too impersonal, really, to be Peter's home away from home. Peter was a collector of many things, from old dictating machines to pinhole cameras to first editions of certain 19th century philosophers. This place had been professionally decorated for professional use, and had nothing of Peter in it.

Peter came around the corner and handed Jacob his drink. "Sit down," he said, "and I'll tell you something about this place and why you're here."

Jacob started to interrupt, but Peter raised his hand. "Please, Ja, this is difficult enough, so just let me get through it. I'll try to answer your questions when I'm done."

Peter took a breath and began. "Ja, you and I have known each other for the better part of our lives. What you haven't known is that for the last several years, since I was recruited at Ann Arbor, I've been an operative for a government agency. I won't tell you which one, and you wouldn't recognize the letters anyway. What's important is, I've lied to you for some time about who I am and what I do. I feel like shit telling you this, but something really critical has come up, and I need your help figuring it out."

"So, this isn't your apartment?" Jacob asked dumbly, suddenly afraid to look past the here and now to what Peter was saying.

Peter smiled. He'd expected a tougher question than that – some question like, "Does Mary know about this, or have you been lying to her, too?" Fact was, his wife knew only half of what his life had really been about. Someday he'd have to go through a lengthy confession with her, as well.

"No, this isn't my apartment. Can't you tell? Even if I could afford it I wouldn't want it, looking like this. This is an agency secure house – it gets used for a lot of things." Peter's voice trailed off sadly, as if he knew more about this apartment than he wanted to.

"And what's it being used for now, Peter?" Jacob's voice was sharp, as he'd got his second wind. "Why am I here, anyway? What do you want from me?"

"First of all, your friendship, if you can find it to forgive me. I really had no choice – you've got to believe me on that. Even Mary doesn't know much about this...."

They sat there quietly for a while, not saying anything. The light from the floor-to-ceiling windows was fading, and a crescent moon hung over the impatient traffic below. Peter realized the big issues, the friendship issues, wouldn't get resolved this evening, and he still had a job to do.

"Ja, when I promised you wouldn't be disappointed about coming here – it wasn't about my career decisions, you know, at least not directly. What we were talking about last night, your work on Genesis? What if I were to tell you there may be life-and-death consequences, if what you say is true."

Jacob laughed out loud. It was such a tension breaker that both of them laughed, and Peter went to the kitchen to grab the bottle and more ice, before going on.

Chapter 13

Maggie poured herself a glass of merlot and went out on the balcony to watch the sunset reflecting over Bangor. It had turned too cold to be gracious anymore, and she wore her insulated jacket and a blue knit cap. "At least I don't have to drink my wine with gloves on, yet," she thought, as she settled into a plastic chair.

Her day had not gone well, not well at all, and Jacob was to blame for most of that. First thing, his phone call had turned their breakfast date into two more classes to teach, while he ran off to New York for no discernible reason. She hated teaching his classes, not because the material wasn't interesting, but because his students were invariably disappointed when he wasn't there. His classes were much in demand, and his students resented every moment he wasn't there with them.

The knock on her door surprised her. She had very few visitors, not counting Jacob, and they always called before coming over. She opened the door to two men in suits and virus masks, who looked so completely out of place she thought they must be Mormons in training.

"Sorry to bother you, ma'am, but we need to ask you a few questions – just for background information," one of them said, and flashed a badge so quickly she did not have time to read it. "I believe you are friends with a Professor Jacob Alexandre?"

A quick series of images ran through her mind, of plane crashes and muggings, and even suicide. She surprised herself with that one.

"Is he all right?" she asked quickly, holding her breath. How could she have been so resentful of him just two minutes ago?

"Yes, ma'am. As far as we know. We're simply doing a background check on him – nothing important, just routine. How long have you known Dr. Alexandre?"

It seemed like she'd known him forever, but in fact it had been little more than a few semesters. It surprised her when she thought about it, but that's all it was, and that's what she told them.

"Has he ever mentioned his political activities to you, who he voted for last time, any clubs, special-interest lobbies, and so forth? Has he ever used hallucinogenic drugs in religious ceremonies, or belonged to a cult?"

Maggie finally pulled herself together. "Alright, who *are* you guys, and where do you get off asking questions like that? Get the hell out of my house!" she almost shouted, and slammed the door in their faces.

Chapter 14

Jacob and Peter sat on a small balcony that extended no more than six feet from the side of the building, watching a steady stream of yellow cabs in pursuit of the elusive fare. It was late enough now to pick out a few stars – about as good as it gets with so much light pollution from below. They'd been talking Genesis again, and together with the Jack Daniels, it seemed like old times, almost.

"The thing is," Jacob was saying, "with multiple creations being discussed, you could have had whole civilizations come and go before the creation of Adam. After all, where were the wives for Cain and Abel and Seth if there weren't people already there? Who did Cain build cities for, if all the housing needed was for his aging parents and their offspring? No, it seems clear to me from the text that Adam and Eve were a special case, and that Eden was set apart not to guard them from the wilderness, but to guard them from people who were already in the world."

Peter looked thoughtful. "So, you would contend that Eden is an actual place, and all we have to do is dig until we find what's left of it?"

Jacob smiled at the thought, which could well be considered a possibility. After all, the text gave Eden's general location by naming the rivers that flowed from it. For most of known history, only the Tigris' and Euphrates' locations were obvious. But with the discovery of the Pishon riverbed, dried up for centuries but still visible by NASA satellite photometry, archaeologists were given the approximate triangulation they'd need. But by now, what could there possibly be to find?

"Yes and no," Jacob said at last. "Yes, because the text itself implies that we should dig."

"What do you mean, the text implies?" Peter asked.

"Well, a long time ago I made the connection. It comes out in Genesis 3:24." Jacob recited it from memory:

He drove out the man; and at the east of the garden of Eden he placed the cherubim, and a flaming sword which turned every way, to guard the way to the tree of life.

"It's the business about the flaming sword. What do you see when you look in that general area of Iraq?"

"Desert," Peter said without hesitation. "So what?"

"Well, I did a word study of the original Hebrew for 'cherubim and a flaming sword," Jacob said. "The word for sword is *chereb*, which means 'cutting instrument' from its destructive effect. It also means 'drought.' It comes from its prime root, which means to 'parch,' to 'desolate.'"

"Are you telling me the text says God has hidden Eden with the desert?" Peter asked.

"Yes, and more than that, because the root of the word for 'flaming,' *Lahat*, means 'enwrapped in magic,' 'covert.' You see, that's where Maggie's thoughts about inter-dimensionality may come into play. After all, we are talking about what the Bible calls spiritual realms – which only means realms the ancients weren't able to explain. But now we've got the beginnings of a handle on time/space relationships, and our fiction incorporates ideas like folding space to move from points A to B without traveling in-between. Well, for instance, take that description of the expulsion from the garden. Even at face value, the phrase 'cherubim, and a flaming sword which turned every way' says that beings guard the garden and the tree in a multi-dimensional way. There is nothing in the text to indicate that Eden is not still there, and the tree of life, whatever that is, is still there, too. But it's probably not in a place where any archaeologist with a pick and shovel is going to find it."

Peter stood up and looked over the edge of the balcony. It was late, and thirty stories below, the traffic was finally beginning to thin. "That's what I hoped you were going to say," he said into space, and turned to face his friend. "Ja, we need your help on a project so problematic that I really didn't want to involve you at all. But if we're successful, it's a project that should confirm to the greatest extent possible that your theories about Genesis are correct."

Chapter 15　　Iraq

The Followers of Paul expedition had traveled a long way to get to what appeared to be little more than a mound in a vast desert of mounds. They had come on foot and by camel, though some were wealthy enough to have brought whole caravans with them, were it allowed. A great effort and much physical stress, thirst, and deprivation were prerequisites for the mystery they were about to undergo. The sun had set an hour before, and the sand had already lost the heat of the day. The wind picked up as the temperature dropped, and the pilgrims huddled by the door they had uncovered in the excavated mound. With the door brushed clean, they could see the raised image of a golden bird in flight. "This is the resurrection bird, the phoenix," one man had said. They had spent the day digging without tools, and their hands were scraped and blistered from the sand they had removed to uncover the ancient portal. Soon, they believed, the door would open to them – though how soon and to what effect, they did not yet know. They did know, however, that the door would be opened from the inside.

Chapter 16

Maggie needed to talk to Jacob, urgently, and yet he didn't answer his cellphone. It had been a bad day, sure, but the visit of those two cops, agents, whatever, had thrown her more than she'd realized. And she had no way of knowing where Jacob was, save for the fact he was meeting his friend in New York.

She recalled his friend's name was Peter, and that they'd been close since high school. She thought he'd even told her Peter's last name, but for the life of her she couldn't remember what it was. She also knew that Peter lived near Stamford, Connecticut, but without his last name, she wouldn't be able to reach him. She decided finally to do something she would never have thought possible – she'd search Jacob's apartment to find a phone number for his friend.

It was after midnight when Maggie left her door, flashlight in hand, and walked the three blocks to Jacob's building. The wind had turned sharp now, the temperature near freezing, and Maggie's jacket, which seemed like overkill with her sunset glass of wine, was now barely adequate. Jacob lived downhill from the seminary – in more ways than one. Though the building was on seminary property, it was not a structure they were proud of, and plans had been made several times to tear the whole thing down. Each time the budget wouldn't permit it, or they couldn't spare the housing, but at the same time no money was spent to maintain it, either. The result was the closest thing to a slum that Bangor had to offer. Bugs that lived nowhere else in Maine lived here; lead paint was the only paint on the walls, and the plumbing still featured lead drains. To top it off, the heating plant was coated in asbestos insulation. If it hadn't belonged to a religious institution, the building would have been condemned by city inspectors years ago.

All this suited Jacob to a T. After all, it reminded him of his student days in New York, where roaches would pour from between the floorboards whenever the boiler came on. In that apartment, the toilet still had a wooden tank on the wall, mounted almost to the ceiling. When you pulled the chain you stood back, since water came over the top of the tank as well as down the pipe.

Maggie had been to Jacob's apartment once before. He had invited her to dinner, but even the dim candlelight could not hide the squalor he was living in. After that, they shared an unspoken agreement that all dinner invitations would be fulfilled in her apartment, whether she did the cooking or he did.

The third-story hallway had one working bulb. That it hadn't burned out by now could be laid to the fact that it was no more than fifteen watts, max. There was more light on the midnight streets than there was in that hallway, and she was glad she'd brought her flashlight. Maggie was relying on the fact that Jacob always kept his key under the edge of the ratty hall carpet. As it turned out, she didn't need the key.

Chapter 17

Peter hadn't been willing to say any more that evening, except for blaming the Jack for saying too much already, so they'd each gone off to their own bedrooms. Jacob took a shower and climbed into bed. For some reason, he couldn't find his cellphone; still, there was a phone right there, next to the bed. But it was after midnight, and he didn't think Maggie would want him waking her so late. After all, she needed her rest if she was going to be teaching his classes for him again.

For all his traveling, drinks and conversation, Jacob couldn't really get to sleep. His life had been so predictable for so long, he couldn't even remember the meaning of adventure. And he wasn't sure he was still up for it, whatever it was, even with his best friend by his side. Life had gotten away from him, somehow. And even now, when his career as a teacher was finally getting off the ground, he felt his life was shutting down, his options closing, his race run. Even his tentative courting of Maggie, a few years his junior, was frightening to him. He didn't want it to mean so much.

But proof of these theories about Genesis! Could it even be possible? Jacob tried to imagine what that would mean. It was one thing, sure, to write yet another book on a well-worn subject. But to offer proof of a radical theory – perhaps even to uncover the physical Eden itself! And what would that mean to the nature of faith?

Tonight, Peter had shown himself to be more serious, more dedicated, than Jacob had ever seen him before. He had kept himself from Jacob, that was certain. The most important part of Peter's personality had been deeply submerged in his secret work, and only the bright exterior had come through. Jacob wondered, as he closed his eyes, that if he'd really known Peter's actual true nature, would he have straightened out his own life sooner than this? As he finally fell asleep, he imagined he could overhear his friend arguing with other voices in a distant room.

Chapter 18

To be safe, Maggie knocked on Jacob's door, and was startled to feel it swing open. The room was dark, and she relied on her flashlight to look around. What she saw was not encouraging. Jacob had never been the soul of neatness, but this was too much. Books had been pulled from the shelves, papers dumped from the filing cabinet, even dishes from the kitchen had been scattered, broken on the floor. She walked into the bedroom, and found more of the same – clothing pulled from drawers and closets, even the bed torn apart.

"Jacob didn't leave this mess," she thought dully, then suddenly remembered the so-called cops who'd been to her apartment. She reached for the phone by the bed, but the wire was pulled from the wall. And a voice in her head was telling her the smell in the place was not normal, not normal at all. "It smells like gas from the cook stove," she thought. That suddenly, she felt herself getting faint, and on impulse, grabbed Jacob's bedside Bible and hurled it through the window. The sound of breaking glass was the last thing she heard as she collapsed on the bed.

Chapter 19

Jacob was letting Maggie's phone ring this time, but again no answer. He still couldn't find his cellphone, and thinking about it, he remembered the man who crowded him on the plane. "That makes no sense," he finally decided. "No one would want my old flip-phone!"

He called her from the bedside landline as soon as he woke up, seven sharp, according to his watch, but she must have gone out to breakfast. "Without me," he thought with regret. He then tried the school to leave a message, but it was too early for anyone to be in the office. Her cell number was on *his* missing phone, so that wouldn't work. Finally, he tried Maggie's landline again to leave a message on the machine.

"This is Dr. Colburn," said her disembodied voice. "I can't come to the phone right now, so please leave a message when you hear the tone." Jacob waited dutifully.

"Maggie, I need to talk to you as soon as possible, but I don't know the number here where I'm staying in New York, and my cellphone's gone missing. I'll call back later. Bye." That was totally inadequate, but at least she'd know he was still alive.

He found the bathroom fully stocked, so he shaved and showered again before looking for Peter. Peter, however, was not there. Instead, Jacob found a note telling him to eat some cereal and read the morning paper, that Peter would be right back.

Jacob stepped out on the balcony and took a deep breath of polluted air. It was New York all right, in all its glory, and Jacob once again felt a rush of enthusiasm. "I wonder if I have time for a walk," he thought, "before Peter gets back to tell me some other ridiculous story."

Forsaking the walk, Jacob opted for Cheerios and his laptop. If they were going to look for Eden, there was the damage caused by the Iraq wars to consider. Though young at the time, Jacob had followed the Iraqi bombing stories closely. He had opposed war in Iraq even as a teen, primarily because he feared for the thousands of crucial archeological sites that could be destroyed by carpet

47

bombing. His concerns had been confirmed already, not only by damage reports, but also by Saddam Hussein's vindictive draining of the marshes, and the wholesale slaughter of peoples who had occupied that mysterious area since before the dawn of history. If any people still knew about Eden, surely it was those marsh dwellers of Iraq. And when Bush picked up the war where his father had left off, many archeologists abandoned hope for the preservation of Iraq's priceless ancient artifacts. Reports of the bombing and looting quite convinced them that much of it was already gone.

Jacob heard the front door open, and the call "Hello!" Peter came into the kitchen with several packages, which he set on the table in front of Jacob. "We have to hurry, Ja," he said. "You have a full day ahead of you."

Jacob was nonplused. "What's in the packages?" he asked.

"A suit, shirts, a choice of ties, some wing-tips, and so forth. I hope you like Brooks Brothers, because they were there early to let me in. You and I are just about the same size, so these should fit just fine. Go ahead and try them on."

For the tenth time since he got there, Jacob stifled the impulse to yell something rude. "What the hell are these for, Peter? What's going on?"

Peter looked Jacob in the eye. "Ja," he said, "you are about to teach the most important class of your entire life."

Chapter 20

Jacob stood in a small anteroom behind the lecture stage on the top floor of the building. He felt like a caricature of a teacher, dressed as he was in the brown tweed suit, oxford shirt and striped tie Peter had picked out for him. "All I need is a pipe to make it complete," he told Peter, who was too preoccupied to be amused.

"Just tell them what you've been telling me – you know, about Genesis," Peter instructed. "No, on second thought, start them off with the basics. This theology stuff is going to be new to them, so you might as well cover the field."

"Who are these people?" Jacob asked. "At least tell me that much, so I know where to start."

"Can't," Peter said. "At least not yet. Make a good case for your theories, though, and you can count on getting to know them – probably better than you want."

A young woman came into the room and whispered something to Peter.

"Hold on," he told Jacob. "Wait right here." A moment later he was back.

"There's been a change of plans," Peter told Jacob. "They first wanted to hear from you, followed by two other speakers. Now we don't have that much time. What they want to do is put the three of you together and watch while you brainstorm it."

"Brainstorm what?" Jacob said with irritation, though feeling somewhat relieved not to be out there alone.

"Genesis, of course," Peter replied.

The room had been darkened, except for directional spots shining on the polished walnut table set in the middle of the stage. It made the audience practically invisible to Jacob, though it seemed to him there were about twenty people, most of them in uniform, seated down front. Three whiteboards had been set up, with packs of colored markers neatly arranged.

Two elderly men were already seated in red leather chairs, facing the audience. Jacob went to the third chair and sat down.

Someone in the audience, a uniformed man with graying hair, stood up. "Gentlemen, I want to thank you for interrupting your busy schedules to come and talk to us today. I know you haven't yet met one another, so allow me to do the honors: Dr. Harold Hopkins, seated to your right, is an astrophysicist; seated in the middle is Dr. Sidney Cantor, theoretical physicist, and on the left, Dr. Jacob Alexandre, theologian. All of you, we know, have been working on problems that seem to have links to the book of Genesis. I can't tell you much about why the U.S. military, and the other government agencies represented here today, would be interested in so seemingly arcane a subject. All I can really tell you is we are, suddenly, right now, intensely interested."

"Maimonides," Jacob said under his breath.

"I beg your pardon, Dr. Alexandre?" the man in uniform said.

"Moses Maimonides," Jacob repeated. "A rabbi and writer of the twelfth century. He said, 'Study astronomy and physics if you desire to comprehend the relation between the world and God's management of it."

"Exactly our thought," the uniformed man said. "If you would, please discuss any ideas you may have on the Genesis story and how it relates to what science tells us about creation. Dr. Hopkins, will you start us off?"

Harold Hopkins cleared his throat. "The first thing you have to realize is the extraordinary chance involved in our existing here at all. If the Big Bang had occurred faster, slower, bigger, smaller, hotter, or colder by the smallest fraction of difference, the universe as we know it and life itself would not exist. It's been calculated that every part of the mix was attuned to one part in ten to the one hundred and twentieth power. The odds of this happening on its own, without an intelligence behind it, are statistically impossible. We are the one in a zillion outcome that God called 'good'."

"And the odds against life establishing itself by chance are almost as great," Dr. Cantor added. "After Stanley Miller's 'primordial soup' experiments of the 1950's proved wrong, the *Scientific American*, in a 1979 retraction, cited Harold Morowitz's book, *Energy Flow and Biology*. He'd computed 'that merely to create a bacterium would require more time than the universe might ever see if chance combinations of its molecules were the only driving force.'"

"Equally amazing," Dr. Hopkins quickly added, "is the knowledge of space-time that is reflected in the six days of creation described in Genesis. Until Einstein spelled it out for us, we thought time was a fixed quantity. The idea that the universe could be created in six days seemed absurd – especially where science was indicating the earth was some four billion years old, and the universe some fourteen billion.

"Then Dr. Gerald Schroeder, a physicist who taught at MIT, reflected on the relation of time and space from God's Big Bang point of view. His math suggested that, given the distortion of time in the Big Bang process, the length of time from the moment of creation to the creation of Adam was the equivalent of Genesis' reference to six days. Of course, from today's point of view, looking back through expanded space/time, the same events happened over roughly fourteen *billion* years. Schroeder called them 'identical realities that have been described in vastly different terms.'"

"Wait a minute," the uniformed man interrupted. "Are you saying there's a scientific point of view that creation actually took place in only six days? How could that be?"

"Look," Hopkins said. "Imagine the moment of the Big Bang, when all matter, space and time, plus several other dimensions, were contained in a speck no bigger than a quark. That's about as far back as our theoretical math can take us. From there we can calculate the expansion and the development of the universe – and it comes out, six days' time from the point of view of the Singularity, fourteen billion years from our vantage point, looking back. This would be almost irrelevant, if it weren't for the fact this ancient text called Genesis was correct, and in multi-dimensional terms that we are just beginning to understand. Now, maybe the theologian can tell us how Genesis could be so accurate on this point?"

Dr. Cantor interrupted, "You know, as recently as 1958, the mid-20th century, a survey conducted by the *Scientific American* showed two-thirds of scientists then believed there *was* no creation – that the universe had always existed. This notion went back to Plato and Aristotle, and yet, remarkably, there was Genesis, describing the creation of everything from nothing, just as we now understand it to have happened. How could this ancient Hebrew story have contained more truth than 3000 years of scientific study? We can blame our errors on the mistakes of Greek philosophy and Ptolemaic science, but that doesn't explain how the Hebrews knew the truth more than a thousand years before the Greeks sent us down the wrong road."

"Finding truth is the goal of both religion and science," Jacob said. "But from the age called the Enlightenment – perhaps even from the early Renaissance – science and the rational have intimidated religion. Once upon a time, mankind took the Bible to be the literal truth. Later on, science became the literal truth, and the Bible became 'mythic.' Now science has matured enough to begin to understand the underlying truths of myth.

"But, of course, this is not the first time people have looked beneath the surface text for some deeper meaning. Maimonides compared the Torah to golden apples in a silver bowl – the superficial reading is beautiful, while a closer look reveals the deeper beauty contained within. Mystics in the Middle Ages, and probably the priests in David's time, 1000 years BCE, were looking at the numerology of the text to see what the numbers mean. For example, the four perfect numbers, 3, 7, 10, and 12, when multiplied together give you 2520. That's also the number you get when you multiply the number of days of the week times the biblical year of 360 days. And I could spend the next hour showing you calculations of years – based on scripture – that demonstrate Ezekiel's prophesy that from the end of the Babylonian captivity to the reestablishment of Israel in 1948 is a period of 2520 bible years. There are dozens of such examples, far greater than coincidence can claim.

"Then there's what is called the 'gematria' of the Torah, the Kabbalistic belief that the numerical values of the Hebrew letters were given to Israel at Mt. Sinai, and that the number values of a word or phrase can be used to prove the internal consistency and meaning of the text. For example, it's been said that in the first words of the Torah, 'In the beginning, God created...', the letters can be divided to read, 'It was created with the head'. An entire book was written to describe all the possible combinations of the letters of the first word of the Torah.

"In fact, mystic Judaism believes that Hebrew letters and words preceded physical reality. Gutman Locks calls them, 'The empirical manifestations of an *a priori* language constituting the inherent spiritual ideas or forms which are at the root of created reality.' Do you remember the opening to John's Gospel – In the beginning was the Word, and the Word was with God, and the Word was God?

"You're probably beginning to realize, like I recently have, that understanding scripture takes place on many levels. To quote the Zohar, 'Woe to the man who says that the Torah merely tells tales of ordinary matters.' It also states, 'The Torah is clothed in garments which relate to this world, because otherwise the world would not be able to contain and absorb it.' And by the way, because the Torah is written without punctuation, it becomes blocks of Hebrew letter/numbers that can be read up or down or sideways or diagonally. To that extent, it's like a giant crossword puzzle that's already filled in. All we have to do is figure out the questions."

The uniformed man interrupted. "Yes, Dr. Alexandre, but before we get into the Bible code thing, I want to hear more about the parallels in the creation story. Dr. Hopkins, what about the details of each day's work during the six days – how does that match up with science?"

Hopkins leaned forward in his chair. "Just remember, big changes in gravity produce time dilation. If you remember that, you shouldn't have a problem. Basically, the force of a gravitational field on any object is inversely proportional to the square of the distance between the objects. Therefore, as we double the distance, the gravitational attraction drops fourfold. Complete that with motion, the other factor in Einstein's general theory, and you can see that time is relatively different for different matter in different locations in the universe.

"Now, the second sentence of Genesis tells us the earth was 'void and waste' – in the Hebrew that's *Tohu* and *Bohu*.

It's appropriate that particle physicists have borrowed the *T* and *B* from those words to label the two foundational building blocks of all matter. Anyway, to quote Schroeder, the 'forces of the Big Bang literally pressed this *T* and *B* into hydrogen and helium – almost no other elements were formed at that time.... it took the alchemy of the cosmos to convert this primordial hydrogen and helium into the rest of the elements.'

"But to answer your question about correlating the six days to science – it seems to work out surprisingly well. Just remember, time relates to gravity, and gravity was reduced dramatically as the Big Bang expanded. God's first day looks to us like the longest – that is, looking backward from our expanded-space point of view – so each 'day' appears *to us* to be half as long as the one before.

"And God said, 'Let there be light.' That's all God did in the first day, and that correlates to the first seven to eight billion years, our time. But remember, 'light' means both particle and wave, and represents the complete spectrum – not just what we see with human eyes. As electrons began to bond with atomic nuclei in this first day, light was released and galaxies began to form.

"Day Two lasted about half as long as Day One, during which the 'firmament' was created. That's the time the Milky Way galaxy, including our sun, coalesced, and the earth was formed.

"Day Three lasted half as long as of Day Two, during which time the dry land and oceans appear, and the first bacteria and plant life, algae, appear. Genetic replication 'after its own kind' begins in Day Three.

"Day Four lasted almost one billion years, during which time oxygen concentrations rose and earth's atmosphere cleared. That's when the sun, moon and heavens became visible from earth.

"Day Five lasted about five hundred million years, bringing us to the Cambrian period. The fossil record demonstrates the fecundity of God's command: 'Let the waters bring forth swarms of living creatures, and let birds fly above the earth....' The Cambrian period was also the basis of Darwin's doubts about his own theory of a gradual evolution. Darwin's theory couldn't account for all the animals appearing at almost the same time, geologically speaking.

"Day Six lasted roughly 250 million years, the day when the Bible indicates Adam was created. Now, here's an interesting problem. About 250 million years ago, science tells us, all life on earth was virtually wiped out by some worldwide, global disaster – most probably volcanos in Siberia. The loss of life was greater even than the Mexico meteor strike of 65 million years ago, when the dinosaurs were destroyed. And the Bible tells us the geologic and biologic conditions at the time of Adam's creation: no bushes, no plants, no farming, no rain. Could this have been the result of this verified major catastrophe? Scripture says it was during this time that the Garden was created and Adam placed in it."

Jacob was jolted by an idea he'd never before considered: "Dr. Hopkins, are you saying Adam, Eve, and Eden were created as much as 250,000,000 years ago?"

"Now you're getting into an area that's more faith than physics," Hopkins said. "But notice how, from Day One on through to Eden, the Bible's perspective takes a closer and closer look at the situation. Schroeder compares it to a zoom lens, beginning with a wide-angle view of the universe on Day One, and zooming closer and closer toward earth. By Day Four you're on the earth, looking up. By Days Five and Six, you've come to mammalian biology, to mankind itself, and then, more specifically, Adam. The events are reported sequentially, but your guess is as good as mine as to when Adam was created."

Dr. Hopkins reached into his briefcase and pulled out a well-worn paperback. "To amplify on that, Dr. Alexandre, let me read you a passage from Schroeder's book, *Genesis and the Big Bang*:

The formation of Adam was qualitatively different from all other events following the creation of the universe. It signaled a monumental change in God's relationship with the universe. We know that all entities of the universe, organic or inorganic, living or inert, are composed of matter, the origin of which can be traced back to the original creation. In this respect, mankind is no different. We are told explicitly that our material origins lie in the "dust of the ground." All animals (Gen. 1:30) including man (Gen. 2:7) were given a soul of life (in Hebrew, the nefesh). *However, Adam alone was given something new, unique in the universe – the living breath of God (Gen. 2:7). It is only at the instant when God places in Adam this breath (in Hebrew, the* neshamah), *that both the created and Creator become inseparably linked. It is at this juncture that one out of billions of possible clocks was irrevocably chosen, by which all future acts would be measured....*

Jacob paused for a moment to consider the idea. It's true the Bible text left open the moment of Adam's creation – and as long as he was under God's protection, Adam could have lived forever. That's why, before the fall, there was no need for Adam or Eve to eat of the tree of life. Meanwhile, who knows what was going on in the outside world, beyond the garden gate? It made sense in light of an idea Maggie had suggested, during one of their discussions, that Adam clearly was not the only man on earth. "Why would God have created a protected place for Adam? What was this 'hedged about' garden guarding him from? Why did Adam and Eve *need* protecting – if not from the other, already corrupted forms of humanity?"

Jacob suddenly realized that the uniformed man was calling for a short recess. The room emptied quickly without the overhead lights coming on, until Jacob and Peter stood alone in the quiet hall.

Chapter 21

"Damn, it's freezing in here," Maggie thought, as she pulled herself to a sitting position on the bed where she had fallen. She dimly remembered staying conscious long enough to throw a Bible through the window, letting the gas escape. "I wonder if they were trying to kill me," she thought, and rubbed her aching head.

Nothing in the room had changed, and in the daylight she could see the totality of the disaster. What had she been thinking, coming in here, since she had seen the place was obviously ransacked. She looked around the floor for Jacob's leather address book, but it seemed to be missing. Last month's phone bill lay open on the floor, and she picked it up. There were several late-night calls to a Stamford number, and she figured it had to be Peter's. She shoved the bill into her pocket, stood up slowly, and headed for the door.

Chapter 22

Jacob and Peter went back to the room, where lunch was waiting for them. "So much for seeing New York," Jacob thought. "Feels like I won't leave this building 'til I'm leaving the city." Peter didn't have much to say about the discussion thus far, but as they got on the elevator to go back up to the hall, Peter quietly asked Jacob to focus on the details of Eden.

The audience was back in their seats when Jacob came through the off-stage door. The table was gone, and so were the physicists. He walked to the lectern.

Jacob, speaking in subdued tones, simply told them what he'd discussed with Maggie – that scripture implied the proposition that civilizations existed concurrent with Adam and Eve and Eden. Adam and Eve were spiritual hothouse flowers, created to learn if matter could be wholly good. It could not, and because it could not, evil entered Eden as it had the rest of the world. Finally, Jacob zeroed in on the vortex of earthly trouble – the tree of the knowledge of good and evil.

"Now, I'm going to talk a lot about duality, because that is the essential nature of creation. It's a simple, logical concept, but you'd be amazed at how people resist it. For there to be good in this world, there has to be evil – by definition. Just as computers run on zeros and ones, just as Eve was divided out of Adam, just as matter is made of *Tohu* and *Bohu,* just as DNA is constructed as a double helix, duality resonates as the essence of our being. It should not be surprising, then, that to the medieval mystics, the spiritual significance of the number two is difference, opposition, and division. And it should not be surprising to us that after Cain murdered Abel, Adam and Eve begot a replacement second child, Seth.

"Turning to theology as well as the Big Bang," Jacob continued, "before the first creation there was unity, there was oneness, and it's to that condition that all of creation strives, to be at one with God. That's one reason the pyramid is such a potent symbol – a huge structure with opposing sides rising to a single point of unity.

"With duality in mind, then, let's look at what happened in Eden. You'll recall Genesis tells us that in the center of the garden stood the tree of the knowledge of good and evil. That was the one tree whose fruit Adam and Eve were forbidden to eat. At the same time, there stood in the center of the garden the tree of life, which was not forbidden to them.

"Now, most translations of the text make little of this apparent locational problem. In chapter two, verse nine, Genesis speaks of 'the tree of life also in the *midst* of the garden, and the tree of the knowledge of good and evil.' Again, in chapter three, verse three, Eve quotes God as saying, 'You shall not eat of the fruit of the tree which is in the *midst* of the garden, neither shall you touch it, lest you die.' And if God said don't touch it, that further confirms a theory of mine, as you'll see in a minute.

"The important thing to remember here is that *both trees are located in the same place.* That's because the locational word in Hebrew is far more precise than 'midst.' 'Midst' connotes somewhere in the general area of the middle, while the Hebrew word, *tavek*, means the 'center,' or 'bisection' of the garden.

"Now this raises an interesting question: How can two trees both stand in the same bisectional point of the garden? And a second question has to be, if both trees stand at the same point, don't they both become forbidden? How could Adam and Eve touch one and not the other? But after they'd sampled one, the other became available to them. You'll recall that after the fall, they were forced to leave the garden to prevent them from eating from the tree of life, which God said would make them live forever. The text tells us:

The Lord God said, "Behold, the man has become like one of us, knowing good and evil; and now, lest he put forth his hand and take also of the tree of life, and eat, and live forever" therefore the Lord God sent him forth from the Garden of Eden...

"The answer to this is not self-evident from the text. There are two ways these two trees could stand in the same spot: One, if they wrap around one another – a double helix, if you will; and Two, if they transcend the three-dimensional world. I have a friend back in Bangor who believes *both* answers are correct. She also believes that by eating of just one tree, Adam and Eve condemned us to our meager, limited existence in just three dimensions. That other, multi-dimensional/spiritual world was lost to the creation." An unusual quiet had settled over the room. Jacob had been a teacher long enough to hear the wheels turning.

"So, what's the solution to this riddle? To the medieval monk, it was simply a matter of accepting our loss as the result of Adam's disobedience. To the 21st century philosopher/physicist, however, the ongoing existence of this site would mean something profound. It would represent" – and here Jacob paused for emphasis – "a fount for the answer to every question, an incredible source of power. For if I'm right, the unity formed of those two trees illumines and overcomes the bonds of our duality. The place of their location would represent an umbilical cord, connecting our world to those dimensions that were lost to us – the double helix of creation linking heaven and earth."

Chapter 23

Maggie was feeling a little better by the time she got home. Walking those three blocks in the cold, sunny air cleared her lungs and cleared her head. As a result, she was doubly furious as she came through the door.

First of all, she was furious with Jacob for leaving her with this incredible mess and no answers at all. The message he left on her machine did nothing to calm her; in fact, it made things worse. "I have to talk to you right away," he'd said, and then never called back, even to leave another message with a number she could call.

Second, she was furious for being used so easily by those so-called cops. She was sure they had lied to her about who they were, and they were probably the ones responsible for destroying Jacob's apartment, and nearly killing her.

And she'd missed her classes – all of them – and Jacob's classes, too. She could be fired for that, and Jacob could lose his job, as well. It was all a complete mess.

The first call she made was to the dean's office, to try to explain what had happened. It was not yet four p.m., and she expected someone to pick up the phone. After a while, someone did. It was Alice Blake, the school president, and she sounded polite, but distant.

"Don't worry about anything, Maggie," she said. "It's all taken care of." Maggie felt a chill creep down her spine.

"What do you mean, Alice, by taken care of?" she asked. "I missed all my classes and Jacob's, as well! Who covered for me, and how did they know I wouldn't be there?"

"We were given plenty of notice, and everyone pitched in. Don't concern yourself. We'll expect to see you soon." And Alice Blake hung up.

The next call was even more frustrating. Maggie phoned the police to report the break-in at Jacob's apartment, as well as the two plain-clothes impersonators who had asked her those questions about Jacob.

The cop on the desk was not sympathetic. "We already went to that building and checked it out," he told Maggie. "Apparently the guy who lives there had a fit and tore the place apart. I don't know about anyone impersonating cops, but if they turn up again, give us a call."

Finally, she tried calling the number in Stamford and got Peter's wife on the phone. No, he wasn't there, she was told. "Who did you say you were again? Does my husband know you? Yes, of course I know Jacob, but he's in Maine, as far as I know. Yes, I'll give my husband the message. Good bye."

It was too early to start drinking, but Maggie poured herself a glass of wine anyway. Then she sat down at the kitchen table, put her head in her hands, and burst into tears.

Chapter 24

"I've heard enough. Put the damn lights on," said an authoritative voice from the back of the room. It startled Jacob, who had paused a moment to figure out what to say next.

When the lights came up, Jacob could see that half his audience was uniformed military personnel, complete with decorations. The rest of them wore suits, and looked like the dark-glasses guys who walk behind the president. One of the military men – a general, by the look of his uniform and bearing – came to the lectern and offered his hand to Jacob.

"I'm Lou Morris," he said. "I want to thank you for coming down on such short notice. Maine is one of my favorite places," he said, almost as an afterthought. "Now that you're here, we'd like to keep you a few more days. We're holding a briefing at 0700 hours tomorrow – right here in the building, so it should be easy for you."

"But it's *not* easy for me," Jacob blurted out. "I'm supposed to be teaching classes in Bangor right now, and a good friend of mine will probably kill me if I don't get back by tomorrow morning."

"That's your friend Maggie?" the general asked. "Don't worry about it. We've taken care of everything. See you tomorrow," General Morris said, walking away. The rest of the audience followed him out of the room.

Peter, of course, was more sympathetic. "Why don't we get something to eat," he said, taking Jacob's arm. "It's time to get out of here and spend some time in the big city."

"Peter knows how to push my buttons," Jacob thought, but didn't say no. He had to admit the last thing he wanted to do right then was catch the flight to Bangor, even though that was the only way he'd ever get back in time for tomorrow's classes.

Chapter 25

Jacob and Peter were sitting at a hole-in-the-wall jazz bar just a few blocks from the apartment. They'd debated going to a restaurant, but opted for a sandwich and bourbon instead. Peter seemed pleased with himself, as if luring Jacob to the city had been some sort of personal coup.

"Well, you seem to have made the first cut," he said smugly. "By tomorrow we'll know if you're on the team, and what the next move will be."

It bothered Jacob to see his friend drinking so much. Peter had never handled his liquor well, but he'd known his limits and controlled the pace of consumption. Jacob had noticed last night that Peter didn't do that anymore, and the way he was talking now seemed dangerous, though Jacob couldn't say why. The whole thing seemed so bizarre, anyway. Giving his talk to a dark room, and then learning the audience had come from a military base to some agency-owned building in New York City to listen to a lecture on Eden? What was *that* about?

"Peter, I should get back to the room and give Maggie a call. It's all very well for General what's-his-face to say that everything's taken care of, but quite another to appease Maggie when she's feeling used. Secret meetings or not, she deserves an explanation."

"Can't let you do that, old boy," Peter said with a smile. "The problem is, my cell and the apartment phone are monitored, so you wouldn't have any privacy anyway. What fun would that be?" Peter spoke as if he knew.

"So, I'll call her from here, from the payphone," Jacob said, standing up. "And don't try to stop me. I could always whip your butt." He smiled, knowing Peter wouldn't try.

Jacob turned the corner to the men's room, where he'd seen an antique payphone hanging on the wall. He dialed the number, and fed in some coins. Maggie's phone rang once, twice, three times. By the tenth ring he started to worry. Now even her answering machine wasn't coming on, and that made no sense at all.

But what was even stranger – when he got back to the table, Peter had disappeared.

Chapter 26   Turin, Italy

It was early morning in the city of Turin as Jack and Philip walked toward each other on the central via 22 Settembre, both on their way to the same small office not far from the Cathedral of St. John the Baptist. Their move to this nondescript building from a secret location in the cathedral itself had been necessitated by a fire, some twenty years before, which damaged the Chapel of the Shroud, home to the most sacred object of veneration in the tradition of the Knights Templar. Now known as the Shroud of Turin, the cloth still held them in its sway, so the thought of abandoning a Turin location altogether was never even considered.

The linen cloth, some fourteen feet long by more than three feet wide, was undeniably the burial cloth of Jesus described in the Bible. His image at the moment of resurrection was burned into the cloth as a three-dimensional portrait of unimaginable suffering, with thorn wounds to the head, more than a hundred, weighted lashes to the back, crucifixion spike wounds in the wrists and feet, and a stab wound to the side. After the disciples found the cloth laid aside in the tomb, it made its way first, it seems, from Jerusalem to Edessa – perhaps as early as 32 AD, to heal the ailing King Abgar V. From there it travelled to Constantinople, where, before the sacking of the Eastern Church by the crusaders, it was on display, around the year 1200, for faithful prayers every Friday in My Lady of St. Mary of Blachernae Church – this according to the diary of a knight, Robert de Clari, who saw it there. There is some evidence that in 1201 the cloth was taken to Athens, before traveling, in the possession of the Knights Templar, to a Templar stronghold in France.

The shroud became *the* object of worship for the Templars, who were said to kiss the feet of the image, and pray to the head. When the Templars were reduced to ruin by the pope and the French king on October 13, 1307, the cloth's ownership went through several hands before ending up, finally, in the Turin cathedral. The Templar veneration continues there, in secret, even to this day.

Public interest in the shroud, however, did not really take off until the growing uses of photography led, in 1898, to photographer Secondo Pia discovering the faint image on the cloth was, in fact, a negative. The positive image he produced with his camera captivated the faith of Christians throughout the world. Clearly, it was a photo of Christ at the moment of his resurrection, a verification of belief for any remaining doubting Thomases. It was easy for the faithful to imagine the moment of resurrection replicating Matthew's description of the transfiguration, when "his face shone like the sun, and his clothes became white as light."

Such declarations of faith brought out the doubting scientists in droves, however. As a result, the shroud became the most studied object on the planet. First, early claims the image was produced by artful pigments, paints, dyes, or stains was proven false. Blood stains tested out to be type AB, human. Moreover, the blood had stained the cloth before the body's image was created, presumably three days later. The fabric was found to have picked up pollen samples from Jerusalem, Edessa and Constantinople. In 1976, the Shroud of Turin Research Project, consisting of Dr. John Jackson and forty scientists, studied every aspect of the fabric and the forensics. It was discovered 3D information was encoded in the shroud. In 1988, the British Museum arranged for labs in Zurich, Tucson and Oxford to do carbon-dating tests. The results reported the cloth dated from the Middle Ages, but later evidence that the samples were mistakenly taken from an area of the cloth *repaired* during the Middle Ages muddied the results. Then a clue to the creation of the image was discovered. In 2011, a 40-nanosecond flash from a vacuum ultraviolet photon laser, with a blast of 30,000 watts at a billionth of a second pulse, seemed to replicate the possible physics of the image that was created on that linen cloth. Finally, new tests run by Padua University in 2013 dated it to the time of Christ.

"Good morning, Jack," Philip said, as he stubbed out a cigarette on the ground and followed him through the door. A handicapped-access elevator to the upper stories had recently been installed, but a second key on Jack's ring sent the elevator in another direction, almost twenty feet underground.

They stepped out into a small office. Phones, recording equipment and computers sat on two metal desks; the rest of the narrow space was taken up with an oak conference table, twelve leather chairs, and a green-shaded banker's lamp at each position. Jack turned on the overhead light, and sat down at a desk.

Almost immediately the phone rang. Jack let it ring again, then picked up. Philip noticed the red light on the recorder come on. "Yes," Jack said. "I understand. It will be difficult but not impossible; we will have everyone together in time. Yes, no problem."

He hung up the phone and turned to Philip. "They want a meeting of the Garden Club tonight at midnight. Everyone should be at Rosslyn Chapel. Apparently, it's begun."

Chapter 27

Jacob waited a half hour for Peter before heading back to the building. Fortunately, he had his own key, and the doorman recognized him from the day before. He took the elevator to the 30th floor and walked down the hall to the apartment. For some reason it didn't surprise him that Peter wasn't there, but he stayed awake until nearly two before turning in. He knew he was expected to be at a meeting at seven, but was he supposed to go alone? He'd been leaning on Peter to guide him through this maze, and he resolved not to make that mistake again.

Jacob slept fitfully, and was up way before dawn. He showered, dressed and waited to see if anyone would call. He'd already decided that if nothing happened by half past seven, he'd board the first train for Boston and get his tail back home. Enough was enough.

At five minutes to seven there was a knock on the door. Two men in uniform, one with a scar on his lip, told Jacob to follow them to the elevator.

The meeting had started by the time they reached the room – the same room where he'd been lecturing the day before. This time, however, the lights were on, and a large conference table had replaced the lectern. A lot of military types were there again, and General Morris seemed to be in charge.

"Come in, Dr. Alexandre, sit down," Morris said. "We've just started." Jacob looked around at the dirty cups, and supposed they'd been there for an hour, at least. He wondered if they'd been talking about Eden all that time.

An army captain poured Jacob some coffee, and handed him a short transcript of what appeared to be conversation between some pilots and a tower. "Take a minute to look at this, and tell us what you think," the general said. Jacob noticed the names had been redacted and replaced with numbers in the document. The room fell silent as Jacob scanned the page:

Pilot 1: Missile one away and tracking... she'll tell us if there's anyone under that dune... whoa, what was that?

Control: We've lost satellite contact, and the camera cut out way before the hit. What's happening?

Pilot 1: I'm not sure, control. Detonation, but there's no trace of damage – it didn't make a dent. For a second, I thought I saw a shadow, a structure or something, but there's nothing there now.

Pilot 2: I saw the same thing, control. Do you want us to hit it again?

Control: It's your call.

Pilot 1: If there's something there, it's damn tough. I don't see a hole in that dune. Let's hit it from both sides and see what happens.

Pilot 2: Acknowledged. Go for it.

Pilot 1: One away.

Pilot 2: Two away.

Pilot 1: My God, it's...

Control: Control to Pilot 1, Control to Pilot 2, do either of you guys read me? You're off our screen altogether. Do you read me....

Pilot 3: Control, this is Pilot 3. What happened to 1 and 2? I had eyes on both of them, and they just disappeared. And their missiles – both detonated, almost on top of each other, didn't scratch that dune. But there was a shimmer or something, looked like a mirage of something, but I couldn't tell you what.

Control: Pilot 3, return to base. Do you read? Return to base.

Pilot 3: Acknowledged. Returning to base.

Jacob looked up, and realized that everyone at the table was staring at him. "I don't know what to make of it," he said. "There's not enough here to tell much of anything, unless you believe in UFOs."

The general shifted uncomfortably in his chair. "This is no UFO – at least, I don't think so. It was something on the ground, and when the missiles struck, there was some form of equal and opposite reaction that took out two of our planes. But what we really want from you is an educated guess as to what might be sitting there in the Iraqi desert that's normally invisible to radar, infrared, and the human eye – and apparently can't be touched, when we *can* see it, by three direct hits. This encounter took place when we were hunting Saddam Hussein, and we had already tried blowing it open from the ground. When that failed, we tried the missiles. After we lost those planes, the dune vanished – until now. Could this be Genesis-text related, and if it is, why has it suddenly returned?"

Chapter 28   In Transit

Jacob boarded a military jet in New Jersey and settled into his seat. In the time it took to persuade him to go on this adventure, they had made travel arrangements, got him his passport, administered certain painful shots, and helicoptered him to this flight to London. He would be met at Gatwick, they said, and transported by helicopter to a meeting of something called the Garden Club.

"Why do I need shots?" They wouldn't say. "How did you get my passport?" Again, they wouldn't say. "Can I call Maggie?" No – everything at the school was taken care of. And they couldn't or wouldn't tell him anything about Peter, either. If he weren't so intrigued by the Eden thing, he'd have told them all to go to hell.

As the jet got airborne, Jacob thought again about the general's strange explanation. It seems they'd explored the site on the ground following the missile strike, but nothing further was done about it at the time.

But why, Jacob wondered, was he being sent to England? That was really the mystery, as far as he was concerned. Yes, he realized he was meeting with a group who called themselves the Garden Club, but there were lots of nutty groups in England who operated without a clue. Why should these guys be any different?

The engine drone was bearable, and Jacob remembered how little sleep he'd had over the last 48 hours. And now, it seemed, he was crossing time zones to get to a meeting with gardeners? All in all, it made good sense to slip into a deep sleep, and that's what he did.

Chapter 29   Roslin, Scotland

They were already on the ground when the pilot shook Jacob awake. Outside, a helicopter was standing by. Jacob instinctively ducked under the rotating blades and climbed aboard. There was still no one to tell him what the plan was, or even where they were going. He assumed it was to some big hotel in London, so he was surprised to find himself flying over the English countryside. It was past eleven, Greenwich time, and there were few lights on in the cottages below.

They landed in the dark in what appeared to be a grassy field. From the helicopter's landing lights, Jacob could see they'd set down near an elaborate stone church. A man carrying a folded umbrella was standing by, and helped Jacob step down to the rutted pasture. Jacob could hear the bleating of sheep from somewhere nearby.

"Welcome to Scotland, Dr. Alexandre," the man with the umbrella said. "My name is Jack."

"Scotland?" Jacob said in a surprised tone, feeling suddenly disoriented. "I thought I was somewhere outside London."

"Actually, we're in Roslin, near Edinburgh. You'll find everything here is on a need to know basis," Jack said pleasantly. "And since I'm still waiting for some of the other Gardeners to get here, I thought you might like to go on inside and look around Rosslyn Chapel."

"*The* Rosslyn Chapel? The Templars' chapel?" Jacob heard himself say, and felt foolish for sounding so reverent.

"Rosslyn spelled the old way – the Sinclair's chapel, actually," Jack said. "The estate's been in the Sinclair, or St. Clair, family since the Norman Conquest. But yes, you're right, of course, to call it Templar. You'll know that as soon as you step inside, I imagine. See you in a few minutes." Jack preceded him inside, and disappeared.

Jacob felt new energy surge up his spine. Since his first explorations into Templar history, Jacob held Rosslyn Chapel as one of his personal seven wonders of the world – one he'd been sure he would visit someday. He just hadn't expected it to be today.

Standing there alone in the dark, Jacob strained to see the ornate exterior of the building, and to remember the details of its history. It was to Scotland that the surviving Knights of the Order of the Temple of Solomon, known simply as the Templars, had retreated in 1314, after they were nearly wiped out by the greed and treachery of King Philip IV of France, who wanted their money to fight the Flemish war.

Until their fall, the Templars had been honored and feared for almost two centuries. The order had formed during the crusades in 1118, when Hugh de Payens and eight other knights joined together to protect pilgrims on the road to Jerusalem. The Templars took their name from the fact they had occupied the Temple Mount in Jerusalem, and legend had it their immense wealth had come from their discovery of the treasure of Solomon's Temple, which they'd uncovered by tunneling into the site of Solomon's stables below the mount. Bernard of Clairvaux drew up the rules of the order, and by 1128 they were confirmed by Pope Honorius III.

Pilgrims of the time took the Al-Aqsa Mosque to be the historic Temple of Solomon, even though Muslims believed it was where, around 621, Mohammad flew from Mecca on his NDE-like famous Night Journey. The Templars took the Dome of the Rock, a Moslem shrine, to be a fitting church for their ostensibly Christian order. The rock housed within the Dome was sacred to many faiths, of course, being thought to be the rock where Abraham offered to sacrifice his son, Isaac. It was on this rock that Hugh de Payens and his fellow knights swore the founding oath of the Templars, and it was the Islamic octagonal design of the building that became part of their sacred geometry. It was intended by William St. Clair that the octagon within a circle design would become the plan for Rosslyn Chapel, though that plan was never accomplished.

Whether it was the temple treasure or simply the many gifts of lands and money they received from their wealthy initiates, the Templars grew to be one of the most powerful organizations in Europe. Since they were accountable only to the pope, their military strength, enormous wealth, and freedom from secular authority made them the chief money handlers, and they soon became a powerful force in banking, and the owners of vast tracts of land. Such wealth and power were bound to create jealousies, and King Philip, with the help of Pope Clement V, finally succeeded in having the members arrested, tortured, and their property confiscated. The leaders of the order, including Grand Master Jacques de Molay, were tried by ecclesiastic judges and burned at the stake. Legend says that as he was dying, de Molay cursed both the pope and the king, and both of them died within the year. Not all of the Templars were captured, however; some escaped, and were said to have brought their remaining treasure – including, some say, the Holy Grail – to Rosslyn.

Jacob entered the chapel, but paused in the doorway. Someone had gone to the trouble of lighting hundreds of candles, and the flickering light danced on the most incredibly intricate stone menagerie Jacob had ever seen. It was madness set in stone, with geometric designs vying with faces, flowers, religious symbols, snakes and crosses, while angels and devils danced between the shadows and the light.

But in all this riot of stone, Jacob's eyes were drawn to one column of a most intricate design. Set on a raised stage, it's vertical fluting was wrapped in beautiful carved stone vines spiraling upward into the treelike crown. And as Jacob stared at it, transfixed, Maggie stepped out from behind the column.

"Hello, Jacob," she said coyly. "Welcome to the Garden of Eden."

Chapter 30

Jacob stood frozen, his mouth open, not saying a word. Maggie walked toward him, smiling. She knew it was cruel to surprise him like this, but he had a lot to answer for.

In fact, she'd had revenge in mind since the moment she agreed with Peter to come to Scotland. "Look, what would you prefer?" Peter had asked her. "Either you go into protective custody in Bangor, Maine, or you meet Jacob in Scotland." Peter had contacts with the seminary, he told Maggie, and through the school he'd heard about the phony cops. Something was wrong, and he wasn't yet sure what it was. In any event, he wanted her out of there for now.

It was only after they'd talked on the phone that Peter began to think he could make use of her training. Her background included extensive studies in archaeology and comparative mythology at the University of Chicago, and some ancient language studies, as well. If truth be told, she'd given Jacob some of his more provocative theories on the meaning of Eden and the trees. Now it was payback time.

"Maggie, I'm so glad to see you, you don't know..." Jacob finally managed to stammer. "Are we both fired now? What's happened to our classes?"

"It's all right, don't worry," Maggie said. She'd known as soon as she saw him come through the door that she couldn't give him a hard time for more than a minute. "Peter has taken care of everything. Apparently, he works for an agency that keeps on hand the biggest bank of substitute teachers in the country."

"Substitute teachers for a seminary? What are you talking about?" Jacob said.

"No, really," Maggie insisted. "I guess they use teachers as spies all the time. Peter says teachers can usually get into politically sensitive areas through their university connections. When they need a specialist, they bring in a substitute to keep the classes going. The schools get paid very well for this arrangement, so they don't mind a bit. In fact, it may even help my tenure track to be on this list. It's like having a chair endowed for us by Uncle Sam."

Jacob looked at her and shook his head. "I still don't know what they expect me to do," he said with frustration. "Maybe you can tell me."

"Let me tell you about this place first," Maggie said. "Ever since I got here, I've spent every waking minute in this chapel. Isn't it incredible? First of all, consider the head of the Green Man, a pagan fertility symbol, possibly Celtic – it appears in here again and again." Maggie pointed out several leering heads, carved from stone. Jacob could see in the flickering candlelight that vines grew out of the Green Man's mouth, and sometimes out of his ears, to spread wildly over the walls. "It seems the Celts believed the head contained the soul, that it promoted fertility and should be preserved. Of course, the Templars were accused by the Inquisition of worshiping heads. Church officials charged they kept a woman's head – Mary Magdalene's, perhaps? – in a silver reliquary, because Templars believed adoration of the head would make the trees bloom and the land germinate. Later explanations for head worship argued the Templars possessed the Shroud of Turin, which was usually kept folded so that only the head of Jesus could be seen.

"And there's another story I've heard about the Green Man symbol. It was said some escaped Templars disguised themselves as gypsies, and for that reason, the Sinclair family protected the gypsies against persecution by the government. In exchange, the gypsies would come to Rosslyn Castle in the spring and perform fertility rites during the month of May, and at the summer solstice. This, coupled with the gypsy belief in second sight, formed the basis for some of the early Freemason practices that grew out of the Templars. That connecting link gets made right here.

"The gypsies were a later phenomenon, too, about the time of Shakespeare. But earlier, it's said, the Green Man corresponded to the serpent in wisdom, fertility. There are at least seventy Green Men in here, and I'd bet every one of them has something unique and meaningful growing out of, or going into, that Bacchus mouth."

Maggie fell silent as they slowly walked around the perimeter of the chapel. Every wall and arch were richly carved with herbs and flowers, snakes and vines, the ceiling covered with roses, and everywhere the faces of the Green Man peered down through the carved stone foliage. It seemed natural for them to be holding hands. The light from the candles flickered on the leaves and vines and faces as they walked by, as if, just by being there, they were animating this garden of stone.

When they'd come full circle, they stopped in front of the strangely ornate column Maggie had hidden behind. "Now, here's a story you'll be interested in," Maggie said. "It's quite incredible, really."

Jacob studied the column carefully, from the bottom up. Eight eight-sided snakes, with their tails in their mouths, surrounded the trunk of this stone tree as it climbed to support the roof above. The symbolism was gnostic, Templar really, but it reminded Jacob of the Norse legend of Yggdrasil, the sacred tree that keeps the heavens from the earth.

"It's called the Apprentice Pillar, named for the apprentice who built it while his master was away," Maggie said at last.

"The story goes there was a column of this design in Rome, and the master mason decided that before he could undertake to copy it, he would have to make the journey to see the original for himself. While he was away, his apprentice carved what you see here. The master returned and was enraged, overcome with jealousy when he saw the beautifully wrought column. In his anger he raised his hammer, struck the apprentice on the head and killed him.

"And there they are," Maggie said, pointing at two stone faces, carved to oppose one another from either side of the room. "The face of the apprentice with his fatal wound, and the face of the murdering master mason, staring at one another through the centuries."

Jacob eyed the column with growing interest. Beyond being a lovely support pillar, there seemed to be something mythic about it. He recalled a rabbinic legend about the building of Solomon's Temple, that the work was accomplished not with iron tools, but by employing the Shamir, a serpent worm whose magic touch could carve and shape stone.

Hiram, who was architect of the Temple of Solomon, was also martyred by a blow to the head – perhaps for not revealing the secrets of the Shamir.

"Just look at this thing," Jacob said with growing wonder. "This gets at what I was trying to describe to those military guys in New York – a single column of two trees grown in the same place – the tree of life and the tree of knowledge. See how those vines climb the central shaft. Don't they remind you of the double helix structure of DNA? And look at the force contained in that central shaft! The fluting shows the energy passing up and down, from the serpents at its base to the heavens above. It keeps heaven from earth, thereby maintaining the inherent duality of creation – what Genesis describes as the knowledge of good and evil."

"There's another Templar legend about this column," Maggie said after a while. "It's said the column was built to house the Holy Grail, that the Grail might be in there today."

"Well, the Grail in medieval symbolism pours out the energy of God's creation," Jacob mused. "That would fit the imagery. Has anyone tried looking inside there?"

"I think it's been x-rayed," Maggie said, "But no one has reported seeing anything, as far as I know. Anyway, it would be like stripping off a Rembrandt to see if there's a painting on the canvas underneath, digging into that beautiful column. You could wind up losing everything in the process."

"Not seeing it on an x-ray doesn't mean it's not there," Jacob said. "Especially if it turns out to be a fragment of stone instead of some fancy, golden cup. And then there's the question of dimensionality...." he said, trailing off. He wasn't sure how Maggie would take to hearing him spout some of his new-found, wilder theories – especially since some had come from her. It seemed to matter to him, suddenly, what she thought of his ideas.

Maggie smiled at him and purposely didn't pursue the point. She felt good, standing there dumbly holding hands and wanting to hang a "do not disturb" sign on her feelings. She knew the moment couldn't last.

"There's another interesting fact about the Roslin area," Maggie said, breaking the silence.

"Do you remember the first sheep they successfully cloned – the sheep named Dolly? It made the cover of *Time Magazine*, and talk show hosts made jokes about it. One of them, Leno or Letterman, I think, said it wasn't hard to believe in cloning, just hard to believe there were scientists in Scotland! Well, Dolly was cloned by the Roslin Institute. How's that for coincidence?"

Chapter 31   Iraq

It was past dawn in the Iraqi desert, but the air was still surprisingly cold. The Followers of Paul had left the shelter of their tents, however, and had assembled by the Phoenix Door once again. Just a half hour before, the man on watch had sounded a horn, to wake and to warn them that something was happening behind the door. It seemed the time had arrived.

They could all hear it now, a grating, ominous sound, like iron wheels of a machine that hadn't worked for a thousand years. Some were afraid, and wondered to themselves what had possessed them to make such a difficult journey, only to face the possibility of a perilous end. Others prayed out loud, confident their faith would protect them from the wickedness of the beast. But the rest, the majority, dreamed of the untold knowledge which, legend said, lay within. Whatever was hidden beneath the Phoenix Door would soon be revealed to them.

Chapter 32

They didn't hear Jack enter the sanctuary, and Maggie and Jacob both jumped at the sound of his voice. "We're ready for you now," Jack said. "We're meeting downstairs in the crypt. Follow me."

The three walked down a flight of stone steps to the large, vaulted basement room below. Jacob was surprised to see a dozen men seated around a circular table, with an octagon inscribed on its surface. There was no door to the stairs, and Jacob realized the men had been sitting there in quiet discussion since he'd entered the chapel – possibly they'd overheard the echo of everything Jacob and Maggie had said to each other, though they didn't seem particularly interested to see them. There were four empty chairs at the table, and Jack indicated they should sit down.

A minute later, a fellow in British military uniform came down the stairs. His bearing indicated he was someone who was used to being in charge; tonight, however, it seemed he was here to conduct a briefing for officials who outranked him. "These guys hardly look like gardeners," Jacob wanted to whisper to Maggie, but didn't.

"I'm General George Collins, gentlemen, Miss, and let me say right off that it's a great honor for me to be here tonight." Everyone remained silent, so he continued.

"As most of you know," he said, looking at Maggie as if this would be news only to her, "there has been some unusual activity in Iraq recently that has created quite a stir in certain circles. During the Iraq wars, we received unusual reports, backed up by video and satellite photography, of some sort of energy anomaly that protects what appears to be a spot of empty desert.

"This was confirmed during the search for Saddam Hussein, who was reported to be hiding in some sort of underground location. We couldn't break in on the ground, so we targeted the spot to learn what a direct hit would accomplish. The answer was, nothing – at least nothing short of dropping a nuclear bomb.

"The worry, of course, was that Hussein had developed some sort of force field that was impervious to direct missile attack. In fact, we had three direct hits that didn't even part the sand. Further analysis, though, confirmed what most of us thought from the beginning – that this kind of technology is generations away from development. In short, our analysis concluded this was not anything that was built on earth.

"Now I don't know what you may know about UFOs, but it's probably more than I do. Obviously, this was going to be our next line of pursuit, and the plan was formulated to send in the regular UFO specialty team of scientists, communications experts, and a unit of special forces under joint US/British command. They would land under cover of darkness, and to that end we were prepared to stage another missile run. But it seems we ran out of time."

"Ran out of time?" Jacob asked.

"Whatever it was, we lost track of it. Suddenly there was nothing there we could detect. The UFO guys thought it might have been a ship that repaired some possible damage and then flew away, but the rest of us weren't so sure. To be honest, W's Iraq war was not only *not* about 9/11 – it wasn't all about the oil, either. We really wanted to learn more about this anomaly, but for all the time we were there, we couldn't find a thing. It wasn't until recently that something new started showing up on US satellite photos. It seems our anomaly has returned."

The general paused for a moment and opened an attaché case he'd brought with him. Jacob detected a subtle electricity at the table, as if General Collins was finally getting to the good part – what the others hadn't yet heard.

"The photos I'm about to pass around are classified Top Secret, and I know you all will respect this confidence." He looked at Jacob and Maggie as he was saying this. "You'll notice the first set was digitally reproduced from the video, then enhanced to show a kind of 'shadow' that both pilots reported seeing from the air."

The photos were passed from hand to hand, still in silence. When they reached Jacob, he glanced at them, then did a double-take. There was a geometric shape that seemed almost imposed onto the photograph, like one of those stereogram, or perhaps Droste-effect pictures that show a different image when you change your point of view.

More than that, though, the shape reminded Jacob of something he'd once seen in a book on the Kabbalah.

Jacob rejected the idea and looked at the photo again. The Kabbalah, after all, was primarily Jewish mysticism from the Middle Ages. And it was symbolic, not to be taken literally. No, the circular emanations that showed in the photo were probably the radiated energy from the exploding missiles; they seemed to flow in ripples, like waves from a stone tossed into a pond. These circles within circles were huge, of course, since missiles pack quite a wallop. But that being the case, why didn't they do any damage? Jacob told the group, "It looks to me like you staged a cross-dimensional attack, and the opposing dimension merely returned the insult."

For the first time since the start of the meeting, one of the twelve sat forward in his chair. He was a man in his late sixties, Jacob guessed, with a graying beard and wearing what must have been a very expensive suit. "Have you consulted the Sefer Yetsirah, General?" the man asked.

"I'm embarrassed to say I don't know what that is, sir," the General replied.

"The Sefer Yetsirah, the Kabbalic book of creation. It surfaced in Provence in the 12th century, but its roots are far older than that – back to Babylon, some believe. Templars returning from the crusades were responsible for its gaining a foothold in France, though they had to be careful, since it flew in the face of Catholicism. In any event, this looks like the manifestation described in the 'Treatise on Emanation' of the four worlds contained within En-Sof. The vibration and power of the rings decrease toward the center, because the outer rings control the inner. Because that's the reverse of how explosions work, it may be canceling out your missiles. I know it's an ancient idea, but they knew more back then than you'd think. Check it out."

Jacob felt pleased with himself. His hunch about Kabbalah might have been right, after all. While General Collins paused to consider the reference, Jacob tried to remember what little he knew about the En-Sof. Maggie felt the General's discomfort, and beat Jacob to it.

"According to speculative Kabbalah," Maggie said quietly to the room, "God manifested four worlds on four separate planes simultaneously." From the shuffling that ensued from the Gardeners, Jacob guessed that a woman speaking out at their meeting might have broken a tradition as old as the church they were sitting in.

Maggie continued, "In the first world, God manifests the archetypes for all of creation. In this first world, God unites with the Shekhinah, his female counterpart and the mother of the three other worlds. The second world houses the purest of spirits and the highest of angels. The third world encompasses formation, and is home to ten hosts of angels led by the angel Metatron, a transformation of the man Enoch. And the lowly fourth world, our world, is our present world of matter, evil, and human existence. Interestingly though, it's this world to which the Shekhinah has been exiled. It's why I've always thought of Christ more as a mother figure, I guess...." Maggie trailed off, having suddenly realized she was not teaching one of her classes.

The General had by now regrouped, sensing the meeting was about to be usurped by a flood of information he didn't understand. "I don't know about any of that," he said, "but I have some more photos to show you. These were taken this morning," he added, passing them around.

Jacob could see these were photos of the same desert site, but with no overlay of emanations or distortions. Instead, there was a large line of camel riders moving methodically toward the spot, while others had already arrived and set up tents around the dune. It looked like a caravan of Bedouins had assembled, but why there?

No one commented, so General Collins reached into his attaché case again. "And these photos were taken a few hours ago," he said.

Jacob stared at the pictures for a full minute before he caught on. Yes, there were the tents, perhaps more than fifty, but it looked as though they'd been blown flat from a sudden wind. And while some camels were tethered, most of the others were wandering away. The problem was there was no one there, not in either the detailed close-ups or the wide-angle shots that covered almost seventy square miles. It seemed as if a tribe of perhaps a hundred people had disappeared off the face of the earth.

Chapter 33

General Collins was packing up his photographs, making it clear to Jacob and Maggie that his part in the briefing was over. Jack leaned across the table and said quietly that it was time for them to leave, as well.

"I've made arrangements at a little guesthouse where Maggie stayed last night," he said. "They have a room ready for you, too, Jacob. You must be tired."

As they stood up to leave, the man who had mentioned the Sefer Yetsirah turned in his seat and touched Maggie's hand. "You should know, my dear," he said to her with the faintest of smiles, "that Dolly being cloned by Roslin Institute was no coincidence. In fact, several such sheep were brought into this very chapel."

"Why?" Maggie wanted to ask, but Jack was already guiding them up the stairs, out of the crypt. The twelve remained at the table, however, and Jacob suspected their meeting had only just begun.

When they got outside, the General was already driving away. "Damn," Jacob said, "I wanted to ask him some questions about that energy pattern in those photos – whether they had enhanced the image in any way, and what the scientific opinion was. I can't believe he came all this way just to hear about medieval Jewish mysticism."

"He didn't come to get answers," Jack responded. "He was a messenger boy to the twelve, bringing them an update they needed to hear." Jacob and Maggie got into the back of Jack's gray Rover sedan, and he started the engine.

"Who are those people," Jacob asked, " and why were Maggie and I invited to the séance?"

"Since they chose not to introduce themselves to you, I can't really tell you their names. Suffice it to say they are brainstorming the situation in Iraq – and when those twelve take the time to brainstorm something, it's usually damned important.

"As to why you two were included – well, we'll know more about it by morning," Jack said, pulling up to the front door of the guesthouse. "Maggie can show you to your room – it's just past hers, down the hall. I'm sure the owners have been asleep for hours, so please be quiet going in. See you about nine o'clock," Jack said, and drove off into the night.

Maggie and Jacob let themselves in quietly, and tiptoed up a flight of creaky stairs. "Can you talk," Maggie asked, when they reached her door, "or are you too tired to bother?"

"I'm fine," Jacob said. "I slept like a stone on the plane. Anyway, I think it's time we compared notes."

They went into Maggie's room and closed the door. The guesthouse appeared to be quite old, 1700's, Jacob guessed, with whitewashed plaster between the gnarled posts and beams of blackened oak. Small pictures of flower gardens hung on the walls, with flowered curtains on the windows and a flowered comforter on the high, four-poster bed.

Maggie took off her coat and sat on the edge of the bed, while Jacob sat in the room's large Victorian chair. "What did you think of that meeting?" Jacob asked. "Are you thinking what I'm thinking about who those twelve guys might be?"

"It's hard to believe there are still Templars around with any credibility," Maggie said, picking up on Jacob's train of thought. "The closest thing to the original group would be the Freemasons, I guess, and I always thought they were just another men's fraternity – you know, a clubhouse with its own secret handshakes, a bar, and no wives allowed at meetings."

"There are different orders and levels, though," Jacob said. "My grandfather was a thirty-something degree Scottish Rite Mason, whatever that is. I do know they helped conduct his funeral when he died."

"What was his name?" Maggie asked suddenly.

"William Orrok," Jacob replied, somewhat surprised at the question. "He was my mother's father. Why do you ask?" He noticed Maggie's eyes had a sudden light in them he hadn't seen before.

"I keep wondering why you're so important to these people that you've been brought all this way, and given this much information. Look, there's something I haven't told you yet – about why I'm here." Maggie paused for a second, trying to choose her words carefully. She didn't want to frighten him.

"The day you left for New York, two guys came to my apartment asking questions about you. They said they were agents of some sort, and even flashed a badge, but the kinds of questions they were asking.... Anyway, I told them to get out, and later I called the Bangor police. It was weird – the police were no help at all." In her mind she was still looking for the words to tell him his apartment had been destroyed, his address book stolen, and that she could have been killed by leaking gas.

"What's that got to do with my dead grandfather?" Jacob asked. He was more put off by the sudden change of subject than by the news that someone was investigating him.

"I'll get to that in a minute," Maggie said, "but listen. When I didn't hear from you, I went to your apartment to try to find Peter's number. Jacob – your apartment – it's been totaled, demolished, all your books and papers gone through. And worst of all, the police think you did it yourself! That's what the building superintendent told them."

Jacob sat silent for a moment. "But that's crazy," he said at last. "Crazy! First of all, I don't have any secrets, any enemies, nothing of value except to me." He thought through his possessions. "And why would I destroy my own apartment – and how, since I was in New York at the time? Why would they even think I would do such a thing?"

"Well, that's not all," Maggie said, and took a breath. "When I went there, to your apartment, someone may have tried to kill me. There was the smell of gas, I was passing out, and I had to throw one of your Bibles through the window to let the gas out," she added, sheepishly. She felt guiltier about that than she'd realized.

Jacob was finally alarmed. "My God, Maggie, I am so sorry! What have I gotten you into? I should never have listened to Peter. We should be in Bangor right now, teaching our classes and drinking merlot. This is just crazy!"

Maggie stepped to Jacob quickly and took his face in her hands. "Listen, dummy, I'm fine, and I've already told you the classes are being covered. The whole reason I'm here is to be safe with you until Peter can figure out who gassed me and tore up your apartment. And I'm sure Peter will get his man, as they say." She bent down and kissed him lightly on the lips – something she'd never done before. Before Jacob could respond, though, she retreated to the edge of the bed.

"Tell me, where did your grandfather come from?" Maggie asked, as if nothing had happened.

"New Jersey, I think," Jacob said, not really paying attention. He could still feel her lips on his.

"Well, his ancestors then, where did they come from?"

"From Scotland, actually," Jacob said. "I don't know for sure, but I always guessed the Orkney Islands in the north, since his name was Orrok. Before that, the ancestors go back to Norway." Jacob could see Maggie was excited, though not by the kiss. "Do you realize Rosslyn Chapel was built by William St. Clair, the Earl of Orkney? You could be related through your mother's side of the family!"

"I suppose it's possible," Jacob said. He'd never had much interest in family trees. It was his observation that every family had its share of heroes and villains; people who did their family trees, however, invariably glorified ancestors who came over on the Mayflower, for instance, but ignored the swindlers and horse thieves.

"Listen, Jacob, blood lines may be more important here than you realize. I know it sounds crazy, but you may have been brought here more for who you are than for what you know about Genesis. So now we have to figure out who you are – or at least who they *think* you are. When we do that, we may be ready to figure out what your connection is to a magic sand dune in Iraq."

Chapter 34

Mulling over his genealogy, Jacob walked down the hall to his room, where he fell into a profoundly disturbing sleep. In his dream, Jacob was back in the crypt of Rosslyn Chapel. The air smelled moldy and damp, and the only light came from a single, guttering candle set in the middle of an enormous round table. The twelve now wore judges' robes, and watched while he shoveled deeper and deeper under the floor of the crypt. At last he reached what he'd been digging for: a trapdoor-covered stone staircase leading downward, with a door at the bottom. He descended the stairs, put his hand on the latch, and suddenly heard a slithering sound, as if he'd disturbed a thousand snakes on the other side of that door. The judges were telling him to open it, to open the door, that he must open the door. He woke up drenched in sweat.

Someone in the hall was knocking loudly on his door. "Dr. Alexandre, wake up please! It's after eight, and your breakfast is waiting. Dr. Colburn is already downstairs in the breakfast room."

He groaned softly and opened his eyes. "I'll be right down," he said, and kept himself from adding, "Just stop that damned pounding!"

The breakfast room was sunny, and Jacob sat down with his back to the window, facing Maggie and a pile of empty dishes. Maggie had already worked her way through an orange, half a grapefruit and a stack of toast, and was just starting in on a plate of scrambled eggs. He poured a cup of coffee, feeling grateful it wasn't tea. "Good morning," he said, speaking softly so as not to disturb his headache.

Maggie smiled sympathetically. "It's a sunny day out there, a rare event in these parts. We should make the most of it.

"I did some reading after you left last night," Maggie went on. "I have a little theory we need to discuss. After your coffee," she added.

Jacob was grateful for any respite. He had not been able to shake the dream, or lose that sensation of digging in the crypt. He decided he had no interest whatsoever in returning to Rosslyn Chapel.

As if she'd read his thoughts, Maggie said, "I think we should go back to the chapel, if there's time. There is something I want to look for in the stone carvings."

Jacob didn't respond, so Maggie continued, "You know, the Knights Templar were meant to be an order of holy monks, practicing poverty, chastity, and obedience. But two corrupting influences got in the way. First, the Templars' spiritual guide, Bernard of Clairvaux, began recruiting from among repentant sinners. Murderers, thieves, even Cathar heretics who confessed their sins, helped fill the ranks of the Templars.

"And then there were the Assassins – fanatical, fiercely loyal Muslim warriors who held strongholds and castles in Syria. They sometimes worked hand-in-hand with the Templars against Sunni rulers, and the Assassins' secret society practices, perhaps even their use of hashish, may have infected the Templars. More importantly, their religious philosophy may have colored Templar thought. The Assassins believed they gained spiritual power through political power, and it didn't matter to them how they got it because they also believed heaven and hell, good and evil, to be one and the same."

"It's no wonder, then, the Knights Templar became as powerful as they did," Jacob said with growing interest. "With such a combination of incredible wealth, personal discipline, an indifference to conventional morality, and no one to answer to but the pope, it's amazing they didn't come to rule the world."

"Perhaps they did, after all," Maggie said. "You know, by the end of the 13th century, the Templars had been pushed out of the Holy Lands as far as Cyprus. They dreamed of one more crusade, and that's where King Philip of France saw his opportunity. In 1307, he and the new pope lured the Templars to Paris with promises of planning a new crusade. Then in the month of October, on Friday the 13th, Philip had every Templar they could catch arrested, chained, and, by order of Pope Clement V, tortured to make them confess heresy. The Knights Templar in England had time to escape here to Scotland, where history says they disappeared. The pope turned over the Templars' lands and estates to their rivals, the Knights of the Hospital of St. John. And that was the end of the Knights of the Temple of Solomon, so they say."

"You make it sound like there's more to the story," Jacob said.

"I think there is," Maggie responded, pushing aside her plate of eggs. "Seventy years later, the famous Peasant's Revolt sweeps across England. Church properties are burned, corrupt officials are beheaded, royalty threatened, and the properties of the Hospitallers – the properties that had been seized from the Templars – are burned, destroyed. History calls the revolt 'spontaneous', and yet it was clearly well planned, with help from the inside. The Tower of London, for example, the most well-defended fortress in the country, went unprotected. Even the drawbridge was left down, to give the rebels access to reach the Archbishop of Canterbury. And when captured rebels were later tortured, after the revolt had been crushed, they confessed to a mysterious Great Society that had targeted those who were to be killed and what was to be burned. And to top it off, the rebels in various cities wore a kind of 'livery,' a hooded cowl of fine white wool, with a red tassel on the point of the hood. There were some 1500 of these uniforms passed out. Each was made from about six square feet of expensive wool, at a time when poverty gripped the land. And they were made in red and white – the colors of the Knights Templar!"

Jacob knew where she was headed, and decided to play devil's advocate. He guessed the coffee was beginning to work. "Well okay, even if I grant you the Templars lasted another seventy years, that doesn't get us as far as the 1400's. Are you suggesting those twelve guys in the crypt are Templars today?"

"Templars, Gardeners, secret cabal – what difference the name, if they occupy a position of unbridled power in some international shadow government? For years we've all heard various conspiracy theories of history, that great wars were orchestrated by financial powers, that secret interests funded Lenin and the Russian Revolution with bars of gold. For a time, every nut in America with a gun and a copier was writing about the evil doings of the Trilateral Commission, the Council on Foreign Relations, and the Federal Reserve. Fundamentalists blamed the Jews and Catholics, Catholics blamed the Freemasons. After World War II, the federal government adopted former Nazis and blamed the Communists; after that, racist militia groups living communally blamed the federal government. Today the paranoia grows exponentially through the tools of social media and the work of Russian hackers and bots, spewing fake news to fuel racism, religious hatred, and other political antagonisms.

"And what's the goal of these accusations? It's almost always us-against-themisms, designed to further divide and conquer. It's power so greedy it always wants more – at everyone else's expense. There's theft through monetary manipulation and rampant money laundering, the tyranny of self-serving values imposed on politics by those in financial control. It was King Philip's charge against the Templars, and probably the Templars' charge against the church and the English government during the Peasant's Revolt."

"Isn't paranoia part of the survival instinct, just another part of our flight-or-fight reaction to the world we live in?" Jacob asked. "Who was it who said, 'paranoia is perfect awareness'?"

"A bumper sticker, I think," Maggie laughed.

"So anyway, let's say these guys in the crypt are a shadow government of retread Templars," Jacob asked lightly. "Why would they need the likes of us?"

"I can answer that," a voice from across the room replied. They turned in their seats, and standing in the breakfast room doorway was Peter.

Chapter 35

They were packed into a blue Ford van and on the road before they had a chance to talk, however, and Peter began with an apology. "Jacob, I'm sorry I abandoned you at the bar the other night, but I'd just got word about Maggie's situation in Bangor, and I had to get her out of there. There was no telling what was coming next."

Jacob sat silent in the front passenger seat, and Peter added they had a plane to catch, that they had to get there right away. Jacob saw this as an opportunity to avoid Rosslyn Chapel, and didn't object. Maggie, however, was not so agreeable.

"All right, Peter, it's time you explain what this is all about," she insisted, as Peter increased speed. "Before I fly away from this tight little island, I want to know where to and why."

"No problem," Peter said. "The Gardeners want you to look into the Iraqi situation yourselves, and let them know what's going on."

"They want us...!" Jacob began, pausing for words. "Why in hell would they send two American teachers to investigate something three missiles couldn't open? Are they crazy?"

"I'm not saying they aren't," Peter answered. "But I can tell you what they told me. They don't seem to feel this is a matter of force, so much as it is for the right person to go in – and it seems you are the right person, Jacob."

"Does this have anything to do with ancestry?" Maggie asked, playing the hunch she'd had earlier.

"Give the lady a gold star," Peter said, not disparagingly. "You've come a long way from seminary thinking, Maggie," he added. "I didn't know that ancestry thing myself until they told me, and I've known Jacob most of his life.

"Look, to make a long story short, the Gardeners believe strongly in genetics, and they have some pretty screwy ideas – but they're not the only ones. It seems there's a second group, a group opposed to the Gardeners – and therefore an enemy to us, for the moment. I think it was those people who showed up at Maggie's, and who destroyed your apartment. And I'm sure that's not the last we'll hear from them," Peter added. "That's another reason we're clearing out of Roslin so fast."

"One secret group is bad enough," Jacob said with some annoyance. "Now you're telling us there are *two*?"

"The Gardeners – I prefer to call them the twelve – go back a long way, a tradition going back to the crusades, and they have sources of information that were lost to history – until recently," Peter said. "For example, they have written records of the so-called lost tribes, after they escaped their Assyrian captors more than half a millennium before Christ. Apparently, they fled through the Caucasus Mountains, intermarried with Indo-Europeans, and traveled west to occupy Europe as the Celts. The twelve know the migration patterns, the assimilation patterns, and – to cut to the chase – they believe that many of us can sing "Father Abraham" and mean it."

"You mean to say we're related to the northern tribes of Israel?" Maggie asked.

"Exactly," Peter said. "They're convinced we are the fulfillment of the promise God gave to Abraham and Isaac and Jacob, that their offspring would be as numerous as the stars in the sky, and would rule the world."

Jacob repeated from memory Genesis 22:15-18, God's promise to Abraham:

By myself I have sworn, says the Lord, because you have done this, and have not withheld your son, your only son, I will indeed bless you, and I will multiply your descendants as the stars of heaven and as the sand which is on the seashore. And your descendants shall possess the gate of their enemies, and by your descendants shall all the nations of the earth bless themselves, because you have obeyed my voice.

"I knew you'd know it," Peter said. "It doesn't take much to prompt you a little."

"But if that's what they think," Jacob said, still annoyed, "then why do they need me? Lots of folks would qualify for having a bit of God's chosen people in their ancestry."

"Because they're afraid their enemies may be right," Peter said.

"What is it their enemies believe?" Maggie asked.

"That to enter the garden, it helps to be a genetic descendant of Jesus," Peter said, after a pause.

Peter drove in silence for a while, while Jacob and Maggie absorbed the thought. They sped down narrow, hedge-lined ways, with few oncoming cars to slow them down. With unspoken but growing concern, though, Peter noted a car in the rearview mirror that had kept pace with them since leaving Roslin.

"I assume you are talking about that fiction that Jesus had a child or children by Mary Magdalene," Jacob said, at last.

"It's based on some old Templar legends, and a theory this enemy team has. Since I don't really know the name of that group, I dubbed them Chaos – you know, from Get Smart," Peter said with a smile. "They may be part of Putin's plan to bring down the existing order. Since Russia can't compete on a level playing field, the game's become 'Let's dynamite the field itself!' The old order has proven surprisingly vulnerable to them, given Chaos' destructive power in the carbon market, on social media, and through the other weaponized technology of the internet. Chaos has been meddling in the economics, politics and stability of the whole world. The twelve suspect it even had a hand in releasing the pandemic," Peter added, "so I think Chaos is the right name for them."

"The Mary Magdalene story – it's a legend that just won't quit," Maggie said, going back to the descendants-of-Jesus conversation. "The theory is, Jesus was married to Mary Magdalene and had children by her. That was the real meaning of the Grail legend, they say – the sacred blood, and so forth. Magdalene *was* the Grail, and the sacred bloodline was brought to Europe when Mary Magdalene and offspring came to France with Lazarus – or to England with Joseph of Arimathea, depending on which legend you opt for." No one commented, so Maggie went on.

"Joseph was supposedly Jesus' wealthy uncle, the man who had Jesus wrapped in the shroud and buried in the tomb. Legend has it that Joseph was a tin merchant, and actually owned tin mines in England. The story goes he brought Jesus to England when Jesus was just a boy. The

English hymn 'Jerusalem' is based on that legend. In any event, the story has Jesus' descendants becoming the Merovingian line of kings in France, and later, a bloodline to the Hapsburgs."

"And you're saying *I'm* part of that bloodline?" Jacob asked, almost laughing. "Give me a break!"

"I'm not saying anything," Peter sighed, defensively. "Those guys do the genealogy, and they say you're the one to go in. I am only following orders." Peter said the last with a trite German accent, but Jacob was not amused.

"This is heresy, Peter. I'm not buying it for a minute. It's just a bunch of sacrilegious claptrap, and about what I'd expect from a group like the Templars, the Gardeners, the twelve, or whatever they're calling themselves this week."

"Whoa, wait a minute," Peter said. "I'm not saying all the twelve believe this – they just want to cover their bases. They don't want you dropping dead at the gate. Don't you see, Jacob? That's why they need you. If there's anything to this bloodline business, you're the safest bet. After all, they think you could be following in the steps of Jesus."

"What are you talking about?" Jacob asked angrily.

Peter took a deep breath. "The thing is, Jacob, this isn't the first time this thing in the desert has opened up – at least, according to the twelve. They claim this is the place where Jesus went after his forty days, the time when he was tempted by the devil. What's the quote from Mark?"

"It was after he was baptized," Jacob said absently:

The Spirit immediately drove him out into the wilderness. And he was in the wilderness 40 days, tempted by Satan; he was with the wild beasts; and the angels ministered to him."

"That's the one," Peter said. "They believe angels might have taken him to Eden to minister to him."

"Iraq is a long way from the Jordan," Jacob said. "Are they saying Jesus went to Iraq, or that Eden came to Jesus?"

"They didn't explain it. They probably don't know themselves. But I know they believe it happened again – a thousand years later. They have a source on that one."

"Who from?" Maggie asked. "The Templars themselves didn't come together until after that."

"Yes, but remember," Peter said, "there was a strong Christian community in Jerusalem in 1099 when the first crusade arrived to trash the place. They had legends and stories to tell the crusaders.

"One of those stories was that a door appeared in the desert, and many attempted to go through. No one who went in ever came out – with two exceptions. It seems there was a Christian pilgrim who traveled with his wife from France to the royal city of Axum, in Ethiopia. They went in search of a copy of the Book of Enoch, which had been banned by the Western church, but remained a part of Christian Ethiopia's sacred scripture. From there they traveled to Jerusalem, and then into the desert, where their caravan came upon the door in the dune. The pilgrim and his wife went through the door, and after some time came out to rejoin their caravan, which fortunately had waited for them. Shortly after that, the door disappeared.

"Think what a long, difficult journey that was in those days! Anyway, the caravan returned to Jerusalem, where the pilgrims told their tale to a secret meeting of the Christian and Jewish communities. The end of the story is, the pilgrim and his wife delayed returning to their home in Provence. They remained in Jerusalem for some years – and get this – they lived together in one cell, in a monastery where only men were allowed. In other words, the two of them together were looked upon as one."

They drove along in silence for a while, watching the flicker of sun and shadow on the hedges and stone walls that lined this stretch of road.

"Did they say what they saw in Eden?" Maggie asked, at last. "Or what happened to the ones who never came out?"

"Not as far as I know," Peter replied. "If the twelve know, they aren't saying. They do seem to think it's necessary for the right people to go in there now, though. They seem quite certain of that. But they didn't say what it was they wanted done in there."

"Right *people*?" Maggie asked sharply. "I hope they don't expect *me* to go in there! I mean, I'm not Jesus' long-lost descendant, *or* the wife of one, nor do I intend to be," she said, looking squarely at Jacob. "So, you can put me on a flight back to Bangor this afternoon."

"Believe me, Maggie, none of this is my idea," Peter said. "I'd like to be on my way home to Stamford right now. Unfortunately, there are people waiting for us in Jerusalem, and that's where we have to go."

The second he said that, a shot smashed through the back window of the van, shattering the rearview mirror. Peter yelled, "Get down!" and floored it. Alone in the back seat, Maggie slumped down and rolled onto the floor. Jacob took a quick look back. A gray Mercedes sedan was following behind, and a man on the passenger side was leaning out the window. He had a gun in his hand.

"Get down," Peter repeated firmly to Jacob, and then as afterthought asked, "Can you shoot?"

"I've done target practice, but never from a moving car," Jacob said, as a second shot slammed into the back door.

"Here." Peter handed him a 9mm from under his coat. "Do what you can. Just stay low and aim low!"

"Jacob rolled down the window and squeezed off a shot. "I think I hit them!" he shouted, but they kept on coming.

Peter did what he could to swerve, but the road curved narrowly. The stone walls made it a hazard to drive under any conditions, with barely enough room for small cars to pass. Peter rounded a curve and suddenly started swearing with conviction. Barely a hundred yards ahead, a low-bed equipment carrier had pulled to the side of the road and unloaded a small, yellow bulldozer. Just beyond was an overpass, a concrete bridge with a narrow ramp leading onto the M8 to Edinburgh. In the oncoming lane, a gravel truck was beyond the overpass, but slowing down to turn.

"Hang on!" Peter yelled, and floored it. With nothing to spare he rounded the carrier, swerved under the overpass, and slid past the truck. The Mercedes was not so lucky. Unable to stop or turn, the driver went the only way possible – up the ramps on the back of the carrier, up some wooden blocking, and over the carrier's cab. For a moment the Mercedes was airborne, and then it came down, smashing headlong into the side of the overpass. Jacob heard a tremendous explosion, saw a burst of flame and then nothing more, as Peter rounded the next turn.

"You're not going to stop?" Jacob asked in a shaky voice.

"We have a plane to catch," Peter replied, and sped on.

Chapter 36   Jerusalem

Deep beneath the Temple Mount, within the heart of Jerusalem's Mount Moriah, the high priest was deep into the ritual of the Yom Kippur atonement before the Holy of Holies. This was a busy day for the high priest. He'd begun preparations the night before, and by the end of the ceremony, blood would be spilled.

The Day of Atonement, the most holy day in the Jewish calendar, had been celebrated in the presence of the Ark of the Covenant once again for a few years now – ever since a powerful, international committee had quietly negotiated over the discovery of the Ark, where it was buried in the rubble of Jeremiah's Grotto by Jeremiah himself in 587 BCE.

For decades before that discovery in 1982 – from the reestablishment of Israel in 1948, and especially after Israel regained the Temple Mount as a result of the 1967 war – it was expected by many that the Ark would be returned from a long exile under the control of St. Mary of Zion Church in Axum, Ethiopia. During times of threat, some people believed, the Ark was moved from Axum to Lalibela, where churches hewn from solid rock beneath the earth proved underground fortresses of protection. Connected by tunnels and trenches, some of these churches still display Templar symbols, leaving many to believe they were carved out of stone by the Templars themselves. During times of peace, it was thought the St. Mary of Zion Christians oversaw care for the Ark. Most Ethiopian Christians still believe the Ark is being tended in Axum, and nearly every Christian church in the country houses a replica. Those replicas are brought out to the streets to parade each January, but the Ark in Axum is never on display, and only one man is allowed to see or care for it.

Now, it seems, the Ark never left the Temple Mount. In 1978, amateur archeologist Ron Wyatt was walking past the place where Jeremiah had hidden the Ark, when, beyond his control, his left arm rose and he heard himself say, "That's Jeremiah's Grotto, and the Ark of the Covenant is in there." The man he was walking with, an official in the Israel Bureau of Antiquities, was startled and delighted. He promised Wyatt the permits necessary to excavate the site. It took more than two years, but Wyatt and his two sons eventually found the grotto cave, the Ark, and several other temple treasures Jeremiah had hidden there to keep them from the invading Babylonians.

Now the high holy days were being secretly celebrated for just a few in this cavern-like place of worship. Space for this new temple had been cleared of the stone rubble that had filled the subterranean excavation, Wyatt claimed, by four angels who appeared to him. And mixing the mystical with the political, Israeli politicos mollified a group of ultra-orthodox Jews who want a third temple rebuilt atop the Temple Mount with "this will have to do for now."

After some heated discussions, the ultra-orthodox had agreed to this secret temple. Building a third temple for all to see could further inflame the Muslims to all-out war, and at the same time trigger Christian endtime fundamentalists' forty-two month countdown to Armageddon. It would become a self-fulfilling prophesy of destruction, with disastrous consequences for the Middle East in general, and Jerusalem in particular. "And after all," the ultra-orthodox reasoned among themselves, "this way the blessed Ark of the Covenant, the mercy seat, is alive in Mount Moriah."

Jacob, Maggie, and Peter stood in the back of this cavern, gazing at the strange scene before them. They had slept through most of the flight from Scotland to Israel, where they'd been met by a military driver. Approaching Jerusalem, Jacob had remarked on the sunlit, golden Dome of the Rock, and they'd stopped the car for a moment to take in the view.

Without prompting, Jacob spoke some verses that came to mind from Psalm 48:

Great is the Lord and greatly to be praised
in the city of our God!
His holy mountain, beautiful in elevation,
is the joy of the earth...
Walk about Zion, go round about her,
number her towers, consider well her ramparts,
go through her citadels;
That you may tell the next generation, this is God....

"Forget travel-agent psalms," Peter had said. "There's no time available to tour Jerusalem." So, Maggie contented Jacob with statistics on the lost glory of the fallen temples. They had been constructed of building stones as long as forty feet and weighing up to a hundred tons. The magnificence of the ascent from the south-west angle, Maggie told them, had astonished the Queen of Sheba. An enormous, arch-supported stone bridge had spanned the valley of Tyropoeon to reach the royal porch of the temple. The porches, or cloisters, which appeared around the inside of the wall had been exquisitely beautiful, with double rows of Corinthian pillars cut from solid blocks of marble forty feet high. The royal porch was especially magnificent, with four rows of forty pillars each. The resulting effect of this porch alone was a central nave forty-five feet wide, edged with pillars one hundred feet high, and side aisles thirty feet wide with marble columns fifty feet tall.

"During Jesus' day," Maggie said, "the only remaining portion of the first temple was the eastern wall porch, known as Solomon's porch. It was there, according to John's Gospel, that Jesus was nearly stoned for saying, 'I and the Father are one,' and, 'I am the Son of God.'"

"There were five outer gates to the temple," Maggie said, "and in a chamber above the east gate was kept the standard measures of the cubit. Once inside, there were nine inner gates leading from the terrace to the sanctuary. The main gate, known as the 'beautiful gate,' was in the eastern wall. That gate was made of richly ornamented Corinthian brass, so heavy it took twenty men to close it. Acts says it was by this gate that St. Peter healed the lame man," Maggie added.

"Well, that magnificence is long gone," Jacob said, as the driver dropped them by a locked door marked as the entryway to Zedekiah's Cave. As the car departed, the door swung open, and a man in orthodox dress let them into a passageway, closed and locked the door, and handed each of them flashlights from an old canvas pouch.

They had followed a circuitous pathway from there, down convoluted tunnels, passed small domed areas and rainwater cisterns, till Jacob's sense of direction grew hopelessly confused. "I hope he sticks around to get us out of here again," Jacob had whispered to Maggie. But then they entered through another door into a surprisingly larger room. It was a cavern room with rough stone walls, and indirect electric lighting that created shadows reminiscent of Rosslyn Chapel. The setup, however, was a tiny layout of the traditional Temple of Solomon, with the cavern walls serving as the outer walls. There was a ramp leading to an altar of sacrifice, and an innermost enclosure to house the Holy of Holies, the newly reactivated Ark of the Covenant.

"This is God's concession to politics," Peter said softly, with a hint of sarcasm. "There was a strong movement to build this up on top of the Temple Mount, where the second Temple of Herod had stood. There was even room for it next to the Dome of the Rock. But Arab-Israeli relations being what they are, it was easier to make do with this for the time being. It meets enough of the qualifications, and gives them a place to follow the ritual sacrifices spelled out in Leviticus." After a moment's reflection, Jacob quoted:

And he shall take from the congregation of the people of Israel two male goats for a sin offering, and one ram for a burnt offering. And Aaron shall offer a bull as a sin offering for himself, and shall make atonement for himself and for his house. Then he shall take the two goats, and set them before the Lord at the door of the tent of meeting; and Aaron shall cast lots upon the two goats, one lot for the Lord and the other lot for Azazel. And Aaron shall present the goat on which the lot fell for the Lord, and offer it as a sin offering; but the goat on which the lot fell for Azazel shall be presented alive before the Lord to make atonement over it, that it may be sent away into the wilderness to Azazel.

"I'll never figure out how he remembers all that," Peter said to Maggie. "A mind is a terrible thing to waste. By the way, just what is an 'Azazel'?"

"The name of a desert demon the scapegoat is sent to," Maggie answered. "Later on, the name was applied to one of the fallen angels, so he could have been one and the same.

"You know, Jacob," Maggie continued, "your quote didn't do justice to the blood that's shed in this ceremony.

First the bull gets killed, with some of its blood sprinkled on the Holy of Holies. The same thing happens to the goat. Blood from those animals gets spread on the altar."

Maggie turned to Peter. "The word 'altar,' by the way, translates from the Hebrew to mean 'slaughter-place.' On top of that, all the sins of Israel get laid on the head of the scapegoat, and that goat is sent out to a devil in the desert – perhaps the original sin-eater. Can you imagine what the Friends of Animals would say about all this?"

"That's another reason this isn't being done in public," Peter said. "There's a strong contingent of Jews who would find these practices unconscionable. To traditionalists, though, this is the ultimate blessing: to be able to fulfill a part of the law here they haven't been able to do for almost two thousand years – some twenty-six hundred years from the destruction of the first temple. Some planned for this since the return to Israel in 1948, raising the special, sacrificial breed of red heifer, reconstructing the details of priestly worship, making the seamless, sacred garments, and getting back some of the temple treasure – from them," Peter said, and gestured toward a dozen observers seated on the other side of the room. Jacob had noticed them when he first came in, but hadn't paid attention. Now he recognized them – it was the twelve from Rosslyn Chapel.

"What are they doing here?" Jacob demanded of Peter.

"You'll know soon enough," Peter replied.

Chapter 37

The ceremony of atonement was now underway, and Maggie, after marveling why she, the only woman in the place, would be welcome here, was preparing her mind for the sacrifice of the animals.

Jacob had been asked by the high priest to stand in front of the tent of meeting, holding the tethers to two identical male goat kids that stood nervously on either side of him. He knew what this was about, but wondered which of the three of them was the real scapegoat. Dressed in his white linen coat, breeches and turban, the high priest cast into an urn two golden lots – identical but for the words *la-YHWH* and *la-Azazel.* The high priest faced the people and shook the urn. He then thrust both hands into the urn, withdrew the lots, and placed one on the head of each goat. The lot fell for the Lord on the goat to Jacob's right, and a piece of scarlet cloth was fastened to its neck. That goat was led away to the altar of sacrifice. The goat to his left, the scapegoat, had a piece of scarlet cloth attached to its horn. That kid was now shaking nervously, and Jacob picked him up and held him in his arms. The goat kept shaking, but didn't struggle against him. Jacob wondered if the goat knew how much they shared in common, as living elements in religious sacrifice.

From where he stood, Jacob had a good view of the sacrifice. Instead, he closed his eyes, following a sudden impulse to say a prayer for the animals and himself. In the sanctuary the high priest cut the throat, then held the animal's head down against the altar while the blood pulsed out in deep, red waves. Maggie caught a look in its eyes before she closed her own.

The high priest brought a censer with burning coals and a container of incense, and went alone through the veil to the Holy of Holies. There was a small fire burning in front of the Ark, and the priest added the incense to the fire. Earlier, he had sprinkled blood from the bull seven times in front of the mercy seat. And now YHWH's goat, the blood sacrifice for the sins of the people, had its blood sprinkled in the same manner as the bull's.

After he'd finished smearing blood on the altar, as well, the high priest returned to Jacob and the scapegoat. The priest had drops of blood on his coat and in his beard, Jacob noted, and on his glasses and turban, as well. "For the life of every creature is in the blood of it," Jacob remembered from Leviticus, and reflected, "Blood sacrifice began with Abel, and his jealous brother Cain killed him for it. Then Abraham was willing to shed the blood of his son. And this is why Christians think Jesus' bloody death became the mechanism for God's forgiveness. Innocent blood spilled for God. We're saved in the blood of the Lamb, we cry, and then celebrate with a communion of bread and wine we call the body and blood. Crazy it is, and yet we still say amen."

The priest laid his hands on the head of the goat; the smell of blood frightened the animal, and he squirmed in Jacob's arms. With prayers and lamentations, the high priest laid upon the shivering scapegoat all the sins and transgressions of the people of Israel. Jacob imagined he could feel the goat grow heavy with the burden of human guilt, until it was quite overwhelmed. Finally, the kid lay still in his arms as if there could be no escape, as if movement of any kind would be too much.

Jacob himself lost track of time until the ceremony was over. An assistant priest led Jacob back to his friends, the kid still in his arms but now fast asleep. "You are the man who is in readiness," the priest had said to Jacob. "Take him to the wilderness and let him go to Azazel."

"Jacob, the Gardeners need a word with you," Peter said. Sensing Jacob's distraction, he added, "It won't take long." Peter took Jacob's arm and led him to where the twelve were sitting. Maggie took the kid in her arms and followed behind, gently petting the goat's head and rubbing his ears.

"Dr. Alexandre," said one of the twelve, "thank you for joining us. You understand by now that you are a very important, very blessed person, but you may be wondering about your role in all this. We realized you deserve an explanation as to why we have brought you here. Please, come with me."

Following his lead, along with the other Gardeners, Jacob, Peter, and Maggie, holding the goat, went through a narrow doorway into a room with a table similar to the one in Rosslyn Chapel. Gesturing them all to sit, the man continued:

"Before you ask questions of us, let me tell you what we know about you and what your assignment entails. Our ancestors recorded some pertinent information about this phenomenon in the desert that General Collins described. It seems to recur every thousand years or so, which was important to the ancients. I am sure you are aware they believed the scriptural assertion that to God, a thousand years is but a day.

"If that's the case, we may assume that this is the sixth day the door has opened. A thousand years ago, two pilgrims from France made the encounter. A thousand years before, we think it was the Christ. I won't trouble you with the detailed calculations of a biblical year of 360 days, but believe me, the figures are basically correct.

"Before that, who of us can say? There are myths and legends that make an approximate fit, but so much can be speculated, and so little confirmed, that it doesn't gain us any ground.

"There are certain qualifications, however, that seem imperative to the success of this endeavor. On occasion, when the door has appeared, some have managed to enter but were lost in the attempt. They got in, to be sure, but then never returned. One of our members here, Mr. Satino, controls a firm in Roslin which explores the genetics of cloning and gene splicing. It's been his theory that bloodline and genetic manipulation are keys to opening the Phoenix Door in safety. Years ago, we learned from bloodstains on the Shroud of Turin that Jesus' blood was typed AB, but we couldn't determine more than that from the sample.

"Then we heard a remarkable claim from Ron Wyatt, the man who discovered the Ark of the Covenant. Wyatt reported that Jesus' blood was spilled onto the west side of the mercy seat. The grotto lies twenty feet below the place where Wyatt determined Jesus was crucified, and Wyatt cited gospel accounts that the ground beneath the cross quaked open when Jesus died. Wyatt theorized blood from Jesus' wounded side bled down through the crevice, and onto the Ark.

"Wyatt claimed to have had a lab test run on the dried blood, and said the lab techs were stunned by the results. First, he claimed, the dried blood impossibly generated living chromosomes 2000 years after it was spilled. Second, it purportedly consisted of 24 chromosomes – presumably 23 from the mother, Mary, and a single Y, to make a male, from God. A normal human would be a product of 46 – that is, 23 from each parent. If such a claim could be verified, it would establish Jesus as perhaps the first case of human parthenogenesis – a true virgin birth – or else, as Wyatt reasoned, it would prove Jesus was the son of God. A term for it is 'haploid,' and interestingly, drone bees, being virgin born, have only half as many chromosomes as other bees. Unfortunately, we have not been able to verify any part of the Wyatt story – the sample, the lab, any of it.

"In any event, we recently commissioned some Pauline Christians to undergo a variety of CRISPR genetic changes to test variations on some of my own theories. We arranged for their pilgrimage, and General Collin's satellite videos showed upwards of a hundred of them recently entered." He paused a second before adding, "Sadly, no one has yet come out. And since the door is still there, it indicates it's still waiting for the right visitors. We think you are the key for several reasons."

"Why would you even think such a thing?" Jacob asked, sensing an opportunity to speak. "Maggie was speculating that you guys imagine I'm a descendant of Jesus – but let me tell you, I find that idea absolutely abhorrent. I can't accept that gnostic nonsense. I believe Jesus came to teach us to love – not to procreate a royal lineage. His sacrifice was to overcome our failings under the law; he embodies God's creative Word; in short, he fulfills the prophesy and promise of Messiah."

"We know you are a faithful Christian, Jacob." The man's voice had just a note of pity in it. "That is, in fact, one reason we chose you. You see, Jacob, we can trace the Merovingian bloodline back to Mary Magdalene, though we can't confirm her children were from Jesus. Still, you can imagine how many share that same bloodline that runs in your veins. Some in our own group qualify on that score. No, your uniqueness is not just that you are related to Mary

Magdalene, or about your theological insights, or that, despite your training, your Christian faith remains intact – although I'll warrant there aren't many all that faithful in the seminary where you're teaching," he added. Jacob only remained silent. Despite his statement of faith, it wasn't so long ago he'd seriously doubted the historicity of Christ.

"In anticipation of Eden's arrival, our group debated what the qualifications for entry would be. You can imagine, I think, how curious we've been, and how much any one of us would like to try entry. We realized, however, how cynical we have become – immersed as we are in the power of the world. And though much of our work has been done in the name of social progress, none of us could admit any sense of faith or the possibility of grace. Gnostic knowledge is not Shekhinah wisdom, I'm afraid.

"But enough of this philosophical self-pity," he said abruptly, pulling himself up in his chair. "We haven't much time. Let me just say that rather than debate the efficacy of sacred bloodlines versus faith, we ultimately decided to send in someone who has several qualifications – just to cover our bases, as you Americans like to say. You have the background and insight to explain what you encounter there.

"Oh, yes, and there is one other thing. In analyzing the situation, it seemed important that there be a woman with you. Ideally, we wanted someone of faith who was also knowledgeable in ancient languages, history, mythology, and so forth. Maggie seems the perfect fit."

Maggie's attention turned from the goat. "Wait just a minute," she said. "Just a damn minute. I don't fit the formula here at all. First of all, I'm not married to Jacob. So just because that pilgrim from France entered Eden with his wife is no indication the same rules will apply to me. Second, Jesus didn't have Mary Magdalene with him when he went into the desert. If that's the case, then why would Jacob need me along?"

"Maggie," the man responded kindly, "Jesus was a special case. He embodied oneness in a world of duality. Even we acknowledge that. Just a moment ago I mentioned Shekhinah wisdom, and as you told us in Rosslyn Chapel, that's the feminine side of God. The Kabbalah describes creation as emanating from the joining of Jehovah and Shekhinah – it's a way of acknowledging the dualistic nature of creation, I would guess. The Kabbalah also postulates four worlds, with Adam existing in all four. In the first three, Adam is androgynous, but in the fourth world, the world of expulsion, gender is a duality. Adam was split to make Eve, and Adam and Eve in the flesh needed one another to procreate. They were the first couple to leave through that doorway, although Lilith left before them. By the way, watch out for Lilith!

"But those four Adams taken together, if such a thing were possible, become the world soul, the *animus mundi*, and so was Jesus. Man in flesh or no, the Shekhinah resided in him. With his baptism, he became home to the indwelling spirit of God, which some teach had been exiled here when God drew back into himself, after creation. In short, then, Jesus housed in his heart the feminine principal of God from whom the worlds sprang into existence. Needless to say, he was complete in himself, and could travel through that doorway alone. Jacob, on the other hand, is not so blessed."

"Nor would I want to be, thank you," Jacob interrupted. "I don't even want to be *this* blessed, if that's what you call it," he said, looking over at the goat.

"What, being goatherd to a scapegoat?" Peter laughed. "You don't even have to keep track of him – just let the damn thing loose. Then pop through that door, take a good look around, and you're done. We'll have you back to the Bangor campus in no time."

"Hold on," Jacob interrupted. "This has got to be more than a sightseeing tour. Why am I going in there – what's this all about, anyway?"

After a moment's hesitation, one of the twelve spoke up.

"Jacob, I'm Satino, and you have every right to know what this is about. My associates were reluctant to tell you, but you should have guessed from the mention that this is the sixth time the door has appeared. You'll recall that scripture described the creation in terms of six days. And it's not a coincidence, we think, that there have been five mass extinctions previously on the planet. The next will be the sixth. Six is the number of man, repeated three times for emphasis, and three sixes together may ring a biblical bell. Given the deterioration of this world, the problems of global warming, alarming population growth, pollution and extinction, we presume this is the last time the door will open on its own. Just three more degrees Celsius, and the world becomes unlivable for us. That rise in temperature is now inevitably close. For several years we have planned for places where select groups can retreat when the time comes. There are fortified defenses in several locations, including miles of construction under the Denver Airport. But it's been my suggestion right along that we explore the possibility of retiring to Eden when the world out here turns to ashes. We don't expect you to gain admittance for us. We just want you to case the situation and see if there is a place in Eden that could accommodate the Garden Club and our associates. Check out the situation for us, and we'll save a place for you and Maggie when the time comes. We're not expecting you to figure out how we get in there. Some of the Gardeners think quantum has given them the dimensional technology to crack the door open and bypass the guardian angel. Personally, I feel certain there's a place in Eden for them, but my associates want to know more, and so they've recruited you."

"Wouldn't it be better," Maggie asked, "if you put your considerable resources into fixing the earth, rather than running away from it?"

"Forty years ago, perhaps," one of the twelve responded, "but we were so busy making money from carbon energy that no one in power was paying attention. The fact is, we were still making big money from carbon when the pandemic hit – the white horse of plague. Anyway, there are already too many people in the world. So, if the disaster is inevitable, isn't it time again for our version of Noah's Ark?"

The twelve, sensing that nothing would be gained by further conversation, got up to leave. "Come on," Peter said to Jacob and Maggie, with sudden seriousness. "We've got to get that goat out of town."

Chapter 38   In Transit

They were outside the entryway again, where three sand-colored Land Rovers were now lined up, waiting for them. It was getting dark, but Jacob could see armed soldiers in the first and third vehicles. They climbed into the middle Land Rover, with Peter at the wheel.

"We need to make several hours' headway tonight," Peter said. "After that, we'll stop and get some food and sleep." The mention of food reminded Jacob they hadn't eaten since Scotland.

"It seems we kept a Yom Kippur fast without even knowing it," Jacob said to Maggie. "You must be starving." Maggie smiled, but didn't answer. She was sitting in the back seat, petting the kid asleep at her side. Jacob figured this goat had been specially raised, perhaps by a family, to feel so comfortable with people. He wondered how the kid would deal with Azazel.

The Land Rovers moved quickly through Jerusalem's streets and onto a well-paved highway. "The roads here are better than Scotland's," Peter commented.

"I'll bet it still deteriorates past the Dead Sea," Jacob said, recalling a trip he'd made to the Middle East some years before. No one responded, and they drove along in silence for several miles, trying to see what was out there beyond the range of headlights. They'd turned south before it occurred to Jacob to ask what destination Peter had in mind. "Where are we going tonight, Peter?" Jacob asked with some trepidation. "It's not as if military escorts are well liked around here, you know."

"We're traveling south, toward Aqaba," Peter responded. Some of it will be fairly rough going, desert track and bring your own gas and water. We'll go off-road in the morning. Tonight we're stopping north of the Gulf of Aqaba, just across the Israeli-Jordan border."

"Do the motels allow pets?" Maggie asked sleepily, stroking the kid's head. "Our motel does," Peter replied.

The soldiers had pitched tents for everyone, and started fires to ward off the cold night air of the desert.

Jacob and Peter sat close to their fire, cooking some skewered lamb, while Maggie and the goat poked around the area, looking for something the kid could browse. He found a clump of dried-out, weedy-looking stuff, and lay down to chew contentedly. A puff of wind on the fire made a shower of sparks that filled the clear night sky, as if in competition with the stars above. Beyond Jacob's fire, the soldiers were gathered around their larger campfire, preparing food for themselves. A soldier on watch patrolled the area. The cooking meat smelled good, and Maggie joined Jacob and Peter in time to claim the first shish-kabob.

"There's something I've wanted to talk to you about since Scotland," she said to Peter, after her first bite. They ate off the skewers, and a trickle of lamb's blood ran down her chin.

"What's the question?" Peter asked, in a tone that suggested he knew what she would say.

"You told me the reason you were taking me away from Bangor was to protect me, so you must have thought I was in some sort of danger. Well, what danger was it, and how on earth could I be safer here? I know those guys came to my apartment to ask about Jacob, but did you think they were coming back? And why am I safer here, with men in Mercedes shooting at us, and soldiers with automatic weapons escorting us into the Saudi desert? I mean, what could be more dangerous in Bangor, Maine than what I'm doing right now?"

"It's very possible those guys at your apartment were from the same team who tried to kill us in Scotland," Peter said, after a pause. "If you'd stayed in Bangor, who knows? They might have killed you first, and then come after Jacob. Or they might have left you alone. I just don't know."

"Well, what *do* you know that you haven't told us," Maggie insisted. "I mean, what reason do they have to kill us?"

"Maggie, I'm telling you the truth – I honestly don't know. The twelve warned me from the beginning that the group I dubbed Chaos would be trying to stop Jacob from completing this assignment, but who they are, or why they care, I can't say for sure. The twelve say the same group has demonstrated combined skills in stirring social division, hacking, trolling and election disruption, so my guess is they're working for Putin, but that just might be my own prejudice. I always said that if Putin isn't the antichrist, he's the nesting doll inside the antichrist. The twelve think it might have been a Putin agent planted in the Wuhan Institute of Virology's P4 lab who released COVID-19. Of course, they may not be objective on the subject – they were hit pretty hard by the pandemic when it reached their base in Turin, Italy. But larger picture, you've no idea how corrupt interests have dismantled intelligence at all levels – especially within the US government. The last few years have been a nightmare. They still call the work I do 'intelligence,' but for the life of me, I feel dumber every day. Moles and traitors are the hardest enemies to understand – especially at the top. You don't know who's got what on whom, or what motivates them. It's the place where frustration marries paranoia. But hey, I'm open to any ideas you may have on the subject," Peter concluded with a grim smile. "It's your life we're talking about, after all."

"All our lives," Jacob corrected, and then changed the subject. "You know, it's interesting one of the twelve referenced the First Seal that opens in Revelation. He called the white horse and rider the bringer of disease. For many centuries, the traditional interpretation about the four horsemen of the apocalypse was that Christ rode the white horse, and that he carried a bow without arrows as a symbol of authority. Over the last two centuries, though, the rider has become the antichrist, bringing infection and pandemic. I didn't really understand it until COVID-19 – his arrows are the invisible, airborne arrows of contagion. Then it occurred to me, the four horsemen might be color-delineated as a prophetic reference, designed for those of us alive today to understand. If that's the case, a white Russian may be more than some barroom racist's favorite. Russians are famous for their use of poisons, so I wouldn't put it past a Russian-born antichrist to kill by disease. Seal Two, the red horse and rider symbolizing war, could be the so-called 'Red' Chinese. China is the only nation with a two hundred million man army, the force described as marching with the fallen angels. Seal Three, the black horse and rider bringing famine, could reference Africa, where drought and plagues of locusts have been provoking mass migrations of starving people toward Europe. And the Fourth Seal, the pale horse and rider bringing death? Well, the word translated as 'pale' from the Hebrew actually means a pale green, or a tan approximating the color we call khaki – the world's favorite colors for military uniforms...."

Jacob trailed off as a silly joke crossed his mind. He thought, "The four horses of the apocalypse walk into a bar and order a White Russian and four straws. The bartender tells them, 'Sorry, but we don't serve straw horses in here.'" Jacob decided an antichrist joke might be in bad taste just then, but was startled to see Maggie smile as if she'd read his thought. "I'm just speculating, of course," Jacob added, lamely.

They sat and watched the fire curling down. The goat came over and lay down by Maggie for warmth, and Jacob threw some dry brush on the fire. A shower of sparks flew high into the night sky, then one by one they fell, faded and died.

"One of my childhood insights came from watching a fire like this," Jacob said reflectively. "We were burning a pile of alders, and after dark I was left there to watch the fire while my parents went in to fix dinner. As I sat there it occurred to me, we are part of a fire like this, burning away in the night. And all those little sparks that fly up by themselves are people who jump out from the source to do their own thing. And see how beautiful, how interesting they are! Look at the variety of patterns they make against the night sky, with all the stars for audience while they do their very own dance. And then they're gone, burned out, while the fire below burns on and on.

"So, my questions there, at twelve years old, were, are we foolish to fly off from the fire, to be ourselves for a moment? The impulse to be our own fire – is it some ego trip like Adam and the forbidden fruit, or is it entirely in keeping with the nature we're born with? Are we flung into space by God, or is it our nature to fling ourselves? And when there is nothing left of us but cinder, do we fall back into the fire again, or land somewhere in the darkness, either to disappear or to watch that fire from a lonely distance? Do we have any control over where we land, or is it just the winds of fate that determine whether we go back to the source or we don't?"

"Hey, you're the Christian around here," Peter said. "Don't go questioning your faith now! Wait until you come out through that doorway before you start messing around."

Jacob smiled. "Faith isn't set in stone, you know. If God had been looking for blind obedience, he'd never have made us like this. In fact, I think he must be amused by the questions of a twelve-year-old. Otherwise, why would he have spent all that time walking around the garden, talking to Adam and Eve? Even at their best I doubt they were what you'd call brilliant conversationalists, if what Genesis tells us is any indication."

Again they sat in silence, watching the sparks and the brilliant stars of the desert sky.

"I had an insight like that at about the same age," Maggie said finally. "It wasn't such a romantic setting, though – it happened in my high school science lab. The teacher played a recording of the radio waves generated by the solar wind hitting the atmosphere, the actual sounds of the Northern Lights. As I listened to the clicks and whistles and chirps and warbles, I realized it sounded very much like another record I'd heard – the bird sounds of the Brazilian rainforest.

"So my question was, 'Did the jungle birds hear and learn their songs from the sun-sounds we need a special receiver to hear, or does God just use the same songs over and over again, so that nature on earth is like a mirror to the music of the spheres?'"

"So, did you ask your teacher?" Peter inquired.

"Are you kidding?" was all that Maggie replied.

"Speaking of unanswered questions," Jacob said, "was I crazy back in New York, or were those guys not interested in what I had to say about the Bible code? After all, I thought that was going to be my big contribution to the conference. As soon as I got close to talking about it, they changed the subject."

"No, you weren't crazy," Peter said. "They know more about that whole thing than we'll ever know." Peter paused for a minute, then made a face.

"I suppose it won't matter now if I tell you some black information. By 'black' I mean top secret, so keep it to yourselves. Let me ask you – have you ever heard of a quantum computer?"

Jacob remembered something he had read. "They discussed the concept in some computer magazine," he said at last. "IBM, as I recall it, was working on a quantum computer that can factor lots of variables simultaneously."

"Not just lots," Peter said. *"Lots and lots* simultaneously, and on different planes of reality. Comparatively speaking, a quantum computer can find answers in half a minute that might take an ordinary computer years to figure out."

Jacob gave a whistle. "How is that possible?" he asked.

"It's quantum," Peter answered. "The idea was first suggested in the 1980's by a physicist, Richard Feynman. Its mechanics are based on some weird subatomic world of particles that can exist in multiple realities at the same time, exploring all possible answers on all possible levels.

"Of course, there were major problems to be solved. For instance, how do you present the question, and how do you know which is the correct answer? It has to do with the way you align the particle/waves, the way you probe them with lasers, that makes the thing go. The machine is designed for analyzing number sequences. It can break any prime-number encryption code in a matter of seconds."

"What do you mean by 'can'?" Maggie asked. "Are you saying this thing is operational?"

"Yes," said Peter. "We've had quantum computers up and running, more or less, for quite a while now."

"That's why they didn't care to hear my little laptop discoveries about the Bible code," Jacob said. "They had already figured it out."

"Jacob, I can't tell you what they've figured out because I myself don't know. What I've heard, though, is that there is enough material in the Bible to keep them busy for the next fifty years. Apparently, it may contain everything."

"What the heck do you mean by 'everything'?" Maggie asked.

"Exactly that. What happened and who did it. What *will* happen, and who will do it. Secrets of the physics of the three-dimensional universe, and beyond. It turns out the

Bible really may be the Book of Life. That's why they think they've found a wormhole into Eden."

"How could it have so much information?" Jacob asked. "It's just not that big a book."

"It is when you consider all the combinations," Peter said. "Consider all the possible combinations of just ten numbers – figure it out. Multiply ten times nine times eight times seven, etc., down to one. You get 3,628,800 possible combinations! Now consider all the possible combinations of all the Hebrew letter/numbers in Genesis alone. It's vast – especially when you realize that by skip-searching different sequences in different directions, you can use the same letter/numbers over and over again. For all practical purposes, the number of combinations possible in the text approaches infinity.

"And then what they did, after going through the flat text, was to stack the blocks of text like pages in a book, reading strings of Hebrew *through* the pages. They did the same through the rolled-up scrolls, as well. That way, they could move back and forth in three dimensions. Before they're done, I daresay they'll figure out how to read it in other dimensions, as well. What's interesting, though, is the coincidence of Eden with the implementation of the quantum computer. It's almost as if this breakthrough technology in Washington was timed to this strange event in Iraq – or vice versa."

"You know," Jacob said, "Bible code makes the text into a book of possibilities, the freedom of choices we were offered. Perhaps the straight text was prophecy of the choices we did make, amid the words describing our better alternatives. Until today, of course, when it seems we're bent on accelerating earth's rush from Eden to apocalypse."

Peter paused for a moment. "There's something else about their quantum research, something I thought the twelve should have told you about, as to why they chose you. It seems there are quantum probabilities that you and Maggie..." and here he paused again, "are reincarnations of that couple a thousand years ago, the ones who entered Eden. Perhaps you've already been there."

Jacob thought about that for a second, then mused, "So, back then, was I the man or the woman?"

At just that moment they were interrupted by a yell from the guard. Immediately the soldiers were on their feet, weapons in hand.

"Get away from the firelight," Peter warned sharply, "Get back behind the tents, and stay down. This may be a diversion for something else." Maggie grabbed the goat, and she and Jacob moved back. Peter unholstered his pistol and slipped into the night, away from the soldiers. Jacob pulled Maggie back until they reached a shallow indentation in the soil.

"Lie down flat," he whispered. "Whoever it is, they probably have night vision goggles, so the dark won't protect us if they want to take a shot. We can't do a thing about heat-sensing devices, but if we're out of the line of fire, that's probably good enough. Unless they kill all the guards," he added, and then wished he hadn't. "I'm sorry. Don't worry. I'm sure we'll be all right."

They lay side by side with the kid between them, like a child. Maggie held on tight to the goat, and Jacob stretched his arm across it as well, with his hand just touching Maggie's back. The goat lay quietly, as if he understood. Across the camp they heard sporadic gunfire, then silence.

After what seemed like an eternity, Jacob risked moving his arm to check his glow-in-the-dark watch. Half an hour had gone by since the shooting, but everything was still strangely silent. A few minutes later, they heard the unmistakable sound of an approaching helicopter.

Suddenly the desert burst into sound. Some gunfire, followed by a hand grenade exploding close by, and then Peter, behind them, yelling in their ears to run, run to the chopper landing by their tent. Clutching the goat with all her might, Maggie ran first, followed by Jacob and Peter. They were aboard in less than a minute, lifting off southward, deep into Saudi Arabia.

"What about the soldiers?" Jacob shouted to Peter above the helicopter noise.

"They can take care of themselves," Peter shouted back. "Besides, those guys weren't gunning for the soldiers – they were gunning for you. Once we got you out of there, the shooting was over. Nice of you to think of them, though. I'll drop them a note," Peter added, with a laugh.

"Your so-called Chaos guys are pretty wide-ranging for a mystery organization – to mount a military attack on foreign soil like that," Jacob said.

"Oh, I know who they are now. I doubt we'll be hearing from them again." Peter seemed pleased with himself.

"Well, who were they then?" Jacob asked. "They sure seemed highly motivated."

"I killed their captain," Peter said, gesturing with his right hand. Jacob could see his sleeve was stained with blood. "I got behind him and cut his throat. I'd take credit, but it was pure luck. By the way, does this mean anything to you?" Peter handed Jacob a circular pin. It was a snake eating its own tail.

"Ouroboros. It's another ancient religious symbol for immortality – first used in Egypt, I think, but later around the world. The modern version is the sideways eight that's the math symbol for infinity."

"That should tell us something, but I don't know what. I took it off the leader's jacket. Some of their men were wearing suicide vests with these on them. So this is the snake who eats its own tail – a suicide squad to preserve the immortality of... what?` Well, this might be the answer!" Peter handed him a second pin, marked KGB in Russian.

"I thought the KGB disappeared with the Soviet Union," Jacob remarked. "Is it the FSB now, or something like that?"

"The initials have changed, but the goal remains the same – to rebuild a new USSR at everyone else's expense. This captain, like Putin, was probably a holdover from the past, and proud of it."

Jacob tried to hand the pins back. "I'll take that old KGB as evidence, but you can keep the snake," Peter said. "I got others." His mind flashed for a moment on the bodies left behind at the camp. "Keep it as one of the spoils of war."

Maggie, who hadn't heard their conversation over the roar of the blades, yelled to Peter, "Where are we going?"

"It's a surprise," Peter shouted, "But I'll tell you this – you couldn't ask for a safer place!"

That was all Jacob needed to hear. He glanced over at Maggie, who was whispering reassurances in the goat's ear; then he settled back in his seat and shut his eyes.

Chapter 39   Saudi Arabia

The first glow of dawn was already coming through the window when Jacob woke and checked his watch. He wasn't sure how long they'd been airborne, and the sunrise revealed more hills than Jacob had expected. They seemed to be flying toward what once might have been a volcanic mountain, bearing on that one particular peak. The sun was rising over the desert to his left, while off to his right, Jacob could see the waters of the Gulf of Aqaba.

"We're almost there," Peter said, when he saw Jacob was awake.

"Where's there?" Jacob asked.

"Mount Sinai," Peter said with a smile.

"Wait a minute," Jacob said. "It can't be. We're on the wrong side of the Gulf of Aqaba – we're in Saudi Arabia. Mount Sinai's off in that direction," Jacob said, gesturing to the west, toward the Sinai Peninsula.

"That's what the Emperor Constantine's dear mother thought, too," Peter said. "And you know, for seventeen hundred years we took her word for it, even though there was no real supporting evidence to prove her claim was correct.

"Constantine told his mother to go find Mt. Sinai, so she didn't have much choice. She probably just got tired of looking at mountains, and had a seer pick one out. You'd think at least the builders of St. Catharine's would have looked in Midian before building their monastery at the wrong mountain. Exodus says quite clearly that Moses went to Midian, that his father-in-law was a priest of Midian."

"Well, you're right on that score," Jacob acknowledged. "Exodus 3 says:

Now Moses was keeping the flock of his father-in-law, Jethro, the priest of Midian; and he led his flock to the west side of the wilderness, and came to Horeb, the mountain of God. And the angel of the Lord appeared to him in a flame of fire out of the midst of a burning bush; and he looked, and lo, the bush was burning, yet it was not consumed.

"But there must have been a dozen sites called the mountain of God," Jacob protested, "and I thought Sinai's Mt. Sinai always won the majority vote in these disputes."

"Not really," Peter corrected. "No one's ever found the archeological evidence for a million-person encampment at the base of that mountain. In fact, they've tried using that argument to prove there never *was* an exodus from Egypt. Look for signs of Moses' people in Midian, however, and you find all the evidence you need. Or look in Galatians, where Paul wrote, 'Sinai is a mountain in *Arabia*.'"

"What's the name of this mountain we're going to, then, and how do you know it's the real Mount Sinai?" Maggie asked.

"The Arabs call it *Jabal al Lawz,* the Bedouins call it the Mountain of Moses, and the military calls it N4," Peter answered. "But no need to take anyone else's word for it – you can explore it for yourselves. We'll be in residence on the Mountain of Moses for the next twenty-four hours."

Chapter 40

Jacob had thought they'd be camping again, but as the helicopter set down inside the fifteen-foot high, chain-link and barbed-wire fence, he realized they were back in civilization.

"In a manner of speaking," Maggie replied, when Jacob shared the observation. "At least we won't have to worry about our goat running away," she added.

"No – but he may get eaten," Jacob said, looking at a cluster of armed Saudi soldiers gathering just outside the circle of turning blades.

To accommodate their guests, the soldiers had moved out of their barracks, and set up tents for themselves within the fenced area at the base of the mountain. Around Maggie's bunk someone had arranged a wall of tattered shower curtains on a rope. The young soldier who carried the goat for her took great delight in demonstrating how the shower curtains could slide open or closed.

"There's a shower stall in the back, if you want to wash up," Peter told them. There's no water heater, but the tank sits in the sun so it's not too much of a shock," he continued, glancing at Maggie.

"Also, they've offered us some spare uniforms, since we lost our gear back there. They've promised to pick up our stuff from the campsite, however, so you should have your suitcases delivered soon."

"Peter makes it sound like misdirected luggage on a flight to Boston," Jacob said to Maggie. "You go ahead and shower first," he added. "I think I'll look around outside."

"I'll give you the tour," Peter said.

Though it was still early, the sun beat down with an intensity unfamiliar to a man from Maine. Jacob pulled his cap down to shade his eyes, and walked toward something he'd noticed during the landing.

"I was wondering if you'd notice the column bases," Peter said, as Jacob headed off in that direction. "Does any scripture come to mind?"

"Exodus 24," Jacob replied, "which also offers another clue that Moses wrote this story in the Torah":

And Moses wrote all the words of the Lord. And he rose early in the morning, and built an altar at the foot of the mountain, and twelve pillars, according to the twelve tribes of Israel.

"That altar is just over there," Peter said, pointing off to their right. "It's next to an old streambed that could be the one mentioned in Deuteronomy."

Jacob stood gazing at what remained of the bases of twelve pillars. The circles stood in a straight row parallel to the mountain, exposed in a careful archeologist's trench marked off by string. Jacob estimated the columns had been eighteen feet in diameter at the base, and spaced about five feet apart.

Maggie, her hair still wet from the shower, joined them by the trench. The goat, without any leash, followed behind her. "This is incredible," she said. "It's just like it's described in Exodus."

"Come look at the altar," Peter said.

"Moses' altar, or the altar of the golden calf?" Maggie asked.

"Let's start with the golden calf," Peter said. "Follow me." Peter led them to a large mound of rocks some thirty feet high, fenced off and standing in an otherwise flat location.

"There's some thought that this is what's left of the altar of the golden calf," Peter said. "Interestingly, there's a local Bedouin legend that a golden *camel* is buried here somewhere. Their exact word is 'calf,' so I guess they assumed it was the calf of a camel. Of course, the Bible story says the golden calf was destroyed by Moses when he came down from the mountain with the stone tablets of the commandments."

Jacob said, "I know two references – this one from Exodus:

And as soon as he came near the camp and saw the calf and the dancing, Moses' anger burned hot, and he threw the tablets out of his hands and broke them at the foot of the mountain. And he took the calf which they had made, and burnt it with fire, and ground it to powder, and scattered it upon the water, and made the people of Israel drink it.

"The other comes from Deuteronomy:

Then I took the sinful thing, the calf which you had made, and burned it with fire and crushed it, grinding it very small, until it was as fine as dust; and I threw the dust of it into the brook that descended out of the mountain.

"You can see from the remains of that old stream bed just above here that the water must have run down right by this spot," Peter said. "If that's the case, it would have been easy to throw that powdered gold into the water supply. Now, look at this." Peter led them around the outside of the fence, and pointed in.

"Petroglyphs!" Maggie said in surprise. "Drawings of bulls, calves – even a man raising a calf above his head!"

"The archeologists say they're done in the Egyptian style – Hathor and Apis – cattle for worship," Peter said. "Now, follow me up the mountain a little way, and I'll show you what might have been Moses' altar." Jacob noted once again how much Peter enjoyed playing tour guide.

As they headed uphill, Jacob noticed the piles of stones all along the base of the mountain.

"And I suppose these rock piles are the 'bounds' God told Moses to set in Exodus 19?" Jacob asked. "Let's see. It goes something like:

And you shall set bounds for the people round about, saying, 'Take heed that you do not go up into the mountain or touch the border of it; whoever touches the mountain shall be put to death; no hand shall touch him, but he shall be stoned or shot; whether beast or man, he shall not live.

"That rule no longer applies," Peter assured them, "unless you're an enemy of the Saudi government."

That reminded Jacob of something he'd meant to ask about. "You mentioned back on the helicopter that the government calls this mountain 'N4'," Jacob said. "What's that about?"

"This is more than a well-guarded archeological site," Peter replied. "This has been a missile defense and radar center for the Saudi government. It's an unusual honor for three Americans to be given free run of this place, but it's only because they want something in return."

"What's that?" Jacob asked.

"They want to know what we plan to do with the Garden of Eden – and they believe you two are going to find the answer to that question."

"Well, that may or may not be the case," Jacob said after a pause. "But that still doesn't explain what we're doing here."

"Some of the twelve thought Paul may have come here during his search for Eden," Peter said, to Jacob's surprise – then added cryptically, "You're here to learn something."

And then, in an abrupt change of subject, Peter noted, "There's that other altar." He pointed out a V-shaped formation of earth and rock. "Now let's get back before we miss lunch."

Chapter 41

"So, when are you going to send that goat to Azazel?" Peter asked Maggie, as they walked Moses' boundary line back to the barracks.

"Forget it," Maggie said. "After all, he's just a kid."

"He's old enough to be growing horns," Peter said, noting the scarlet cloth from the high priest was still attached to one. "Besides, you're hauling all the sins of Israel around with you."

"Hey, all we promised was to take the goat to the wilderness," Maggie said, "and if this isn't wilderness, I don't know what is. It's not my fault if Azazel can't get through the Saudi defenses."

"Shouldn't we give him a name?" Jacob asked. "We can't keep calling him 'the kid' forever."

"I'm sure the right name will come along," Maggie said, as they reached the mess hall door.

A Saudi guard stopped them from entering, and gestured toward the goat. "No, no. Goat not permitted," he said. "Must be outside."

"You go ahead," Jacob said to Maggie and Peter. "Save me a sandwich. The kid and I want to take a walk up the mountain."

The first part of the climb was rough but not too steep, giving Jacob time to reflect on what he was seeing. "The Bible says Moses brought 600,000 *men* out of Egypt," Jacob thought, "meaning a total population of more than a million – not to mention all their flocks and their herds. The St. Catherine site on the Sinai Peninsula had no viable campsite for such a population, or grazing land for such a herd. No grazing there, no water, and yet here all that was available." He paused and looked south, over a flat plain where Moses might have stood all day, watching his men defeat the army of the Amalekites. "Hell," Jacob thought, "this sure is where *I* would have brought them. The St. Catherine's area of the Sinai Peninsula wasn't even 'out of Egypt.' It was territory controlled by pharaoh, an area where the Egyptians mined turquoise and copper, and no place for the Israeli people to feel safe. Midian, on the other hand, *was* out of Egypt; it was where Moses had left his wife and family. It was his home.

"Besides," Jacob thought, "this location ties in with that ancient, shallow wading-path that crosses the mouth of the Gulf of Aqaba. Moses lived in Midian for forty years. He no doubt knew about that shallow-water shortcut from Sinai to Midian, and probably led his people down the eastern shore of the Gulf of Suez to get there. They crossed the Red Sea at the Gulf of Aqaba – and it was the Gulf of Aqaba, with God's help, that drowned pharaoh's army. And that path would have led Moses right home to this mountain."

A while later, the walk became more of a climb. Jacob used his hands to pull himself along, but the goat had no trouble keeping pace. It was almost three o'clock when they neared the top of the mountain. Jacob marveled at the blackness of the rock up here – quite different from the buff-colored stone of the mountain below. "Could this still be black from the days of Moses?" Jacob asked. "How could that be possible?" He thought about the passage from Exodus 19:

And Mount Sinai was wrapped in smoke, because the Lord descended upon it in fire; and the smoke of it went up like the smoke of a kiln, and the whole mountain quaked greatly.

"This could have been an active volcano in Moses' day," Jacob thought to himself. "That would be a scientific explanation for the fire, smoke and shaking. It also might have been the source of the smoke by day and the fire by night that guided the Hebrews out of Egypt."

Jacob and the goat stood side by side, quietly observing the scene. There were two peaks at either side, with a large, rock-strewn plain between. To one end, Jacob could see a prominent cleft rock, perhaps the spot where the text says God protected Moses so he wouldn't be incinerated.

And the Lord said, "Behold, there is a place by me where you shall stand upon the rock; and while my glory passes by I will put you in a cleft of the rock, and I will cover you with my hand until I have passed by; then I will take away my hand, and you shall see my back; but my face shall not be seen.

Jacob walked around the plain, but didn't see anything more notable than the strange, blackened color of the terrain. Finally, he found a shady spot and a comfortable rock to sit against. The goat lay down by his side, and both of them dozed for a while.

When Jacob woke it was after four, and he realized they'd be sending a search party for him if he didn't hurry back. He was halfway down the mountain before he even noticed the goat was gone.

"Uh-oh," he thought, imagining how he would ever explain to Maggie if he lost her kid. He backtracked toward the top until he came to a side path, leading off on a level around the face. He hadn't noticed this path before, but thought the goat might have turned that way out of curiosity.

Walking cautiously along this boulder-strewn track, Jacob rounded a turn and came upon the mouth of a cave hollowed deep into the mountain. He wished now they had named the goat *something*, so he could at least call to him. It seemed impossibly stupid to be standing on the Mountain of Moses, calling out, "Goat! Oh, goat!"

Jacob stepped into the cave, and was overwhelmed by blackness. He hadn't realized how blinding the afternoon sun had been. He froze, afraid to take a step until his eyes adjusted to the dark. As he stood there he thought, "My God, could this be Elijah's cave? In First Kings they talk about an angel bringing cakes and a jar of water to the prophet Elijah:

And he arose, and ate and drank, and went in the strength of that food forty days and forty nights to Horeb the mount of God. And there he came to a cave, and lodged there; and behold, the word of the Lord came to him, and he said to him, "What are you doing here, Elijah?" He said, "I have been very jealous for the Lord, the God of hosts; for the people of Israel have forsaken thy covenant, thrown down thy altars, and slain thy prophets with the sword; and I, even I only, am left; and they seek my life, to take it away." And he said, "Go forth, and stand upon the mount before the Lord." And behold, the Lord passed by, and a great and strong wind rent the mountains, and broke in pieces the rocks before the Lord, but the Lord was not in the wind; and after the wind an earthquake, but the Lord was not in the earthquake; and after the earthquake a fire, but the Lord was not in the fire; and after the fire a still small voice. And when Elijah heard it, he wrapped his face in his mantle and went out and stood at the entrance of the cave. And behold, there came a voice to him, and said, "What are you doing here, Elijah?"

Jacob felt his way into the cave, and made an executive decision. "I am naming the goat. The goat's name is now Elijah, and I'm going to call him by name and I'm not going to feel like a fool." He sat on a rock in the blackness, and after a moment called softly, "Elijah! Here goat, come here." There was no response, not a sound but the echo of his own voice. He tried again – this time a bit louder: "Elijah! Come here! It's time to go down the mountain!"

This time he heard a voice right inside his head. It said, "Thank you for protecting me." And coming out of the darkness, the goat nuzzled his hand.

Chapter 42

It was after dinner, and Jacob, Peter, and Maggie sat in chairs outside the mess hall, finishing their coffee and talking about tomorrow morning's departure into Iraq. Their bags and camping gear had been rescued and delivered by a unit of Saudi soldiers; they agreed they were pleased to have their toothbrushes back, with changes of underwear running a close second.

During dinner, Maggie had asked Jacob what his impressions of the mountain had been, but he was strangely reticent, giving only a sketchy description of the landmarks he'd seen.

During a lull, Jacob asked Maggie, "Do you remember the Bible story of Balaam's ass?"

"Sure," she said. "It's about a talking animal that can see angels. It comes from the Book of Numbers, and tells how the King of Moab was feeling threatened by the people of Israel, since he'd seen how they trashed the Amorites. So, he sent for a holy man named Balaam to put a curse on the Israelites. God tells Balaam not to go. But the king would not take no for an answer, and this time he sends princes to persuade Balaam. They promise him great honors, and Balaam is tempted to disobey God. Balaam saddles his ass, but God sends an angel to block their way."

"The ass saw the angel standing in the road with a drawn sword," Jacob quoted,

and the ass turned aside out of the road, and went into the field; and Balaam struck the ass, to turn her into the road. Then the angel of the Lord stood in a narrow path between the vineyards, with a wall on either side. And when the ass saw the angel of the Lord, she pushed against the wall, and pressed Balaam's foot against the wall; so, he struck her again. Then the angel of the Lord went ahead, and stood in a narrow place, where there was no way to turn either to the right or to the left. When the ass saw the angel of the Lord, she lay down under Balaam; and Balaam's anger was kindled, and he struck the ass with his staff. Then the Lord opened the mouth of the ass, and she said to Balaam, "What have I done to you, that you have struck me these three times?" And Balaam said to the ass, "Because you have made sport of me. I wish I had a sword in my hand, for then I would kill you." And the ass said to Balaam, "Am I not your ass, upon which you have ridden all your life-long to this day? Was I ever accustomed to do so to you?" And he said, "No." Then the Lord opened the eyes of Balaam, and he saw the angel of the Lord standing in the way, with his drawn sword in his hand; and he bowed his head, and fell on his face.

"That's a great story," Peter said, "but what the hell has it got to do with tomorrow's trip?"

Jacob decided this was not a good time to announce that Elijah the goat had spoken to him. "Nothing, I suppose," said Jacob. "Nothing at all." Then after a minute, as if in reply to Peter's question, Jacob asked, "Peter, why did the Saudis allow us on this mountain? Was it just a request from the twelve to their oil buddies, or is something else going on here?"

"Actually, it was a little of both," Peter said. "When the Eden thing showed up on our equipment, something turned up on the Saudi sensors on this hill. I don't know what exactly – they call them anomalies, just like our government does. It's as if the two places are connected, somehow. Anyway, the twelve wanted you to stop here. They thought something important might happen. I guess they were wrong."

Jacob glanced at Elijah the goat, who seemed to be watching him. "I guess they were," Jacob said.

Chapter 43   Iraq

Peter shook Jacob awake. Outside it was pitch black, and Jacob groaned. "Is this some kind of cruel joke?" he asked mechanically, as he pulled on his pants.

"The plane will be here in a minute," Peter said. "Maggie is already up and dressed."

They walked down through the gate and stepped into the wilderness, away from the Mountain of Moses. Maggie had already nicknamed the goat Eli, and made a leash from the rope that held the shower curtains around her bunk. Like a trained dog, the goat trotted happily by her side.

There was a sudden roar in the air above, and an unlit Harrier jet descended vertically in front of them. "Isn't this a bit of overkill – transportation-wise, I mean?" Jacob yelled above the roar.

"Helicopters are too slow and way too obvious," Peter shouted back. "This Harrier II is built with some stealth technology, so we should be able to get you two into Iraq – and us out again – undetected."

It proved a surprisingly short flight, given the build-up, Jacob reflected, as he, Maggie, and Eli stood watching the Harrier lift off from the Iraqi desert. They had agreed with Peter to wait in one of the tents left behind by the pilgrims who'd entered the door, until there was daylight enough to see what to do. They had radio communications, flashlights, first-aid kits, dehydrated food, and water for a week, and all contained in relatively comfortable backpacks. The goat, Peter said, would have to fend for himself.

"That's a better deal than if I told them he spoke to me," Jacob thought. "If I'd said anything like that, they'd have Eli in transit right now, back to some lab cage in Washington."

Just before he left, Peter handed Jacob his missing flip phone, much the worse for wear. "The pilot gave it to me," Peter said. "It got blown out of that Mercedes when it wrecked, so they knew who they were after. It was time for a new phone, anyway. That one went out of style years ago."

Peter also gave them one final suggestion. "While you two are sitting in that tent waiting for daylight, you should compare notes on what you know about evil."

"Why?" Maggie asked. "What do you mean?"

"It was something the twelve suggested to me in their call this morning. Apparently, they are thinking you could encounter evil in Eden as well as good. They don't want you caught off guard."

It was a little after four in the morning when they felt settled enough to consider Peter's suggestion. Within a partially collapsed tent they'd found a lantern, cushions, and the comfort of an ancient, beautiful Bedouin carpet. Maggie, Jacob, and the goat lay relaxed on the rug, while the lantern flame highlighted the reds and blues of the carpet and threw strange, ghostly shadows on the canvas sides of the tent.

"So, what do you think caused the origin of evil?" Maggie asked. "Do you believe that evil is real, or just a name for the absence of good?"

"I would call something like the holocaust more than the 'absence of good,'" Jacob replied. "No, I would say that something happened early in the history of creation that made things what they are today. I disagree, though, with putting the blame on Adam and Eve. They disobeyed God's command not to eat of the tree of knowledge, but *until* they ate it, they didn't really comprehend the meaning of right and wrong. It was a catch-22, but not what I would call evil.

"No, it wasn't until they were out of the garden that bad behavior flowered in Cain's killing of his brother, Abel. But it seems to me the world had already been corrupted by then. I have to admit, I agree with you now that whole civilizations existed outside the protective garden God made for his special creations, Adam and Eve. Personally, I think the embodiment of evil in the world is described in Genesis 6, the passage about the fallen angels:

When men began to multiply on the face of the ground, and daughters were born to them, the sons of God – angels – saw that the daughters of men were fair; and they took to wife such of them as they chose. Then the Lord said, "My spirit shall not abide in man forever, for he is flesh, but his days shall be a hundred and twenty years." The Nephilim were on the earth in those days, and also afterward, when the sons of God came in to the daughters of men, and they bore children to them. These were the mighty men that were of old, the men of renown.

The Lord saw that the wickedness of man was great in the earth, and that every imagination of the thoughts of his heart was only evil continually. And the Lord was sorry that he had made man on the earth, and it grieved him to his heart. So the Lord said, "I will blot out man whom I have created from the face of the ground, man and beast and creeping things and birds of the air, for I am sorry that I have made them." But Noah found favor in the eyes of the Lord.

"I think what we're being told is that angels and women had children who were the superheroes of the day. They were the ones who probably became the cross-bred gods of Greek and Roman legend, such as the Greeks' Heracles, Hercules to the Romans. They were out of balance with God's creation, doing major damage. At first, God limits life spans to 120 years. When that's not enough, he decides to flood the earth and wash it clean."

"Okay," Maggie said, "let's say angels did seduce human women. Why were there angels here on earth? Was it because there was a rebellion in heaven, led by the prideful angel Lucifer? That story says a third of the angels followed him and got thrown out of heaven, down to earth. Or is it the other story – that there were innocent angels on earth, assigned to watch over us, who then seduced – or were seduced by – the daughters of men? You know the Hebrew word *ir*, 'watcher,' is used to describe angels in Daniel. It comes from the term for city lookouts, who were to keep their eyes peeled for danger. And 'watcher' is used in the Book of Enoch, where the fallen angel stories seem to come together in one telling."

"Well, however angels got here," Jacob said, "their breeding with human women and having children by them seems to be where the line got crossed. After all, Adam and Eve ate the forbidden fruit, Cain killed Abel, and every other form of sin got committed in the world. But it was this interbreeding of species, this crossing of kinds, that broke a fundamental law of creation: *Let the earth bring forth living creatures according to their kinds.* In other words, don't be messing with the DNA. Bringing them forth *not* according to their kinds was what made God regret his creation and want to destroy it.

"Maggie, remember the story of Leda and the swan? That might be a mythic memory of pre-flood genetic tampering. There was Zeus, presumably a fallen angel playing god, who lusted after a human woman, Leda. So to seduce, or some say, rape her, Zeus becomes the image of a swan, and impregnates her with Helen, later known as Helen of Troy, and her twin, Pollux. And both of them are born in egg shells! Because a swan was the father, Leda laid eggs that these two semi-mortal humans hatched from. I think the telling and retelling of that story over millennia may have scrambled those eggs, so to speak, but the genetic elements are all there – cross species breeding of angel and human, combined with a swan to explain the notion that human women carry eggs to be fertilized. Greeks and Romans didn't have that understanding, but a pre-flood, advanced civilization could have been deep into God-offending, petri-dish experimentation. The details of the story may have gotten scrambled, but not the warning."

"So, you think it's genetic tampering that spiritually pollutes the earth," Maggie replied. "I wonder what mixing sheep with goats, putting fish genes in tomatoes, sticking weed killers in genetically modified foods and human genes in pigs, is doing to God's opinion of us?"

"Not to mention those Pauline Christians the twelve said they genetically modified. To tell you the truth," Jacob said, "I think we're about to find out."

They agreed it was way past time to get some sleep. They had unrolled their sleeping bags on opposite sides of the tent, and turned off the lantern, when Jacob felt something square and hard under his back. Turning over, flashlight in hand, he uncovered a carved wooden box with a diary inside, and read a few pages.

"Maggie?" he said, hoping she wasn't already asleep. "How do you feel about the notion that we meet the God we believe in?"

Half awake, Maggie responded with a thought she'd had about near-death experiences. "I always thought the NDE stories I read about were quite personal, theologically speaking. That is, Christians often meet a loving being they call Jesus, while people of other faiths meet the being they have been praying to. Is that what you mean?"

"Maggie, these people who got here before us – they call themselves the Followers of Paul, and they seem to believe what Marcion of Sinope believed – that the God of the Old Testament was a lesser God than the God of Jesus."

"Wasn't Marcion a gnostic?" Maggie asked.

"Similar. He had nothing but scorn for the Hebrew Bible, the Old Testament, but he didn't believe in gnostic secret knowledge. He built a canon based on Luke's Gospel and Paul's letters, but he saw the Old Testament God as totally incompatible – wrathful, tyrannical, an unmerciful demi-urge – really, God as the devil. And yet, nevertheless, he believed that God was the creator of the world."

"Marcion..." Maggie said, now fully awake. "Marcion was declared a heretic and excommunicated in the second century, and all his writings were destroyed. How can there be Marcionites still running around, and why would they come here? To their way of thinking, Eden would be a creation of the God of the devil, wouldn't it?"

"Maggie, remember my theory that Paul came out here and spent as much as three years looking for the *Gan Eden*, the third heaven he saw during the vision of Jesus that brought on his conversion? What if these Paul people are attempting to trace his footsteps during his quest?"

"Did Paul actually find the door to Eden?" Maggie asked.

"I don't think so," Jacob said. "My hunch is his search was based on a misunderstanding. Paul may have been told by Jesus that he would visit Eden again before he died – but not this way. Years after his first vision, Paul was stoned nearly to death by a crowd. I believe that stoning triggered his second near-death experience, and a second visit to the Eden he longed to see again."

"But now, two thousand years later, Paul's followers have made it through the door," Maggie responded. "What do you suppose that means?"

"I don't think it's good," Jacob said. "That's why I woke you up with the question, do we meet the God we believe in? If that's the case, they have entered the realm of the creator God, Marcion's devil God of the Old Testament, and that may have sealed their fate."

Chapter 44   The Phoenix Door

It was the first light of dawn. Jacob walked cautiously around the fallen tents, camp gear, and abandoned supplies that littered the desert floor, while Maggie, holding the goat, followed behind. The mound of wind-shaped sand was not particularly unique, except for the wooden door that stood on its eastern side. The door leaned into the mound "like a bulkhead," Jacob said to Maggie. Its pitch reminded him of the wooden basement entry to the house he'd grown up in. His family rarely used it, and it was something of an adventure when it was opened for the plumber, or the man who cleaned the furnace.

The raised, golden phoenix made *this* door, however, like no other door Jacob had seen. He looked carefully before touching it, noting there were no handles, bolts or hinges visible, and any evidence of a frame seemed covered by the sand. It appeared some of the other visitors had attempted to dig holes in the sand on either side of the door, but all they found was more sand, as if the door simply lay against the mound, and opened to nothing at all.

"For some early Christians, the phoenix symbolized resurrection," Maggie commented.

"Yes, the story goes the bird burns up and resurrects new from the ashes every 500 years or so," Jacob replied. "There was a poem in the ninth century Book of Exeter, with the line, 'This bird's nature is much like to the chosen servants of Christ.' References to the resurrection bird go back as far as written history, with corollaries such as the Persian simurgh. The Egyptians believed the phoenix flew from Arabia to an altar in Heliopolis to deliver the ashes it sprang from, wrapped in an egg of myrrh. An interesting parallel, since that's the spice the wise men brought to the infant Jesus."

"Those Persian stories *are* interesting," Maggie said. "They say the simurgh was around to see the destruction of the world three times over. They said it nests in a tree of life that stands in the middle of the world seas, and when it takes flight, the seeds of that tree and the seeds of every plant fall out, healing the world. The simurgh represents the union between the earth and the sky, and serves as a messenger in-between."

"But there's an ominous note, as well," Jacob added. "In Islamic myth the simurgh was created perfect by God, but later on became a plague, and was killed." They both fell silent for a moment.

"But wait," Jacob suddenly remembered. "There's a remarkable story in the Greek Apocalypse of Baruch, which may have been written as early as 70 AD, the time of the temple's destruction by the Romans. Baruch visits the third heaven, and there is shown the phoenix. And guess what the phoenix does!"

Maggie was nonplused.

"No, seriously," Jacob said, suddenly quite excited. "It's the phoenix' job to protect the earth from the rays of the sun! The bird's giant wingspan shades the earth! Baruch is told, 'Unless his wings were screening the rays of the sun, no living creature would be preserved.' Don't you see? Somehow, perhaps, this phoenix door contains our answer to global warming!"

"Unless we can get through this door," Maggie said, "I don't think we'll get an answer to anything. So, what do we do now?" Maggie asked the bird on the door, not expecting an answer.

"By the looks of the camping gear, the others had to wait awhile," Jacob said. "But I don't think we have the luxury."

"I wonder what's happened to the others," Maggie said.

As if in answer, the door slowly swung in, revealing a flight of steps downward. Against the glare of the rising sun, the opening seemed almost totally opaque. Jacob remembered his vision of the black cormorant door on Penobscot Bay, and didn't hesitate. With flashlight in hand, he led Maggie and the scapegoat slowly down the stairs.

As their eyes adjusted to the dark, the answer to Maggie's question became apparent. The fate of the Marcionites was written on each step in discrete piles of ash, as if, phoenix-like, they had self-immolated. Jacob let the flashlight play over each mound, though the breeze from the open door was already mixing them, blowing them away. Jacob glanced at Maggie. She looked terrified, and Jacob was sure she was about to panic back up the stairs and out into the sunlit world above. "Looks like this happened to them as soon as they came through the door. At least they got the first half of the phoenix experience," Jacob joked grimly.

That's when the goat made Maggie's decision for her. In an instant he struggled free from her arms, and went trotting down the stairs into the blackness below. "No!" Maggie cried, and went plunging after him. Realizing what had happened, Jacob turned his flashlight to the path ahead as well as he could for Maggie, who was nearly running down the dark stone corridor. "Maggie," he called out, suddenly in pursuit, "Slow down! Be careful! Just let the damned thing go!"

"No!" she cried. "He can't have gotten far!" Behind them, Jacob realized, the Phoenix Door, of its own accord, was swinging closed.

As the glare from the doorway disappeared, Jacob began to see more clearly. There was writing on these ancient walls, but not a writing Jacob recognized. Was it cuneiform, some form of Sumerian, Sanskrit – or variants of all three? He made a mental note to check it out when they'd caught up with Eli, but no time for it right now. He sprinted down the hallway, trying to throw some light for Maggie to see by.

"Where is he?" Maggie asked, and Jacob could hear the panic in her voice. "Could we have missed him back there?"

"No," Jacob said, "He must have run ahead. But why? You'd think with that sin-load, he'd be more panicked than we are," Jacob said, and squeezed her arm. "That was a joke, lady," he added, to break the tension. But Maggie was ignoring him, peering into the blackness.

"Look!" she said suddenly. "Isn't that a light down there?"

Jacob stared down the dark corridor. A pale, reflected light pulsed on the right wall about three hundred yards ahead. "It looks like the tunnel turns to the left down there, and it must open out into something. I'll bet that's where we'll find Elijah."

They ran together down the length of the tunnel, their footing surer as they approached the light. They turned the corner, and were nearly blinded by the glow. It was a flashing light, like the beacon of a Maine lighthouse, Jacob thought, but muted, diffused by a heavy fog, a kind of dry ice mist that billowed and swirled around the opening.

"Take my hand," Jacob said. "We could lose each other in this."

As they stepped into the fog, everything around them disappeared. Jacob couldn't see a thing, nor could he hear. The only sensation he remembered from before was the grasp of Maggie's hand in his. "Maggie?" he asked out loud, but realized as he said it that she couldn't hear, either. He couldn't pull her closer, and he couldn't let go. Their walk had slowed, stopped, and yet they were still moving forward, like on a moving walkway, yet not like that at all. Jacob cleared his mind of analogies, and let himself relax into the undifferentiated light. There was nothing to think about at all.

Time passed... away. Maggie thought she heard music, but without a rhythm, no beat, no time. "I am imagining this," she thought, and then rejected the idea. She knew the limits of her imagination. Maggie guessed Jacob's hand was still in hers, but she couldn't see him, couldn't hear him, couldn't even read his mind. She suddenly realized she did read his mind, all the time, and never knew it until the link had been removed. She realized that she read minds everywhere, and that others must read her mind, as well. What at any other time would have seemed invasive, threatening, now made her feel incredibly alone, alone with herself; that spark that jumped from the fire had jumped farther than any spark should go. She suddenly knew what it meant to be lost, really lost, and she grasped Jacob's hand with all her strength.

Jacob felt at one with his aloneness, as if the isolation fulfilled a longing that had been there all his life. It wasn't about him, really, not his learning or his ego or his life. It was about being, being a mirror to the singularity of God, a small sliver, a fragment of broken mirror, no doubt, but one that caught the great image for a fraction of a second of infinity.

And then they were through, out of the mist, and the pulsing light had disappeared, as well. Through it all, Jacob and Maggie had kept hold of each other, as incredible as it seemed. Maggie looked at Jacob, and Jacob at Maggie, with unembarrassed love. They looked deep into one another's eyes, deep into one another's souls; they could hear the thoughts of one another once again, and they were not ashamed.

"That was the angel with the flashing sword," Jacob said, answering Maggie's question even before she asked. "Did you feel it looking at us, through us, into all the nooks and crannies? That's the best bouncer I've ever run into." Jacob smiled, thinking, "I guess we don't need to leave our sense of humor at the door." Maggie laughed at the joke he'd thought.

"We still have to find Eli," Maggie thought, but as a fact, not as a fear. They began to look around in ways they'd never done before.

Jacob realized at once that he was no longer seeing with his eyes, as such, but with some other organ of recognition. When he communicated with Maggie, the image of her eye/soul filled his perceptions, and it was all he saw. When Maggie recalled Eli, however, it drew him out of her and into their surroundings once again.

"Look at this place," Jacob thought to Maggie. "Look at this flower!" It seemed to Maggie rather like a cosmos, a pinkish purple color which burst from the stamen like an exploding universe. Both of them stared into the flower, and the image in their minds amplified the flower itself – though how, they couldn't understand. After a minute, Jacob broke the connection.

"Do you suppose the flower sees us seeing it?" Jacob whispered. The whisper seemed deafening, compared to thinking it.

"And we see the flower seeing us seeing it," Maggie replied with certainty. "It's like ripples in a pond, except they flow both ways, out from the stone you've tossed, but in again, as well. It's an action-reaction that never ends. But that's physically impossible, isn't it?" They both knew that here it wouldn't be, and said no more about it.

With effort, they turned from the particular and looked around. "It's like looking in stereo," Maggie thought. "I'm perceiving my perceptions and Jacob's, as well."

"We normally see in stereo," Jacob responded gently. "We've gone beyond, into surround, or echo chamber, or something else. Look at the green of the trees! It's the greenness of green, the essence of color, the Platonic ideal of green, its...." Jacob grew vexed with trying to label the unspeakable. "It's just beautiful."

"Yes," Maggie echoed, "Just beautiful."

They stood in a small, round field, filled with sweet-smelling grasses and wildflowers. Along the edge of the field they could hear a stream as it ran splashing over stones. Beyond the stream, a forest of giant trees, tall as any redwoods, seemed to spread in all directions. The vast forest floor reminded Maggie of the space in a cathedral, the giant trunks like black columns supporting the vaulted canopy above.

"The Hopi believe there have been four worlds," Maggie thought, "each one a lesser version of the one before. Each time, mankind lays waste to the gift until, like Noah's family, only a few survive the inevitable destruction. Perhaps we went through some sort of time warp and entered one of those former worlds?"

"I suppose it's possible Eden was a portion of that third world that God decided to preserve," Jacob thought, "like we've tried to preserve our national parks. The Hebrew meaning of 'garden' is a protected place, hedged about to keep away the degraded world outside. Clearly the hedge is not a hedge as we understand it, and there's no way of knowing how big this garden is. I guess if we're going to look around, we'd better try to remember how to get back here. I don't see any path through the forest, so there won't be markers unless we make them. I only wish I knew what we're supposed to do."

"We are supposed to find Eli," Maggie said. "I know now we were supposed to let him go, but like those ripples I mentioned, we have to find him, as well." She reasoned with authority, and Jacob didn't presume to question her. It was hard to think about anything, in a clearing as radiant as this. They quickly crossed the stepping-stone brook, and walked, like Hansel and Gretel, into the forest beyond.

Chapter 45

Elijah the goat was surprised to find he was aware in ways he'd never known before. He'd always been able to feel I'm hungry, I'm bored, I'm afraid, I'm energized, I'm tired, and that was enough to survive. His life until a few days ago had been easy. The two-legged creatures had kept him penned, but in exchange they fed and watered him, and let him play with the children.

Then there was the crowd, the altar, the blood, his brother destroyed, the smell of death and the hands of the priest on his head. He didn't understand the hands, or what they meant, but it was a burden on his heart, a pain that hadn't gone away until he'd raced down the dark tunnel, through the mist and into the field of light. Then, suddenly, everything had come clear. It's not only that he had the words to say things; rather, the images that now came to his mind were not just to react to, they were something more. It was as if a door kept closed in his mind had opened for him. He was more than he'd ever realized. He wished there were another goat, a herd of goats there with him to share.

Eli thought to linger in the sweet field, to graze on grasses and drink from the stream. He did that for a second, but felt called to go farther when he saw his reflection in the water. Perhaps he was afraid the two-legged creatures would take him away, take him back to the heat of the desert. After all, they had chased him through the dark tunnel, hadn't they? These two-legged creatures were well meaning, but weird.

The forest was overgrown and tangled, but not as dark as he'd expected. There seemed to be an ambient glow that emanated from nearly everything – from the tree trunks, the stones, even from the soft moss of the forest floor. Almost immediately, Eli came to a smooth, well-worn path. The path smelled strange to him, like dead skin. He looked for another way, but realized he could never run through the dense woods except by the path. He'd never been free, and now he was freer than any goat, even the wildest of mountain goats, could possibly imagine.

Chapter 46

The forest was grand but uncared for, littered with a tangled mass of broken branches and trees that had splintered and crashed onto others fallen centuries before. By contrast, the forest floor itself was soft with the thick carpet of decomposition, topped with the greenest mosses Jacob had ever seen. It would have been tough going, but they soon came to a smooth, well-worn path that stretched in both directions. They paused for a second, peering right and left down the shaded alternatives.

"Eli went this way," Maggie suddenly thought with authority, and without explanation turned right and started down the trail. Jacob didn't see how she knew, and was annoyed he had to ask. After all, she could share every secret of her mind with him when she wanted to. He was chagrined to discover that with practice, people could learn to shut one another out – even in Eden.

"Well, what do you think happened to Adam and Eve?" Maggie thought, in answer to his thought. She'd opened the door as easily as she had closed it, making Jacob feel clumsy and vulnerable.

"Cut that out," he said out loud, and was startled by the sound of his own voice. "What happened to Adam and Eve was Eve not playing by the rules. She was the reason we got evicted from here in the first place."

Maggie knew Jacob didn't blame Eve for the fall. Back in Bangor, during some of their best wine-soaked theology discussions, Jacob had gone too far the other way, in fact, until Maggie felt he was implying Eve hadn't been a fully responsible adult. "Say what you will about Eve being up against the guile of Satan," Maggie had insisted. "You know she'd been told by God not to eat from that tree, and she did it anyway. I say that's her fault. Now Adam, on the other hand, was persuaded by Eve. She was hardly a Satan-class seducer, so Adam must have been a real pushover – the Homer Simpson of his day," Maggie had said.

Maggie turned to Jacob and said simply, "They both were warned that the knowledge of good and evil would lead to death, and so it did. End of story."

Jacob had calmed enough to reflect on what Maggie was saying. "You're right," he thought, "I'm sorry." He paused for a moment, then continued, "Maggie, I know you're anxious to find Eli, but perhaps we should stop for a minute and figure out what we're doing here – and what we're *supposed* to be doing. Obviously, those guys back at the door made a big mistake. We should go over what we know about Eden, just to figure out what we might be up against – and to figure out why we're here."

Jacob walked over to a large tree and sat down, letting his back settle against the ancient bark. Maggie looked down the path, trying to gauge if her sense of Eli's trail would stay with her. She couldn't be sure, but joined Jacob on the forest floor. The canopy was high above them, but a huge, fallen tree next to them revealed a readable portion of its growth rings. The tree's trunk was twelve feet across, and Maggie did a quick estimate. This tree had lived at least five thousand years. It would take hundreds more before this monster turned to moss.

"We'd better pool our theology and figure out if this garden is as benign as it seems," Jacob said. He could feel his rational mind fighting desperately against the euphoria of sensation. After all, God may have created this paradise to protect Adam and Eve, but look what happened to them – and to it. Death had entered the garden.

"Genesis tells us God created Adam from the dust of the earth, and enclosed him in a garden, a protected place," Jacob went on. "That implies Eden was a place of safety. What was Adam being protected from?" Maggie could feel a lecture coming on, but suddenly felt too comfortable to object. She was only half listening.

"There's another way of reading the text besides Schroeder's six-day/fourteen-billion-year equation. Look at it this way: We have a description of a creation that could have been a re-creation – a restoration, really – that could have followed a conflagration that took place as recently as 10,000 BCE. You know how Genesis tells it: the first day brought the differentiation of light and dark, as the volcanic mask of airborne debris begins to settle; the second day, a super-saturated atmosphere and glacial melt give up their water to the ocean which covers the surface of earth; the third day the dry land emerges as the oceans recede, followed by the regrowth of grasses, herbs and trees; the fourth day the sun, moon and stars become visible as the atmosphere clears completely; the fifth day, surviving fish and birds come forth; and the sixth day, surviving animal and human species – the remnants of whatever disaster it was that befell Earth – come out of their caves and hiding places. 'And God blessed them, and God said unto them, replenish the earth, and subdue it.' Some claim that because the King James says 're-plenish', and not 'plenish', that this makes the case. Unfortunately, it's a distinction without a difference in the original Hebrew. Nevertheless, God *may* have meant restock the earth, like it was before the disaster. Peter's Epistle reminds us that for God a single day is a thousand years, which may give us a way to calculate a date for the creation of Adam."

Jacob paused, lost in thought for a moment. "Now why, if everything was so good, did God decide to build a protected place and a new man – and from scratch, rather than from the sperm-and-egg-bank already flourishing outside the garden wall? Was there something special about Adam and Eve, or had things just gone terribly wrong outside? Maybe those men and women that God told the earth to bring forth – 'in our image, after our likeness' – were already in the process of being polluted and corrupted by superior powers also made in God's image."

Maggie knew where Jacob was going, but hesitated. "That timeline would better fit the four worlds of the Hopis, and the three world destructions the simurgh was witness to. But you are still trying to fit spiritual events to our old understanding of time. You're talking fallen angels again, aren't you? The third of heaven's population who followed Lucifer's rebellion down to earth. But you see," Maggie reminded Jacob, "our clock and calendar may not corollate well for these sets of circumstances."

"Yes," said Jacob, "but for our immediate circumstances, like we were saying last night, it may be Genesis' chapter six that's key: 'There were giants in the earth in those days; and also after that, when the sons of God came in unto the daughters of men, and they bore children to them, the same became mighty men which were of old, men of renown.' It took flooding the whole world, according to Genesis, to wash things clean again."

"And even that didn't work completely," Maggie added, suddenly realizing this wasn't a philosophical discussion anymore. If there were giant trees in this paradise, was it possible there could be giant people, the children of angels, surviving here as well?

"But we haven't seen animals of any size," Maggie remarked, "let alone giant people. And if this is a protected place, why would God have let giants in here?"

Jacob looked at her. He had a response, but not an answer. "If this place was such a fortress, what was the snake doing in the middle of it, just waiting for the chance to screw things up? The serpent was here from the beginning, and only God knows why. We won't discover the answer to that one, sitting here. That way madness lies.

"So, let's approach this from another angle. We came here by way of a door, down a tunnel and through a mist. Reason would tell us that we went underground, but that can't possibly be true. You can't grow trees hundreds of feet tall in a basement, and even though we can't see the sky right now, the sun was shining in that field back there. So, where are we?"

Maggie was getting into the workings of Jacob's mind. "Okay, well, let's see. We could be drugged, or hallucinating. Since we seem to be linked psychically, perhaps we're in some kind of drug-heightened holographic image together. You don't suppose Peter's government buddies are doing this, do you, like the CIA gave LSD to soldiers in Vietnam?" Maggie had been joking, but saw that Jacob took the suggestion seriously. He sat quietly for a few minutes, exploring the possibility.

"I could see them choosing people like us for that kind of experiment," he said softly. "We're both good examples of the true believer type. People with faith take a lot on faith, and frequently get burned in the process. Christianity always has its children's crusades...." The thought trailed off.

Maggie shook her head. "No, that's not what's going on," she decided. "If they had this kind of technology, they wouldn't need to drag us into the middle of Iraq to test it.

They could have created Easter Island in the middle of downtown Bangor and convinced us it was a miracle. No, this is irrational but real, like the disciples witnessing the transfigured Jesus, speaking on the mountain with Moses and Elias."

"But that wouldn't preclude a multi-dimensional state," Jacob added. "Some doorway we've crossed through to some parallel space. There are two possible meanings for the word Eden. In the cuneiform texts, in Akkad-Sumerian, it's *edin*, the fertile plain. In Hebrew it's *eden*, paradise, and I'd say that's where we are. The key questions are, why are we meant to be here, and who's here with us?"

Maggie had enough. "We'll never get the answers just sitting," she said, getting to her feet. "Besides, I want to find Elijah." They set off again, continuing on the path through the jumbled, self-illuminating forest.

Chapter 47

Eli had kept to a steady trot through the forest for over an hour now, and every step had been a marvel to him. Every time he noticed something, he noticed that he'd noticed. He was building a context of recognition – consciously! He was observing himself observing.

And it seemed so natural! Where had his mind been all this time? Why, if he'd had these powers back in Jerusalem, he might have been able to save his brother! He discovered the feeling of regret, and his eyes grew moist. His brother had been cut and killed by that priest, and the blood had pulsed onto the altar in rhythm with his brother's heart, and in rhythm with his own.

He came to a small opening in the forest where the canopy divided, and sunlight poured through. The terrain had turned hilly, and a spring flowed from the side of a rise to form a little pool that reflected a patch of blue sky above. Eli remembered the quick glimpse of himself he'd seen in the stream in the field. It had frightened him, and he'd turned away quickly, before he saw too much. This time he approached the pool deliberately, looking hard and long at his own reflection.

A goat stared back at him from a mirror of the deepest, purest water he'd ever seen. The fine white coat had an aura about it that fluoresced reds and yellows, and his bony legs seemed infused with a strength far beyond their ordinary capacity.

But it was the reflection of his eyes that captured the goat's full attention. His brother's eyes had seemed flat, with a brownish yellow color like the ground cornmeal they'd been fed. These eyes, staring back, were nothing of the sort. They echoed with a resonance deeper than the pool itself, an echo of Eli, and a time before Eli, that made the scapegoat's tender mind ache.

An iridescent hummingbird entered the reflection, and hovered by Eli's right ear. The goat did a double-take; he'd seen no other animals in the woods until now. Moreover, it seemed as if the bird had sprung from the emanations of Eli's own aura.

"You're going in circles," the hummingbird told him, or rather, thought somehow into Eli's mind. The goat barked in surprise, jumped back from the pool and looked around. The bird hung glistening in the air above his head.

"I'm right here, silly," said the bird, flitting within an inch of Eli's nose.

"How do you talk inside my head like that?" Eli thought. "Can you hear my thoughts, too?"

"Of course," said the bird. "I'm your guardian angel, and I'm telling you you're going in circles."

"What's a guardian angel?" Eli asked, and then added, "I already have a good sense of direction."

""You're in new territory now," said the bird. "If you didn't need me, I wouldn't be here."

"How did you know I needed you?" Eli persisted.

"*You* knew you needed me," the hummingbird replied.

"I didn't think I needed you," Eli responded, growing annoyed. "Why did you think I did?" The stubborn goat nature was beginning to show.

"Look," thought the bird, "I'll make it easy for you. Don't think of me as anything other than a part of you. I know I said I was an angel, but I'm also called an elemental, a spiritual creation of your own goat-headed nature. It's just that here, in the garden, I can manifest myself as something other than you. Look at me! Don't you think the hummingbird suits my nature?"

"Whatever," thought the goat. This was getting more complicated than it was worth.

"Tell me why I'm going in circles."

"Because the garden is round, and it's the nature of things to move in circles. Right now, you're following a path around the outer edge – it's the way most living things spend their lives. Eventually you'll come back to the beginning, to where you came in. Unless you make a radical diversion, you'll never get to the heart of the garden, or learn what brought you here in the first place."

"What if I don't want to?" the goat asked obstinately.

"Then continue on the course you're following," said the bird. "I can't stop you."

Chapter 48

Lost in her own thoughts, Maggie had lost track of his. "What are you thinking about?" she asked. They'd been walking in silence for almost a mile.

"Now I'm thinking about Lilith," Jacob said. "When the twelve warned us about her, I thought it was a joke. After all, Lilith has always been considered a figment of the medieval Jewish mind, with little mention in the ancient texts. The name does appear in Isaiah 34, describing the desolated country of Edom: 'Wildcats shall meet with hyenas, goat-demons shall call to each other; there too Lilith shall repose, and find a place to rest. There shall the owl nest and lay and hatch and brood in its shadow.' But as far as I know, the Lilith idea only got popular after it appeared in the Alphabet of Ben-Sira stories, which were little more than bizarre folktales – a sort of Jewish Brothers Grimm."

"The feminists like her," Maggie responded. "Legend says she was Adam's first wife, created by God from the dust of the earth, like Adam, and she wanted equal status. When Adam tried to dominate her, she flew off in a rage, and three angels sent by God found her by the Red Sea, taking on demon lovers and birthing demon offspring. The angels sent by God could not persuade her to return. By her disobedience she became a demon, too – a seducer of men, a killer of babies, the wife of the angel of death. Amulets to protect the newborn from Lilith were common in medieval Jewish communities. Of course, feminists reply that's what all patriarchal religions believe – that uppity women are evil. I remember seeing a copy of a Jewish feminist magazine titled *Lilith*, in her honor."

"Do you subscribe to that?" Jacob quipped. The double meaning was lame.

"Keep that up and I sure will," Maggie said. "Seriously, though, there is a very early reference to Lilith in the Epic of Gilgamesh, according to Kramer and Wolkstein. It seems the goddess Inanna, named the queen of heaven 4000 years before Mary, was tending a huluppa tree she wanted for the wood to build a throne and a bed. But when she returned after ten years, she found a serpent 'who could not be charmed' had made its nest in the roots of the tree, the storm-bird Anzu had nested in the branches of the tree, and the 'dark maid,' Lilith, had built her home in the trunk. Fortunately for Inanna, Gilgamesh came to her rescue and chased away the riff-raff. But seriously," Maggie concluded, "Why would you think there's any truth to these stories?"

"Because of where and when they originated," Jacob said. "Before all this began, I'd have written Lilith off as a folk tale. But now, consider the source. There are some surprising parallels between Cathar Christian beliefs and Jewish Kabbalistic demonology. Or maybe it's not so surprising. After all, they had a common meeting-place in medieval Provence, before the Templar fortress was destroyed. And if the twelve have some records from the pilgrims' visit here a thousand years ago, it would have come through Provence. Perhaps the Cathars knew something about Lilith firsthand that the Kabbalists had recorded in their medieval writings."

"I hope you're wrong about that," Maggie said softly. "The King James translates Lilith as 'screech owl,' while the Douay prefers 'lamia', a female vampire, a sucking mouth – not a happy picture. I'd just as soon not run into anything like that."

"Michelangelo portrayed her as half-woman, half-snake, wrapped around the tree of knowledge," Jacob added. "I'd rather not run into that, either."

They came to a clearing, where a small pool reflected the sky. "Look there!" Maggie shouted excitedly. "Those are Eli's hoof prints!" In the soft mud, quite close to the edge of the pool, the deep outlines of goat hooves were clearly visible.

Jacob knelt by the pool and scooped up some water in his hand. "This is the sweetest water I've ever tasted," he said. "I can't believe anything as dangerous as a Lilith could live in a paradise like this."

"Don't forget the serpent," Maggie muttered, studying the tracks. "Jacob, it looks like Eli turned here – his tracks are leading off at right angles to the path we've been following. We'd better hurry, don't you think, before it gets dark."

She looked at Jacob, who was sitting beside the pool with a troubled look on his face. She sat down on the soft earth next to him, and dipped her hand in the pool. Her fingers looked unnaturally white under the clear blue of the water.

"What's wrong?" she asked.

"'Don't forget the serpent', you just said. That's what's wrong. I've been so preoccupied with Lilith that I forgot another, earlier tradition the twelve didn't mention. Gnostics and second century Jews spoke of the devil Sammael, the blind demon, the angel of the planet Mars. Sammael and Lilith were the demonic couple placed over the hierarchy of darkness. And traditions reported by Isaac Cohen in the Middle Ages also identified Sammael with Leviathan, the blind dragon."

Maggie looked thoughtful. "Isaac Cohen. Wasn't he the one who made that crack about goats?"

Jacob smiled. "He collected tales. Cohen hung out in the western Languedoc, Cathar territory, and probably knew a lot of sheep herders. He said something like, 'He who lives with herds of sheep has no need to fear Satan and the evil powers, for no evil spirit rules among them. But he who lives among goats – even when surrounded by ten houses and a hundred men – is ruled over by an evil spirit.' It should have been a warning to us."

"So, this is all Eli's fault after all," Maggie said with a smile. "It's the fate of a scapegoat, I guess. But what about what you said before? Why should such evil exist in a place as beautiful as this?"

Jacob frowned. " The Kabbalists believed that Sammael played a legitimate role in the creation, and that even though he'd been cut off, his position would be restored during the Messianic age. Kabbalah-wise, his territory was the left emanation of the ten sefiroth."

"You know how much I don't know about the Kabbalah," Maggie remarked. "Let's just find Eli while it's still light."

"And before the blind dragon and his wife get hold of him," Jacob said under his breath. As they turned to follow Eli's prints, what had seemed like rough brush parted to reveal a path as wide as the one they'd been on.

"How could we not have seen this path?" Maggie asked in surprise. "Do you suppose there were other paths we missed back there?"

"Could be," Jacob responded. He stopped to retrieve the flashlight from his backpack. "It's easy to miss things in the woods." He glanced at his compass again, as he had every half hour or so. It was worthless, with the needle rotating in full circles, first one way then the other. He hadn't mentioned that detail to Maggie. "We'll keep going until the batteries start to weaken. I have spares, but I'd rather save them for another time." Maggie knew he was thinking, "to get the hell out of here."

Chapter 49

The bird and the goat entered the clearing just as the sun was starting to set. The sunset was intensely beautiful, with the entire sky turning from deep blue to fire red in the time it took Eli to eat a peach. Indeed, since they'd turned by the pool, the trees had turned from forest to orchard, with every kind of edible fruit one could imagine. Eli had slowed almost to a standstill, and the hummingbird was impatient, to say the least.

"Come on. It's getting dark. You can eat any time. Don't bother with that now!"

"This bird is more a goat than an angel," Eli thought, forgetting for a minute the bird knew his thoughts.

"That's just what I've been telling you," replied the hummingbird. "I'm every bit as goat-headed as you can be. Welcome to the heart of the garden. Pay attention and you might learn something!" And suddenly the bird was gone, as quickly as she'd appeared.

"Now what am I supposed to do?" Eli thought, and glanced around in the fading light. He stood at the tree line of a large hill. It was not particularly steep, but the goat thought it had to be the highest point in the garden. The fields to either side were choked with scrub growth and weeds, but the path led arrow-straight to the top of the hill. In the twilight, the goat thought he saw an enormous tree at the top, but the path smelled more strongly now of decayed flesh, and Eli decided he'd rather find a sheltered nest in the field, away from the path, where he could bed down for the night.

Twenty feet off the path, Eli found what he wanted – a rounded, grassy patch of earth free from bramble and deadwood. He circled round and round, walking down the grass, and eating a few bites, as well. But he was more tired than hungry, and he quickly settled into his soft, grassy bed. As he dozed off, he could hear the footsteps of the humans walking by on the path, passing his nest on their way up the hill.

Chapter 50

Maggie and Jacob had not walked far before they discovered the orchard, overgrown yet overflowing with peaches and pears, apples and pomegranates. Everywhere they looked in the fading light, in fact, they'd discovered yet another kind of luscious fruit. They ate hungrily and quickly, aware that their flashlight would soon be their only guide.

"Come on," Jacob said at last. Let's go a little further and see where it comes out. We still have to set up camp for the night."

"At least we won't have to cook," Maggie said, speaking through the juice of an orange. This sure beats the rations you've got in that sack." They made their way back to the path, and soon found themselves walking up hill.

"This is the first real hill we've come to on this trek," Jacob said. "Let's keep going. I'd like to see if I can spot some familiar stars." They walked in silence, watching their step in the limited beam of light. At length they came to a steep-sided mound, capped by what seemed like an enormous tree.

"I don't see any stars from here," Jacob said. "Maybe the tree blocks the view."

"Frankly, I don't care," Maggie said. "I don't want to take another step. Let's just make camp here and call it a day." Camp consisted of two sleeping bags, and a bit of tarp Jacob had crammed into his backpack. They'd assumed they'd be in paradise, and were traveling light on that account.

"Look, Jacob," Maggie said, as she played the light around. "There's an opening in the side of this mound. Oh look, it's a cave!" she exclaimed, and poked her head inside. She turned the light to the roof of the cave, and recoiled in horror. What looked like ten thousand snakes were twisting out of the ceiling, just inches from her head. Maggie fell back with a scream.

Jacob grabbed the flashlight and peered cautiously through the opening. And then he laughed – the first good laugh he'd had in Eden. "It's all right, Maggie," Jacob said, and laughed again. "Those are just roots coming through from the tree up there. Nothing dangerous here," he said, and crawled inside.

Somewhat embarrassed, Maggie followed him through the hole. "We might as well camp right in here," Jacob said. It's protected, and there's plenty of room to spread out the bags. This way we won't have to build a fire."

They stripped down to their underwear and climbed into their sleeping bags, which they'd placed close together – not for warmth, but for company.

"It's been quite a day," Maggie said, after a minute.

"One in a thousand years," Jacob said. "I wish I knew what we're supposed to do."

"I think we'll know when we're supposed to know," Maggie said. "And we probably won't know until then."

Their faces almost touched, they lay so close together. "These bags are this century's answer to bundling," Jacob said softly.

"Yes," said Maggie, "but I know their secret."

"What's that?" Jacob asked.

"They zip together," Maggie said, and kissed him on the lips.

"I'm so stupid sometimes," Jacob said.

"I know," Maggie said, as she zipped the bags open on one side, then zipped them together.

"It's not that I haven't thought about this," Jacob said, almost apologetically. "I just didn't want to ruin a perfect friendship."

"Shut up, Jacob," Maggie said, arching her back to slip out of her underwear, "or recite me something from the 'Song of Songs.'" They lay there touching each other, hardly moving, feeling together and alone while their fears and memories melted away. Maggie still smelled of oranges.

Jacob, reluctant to speak the words aloud, thought:

You have ravished my heart, my sister, my bride,
*   you have ravished my heart with a glance of your eyes,*
*   with one jewel of your necklace.*
How sweet is your love, my sister, my bride!
*   how much better is your love than wine,*
*   and the fragrance of your oils than any spice!*

Your lips distill nectar, my bride;
  honey and milk are under your tongue;
    the scent of your garments is like the scent of Lebanon.
A garden locked is my sister, my bride,
  a garden locked, a fountain sealed.
Your shoots are an orchard of pomegranates
  with all choicest fruits,
  henna with nard, nard and saffron,
  calamus and cinnamon,
  with all trees of frankincense,
  myrrh and aloes, with all chief spices –
a garden fountain, a well of living water,
  and flowing streams from Lebanon.

And Maggie, reading the Song from Jacob's mind, thought back to him:

As an apple tree among the trees of the wood,
  so is my beloved among young men.
With great delight I sat in his shadow,
  and his fruit was sweet to my taste.
He brought me to the banqueting house,
  and his banner over me was love.
O that his left hand were under my head,
  and that his right hand embraced me!
Awake, O north wind,
  and come, O south wind!
Blow upon my garden,
  let its fragrance be wafted abroad.
Let my beloved come to his garden,
  and eat its choicest fruits.

And Jacob answered:

I come to my garden, my sister, my bride,
I gather my myrrh with my spice,
I eat my honeycomb with my honey,
I drink my wine with my milk.

And Maggie thought:

I slept, but my heart was awake.

Hark! My beloved is knocking.

And Jacob thought:

"Open to me, my sister, my love,
  my dove, my perfect one;
  for my head is wet with dew,
  my locks with the drops of the night."

And Maggie thought:

I had put off my garment,
  how could I put it on?
I had bathed my feet,
  how could I soil them?
My beloved put his hand to the latch,
  and my heart was thrilled within me.
I arose to open to my beloved,
  and my hands dripped with myrrh,
  my fingers with liquid myrrh,
  upon the handles of the bolt.

And Jacob thought:

Behold, you are beautiful, my love,
  behold, you are beautiful;
  your eyes are doves.
Behold, you are beautiful, my beloved,
  truly lovely.
Our couch is green;
  the beams of our house are cedar,
  our rafters are pine.

And Maggie thought:

While the king was on his couch,
  my nard gave forth its fragrance.
My beloved is to me a bag of myrrh,
  that lies between my breasts.
My beloved is to me a cluster of henna blossoms
  in the vineyards of Eden.

Chapter 51

Maggie awoke to a wet nose in her face and a tongue licking her cheek. "Elijah," she laughed with delight when she realized who it was, and pulled him into the crowded sleeping bag. "Jacob, wake up! It's Eli!"

"I don't want a goat in my sleeping bag – even Eli," Jacob said, half asleep, but he turned over to pet the creature who had led them to this place. It was too warm in the bag, and Eli scampered out again. The humans wouldn't notice, Eli knew, but he smelled danger in the cave and went out into the sunlight. "Don't you run away again," Maggie called to the goat sleepily, but without concern. Everything seemed just as right as could be.

By the light that streamed through the opening, Maggie sat up and looked around the cave. The roots of the tree above them hardly looked ominous by daylight, and the space had a rounded, cozy feeling, like a yurt or a geodesic dome. In the back of the cave, however, Maggie noticed what looked like a hole. Curious, she pulled on her clothes and crawled over to take a look. It was a perfectly round hole, no more than three feet wide, with smooth earthen sides. Maggie took a mirror from her pack and reflected a stream of sunlight down the hole. It was deeper than the light could reach. "Jacob, you should look at this," she said, after a minute. "Here's a hole that seems to drop forever. I'm sure glad we didn't stumble back here in the dark last night."

"We had better things to do," Jacob said, giving her a hug. He peered into the pit, moving the mirror for light but gaining no view. Leaning down, he cupped his hands to his ears and listened. From far below he thought he caught the deep rumble of something. "Let's go outside," Jacob said, suddenly subdued. "We may not want to know what lives down there."

"You think something lives down there?" Maggie asked. With all the beauty of the garden, why would anything want to live down in there?" Maggie suddenly caught Jacob's thought, and backed away quickly. "Oh," she said. "Yes, let's go outside."

They gathered up their gear and left the cave. As she went through the entrance, Maggie reached back and broke off a piece of tree root that dangled from the roof of the cave. "A souvenir," she said to Jacob, and slipped it into her pocket.

Outside, the morning sun threw a dazzling light over the garden. They had climbed higher last night than they'd realized, for they could see well over the fields and orchards to the giant forest trees beyond. Eli lay quietly by the mouth of the cave, quite content since he'd browsed his breakfast before coming to find them.

Jacob, however, had turned from the view. "Look, Maggie, look at the tree," he said with quiet amazement. "Or rather, I should say trees." Indeed, it was clear there were two trees coming out of the earth, two that had grown like one, coiling around one another like snakes, climbing into two canopies of foliage where the branches wrapped and choked each other, vied with each other for the sunlight, fought their imperceptible struggle on a scale and in a time not visible to people or goats. Yet the results of this convoluted battle were powerfully frozen in the trees that loomed over them.

"Could it really be?" Maggie spoke for both of them. "The tree of life *and* the tree of knowledge, bound and twisted together so completely only God could separate them. No wonder Adam and Eve never ate from the tree of life. You could never tell which was the forbidden tree and which was the other."

"But once they ate from the one, it was only a matter of time until they ate the fruit of the other – and then they'd have lived forever," Jacob said.

"You know," Maggie said after a minute, "Satan could have told Eve to eat from the fruit of both trees. He must have differentiated one tree from the another, or else had her eat from the fruit he chose."

"Of course," thought Jacob, "since Satan didn't want mankind to be immortal, either. What would he and God have to wrestle over, if not us?" They stared at the coiled trees in silence for several minutes.

"What do those twisting trunks remind you of?" Jacob asked as last.

You're right!" Maggie said in amazement. "It's a giant version of the curves in the Rosslyn column."

"No, the Rosslyn pillar's curves are a tiny version of this," Jacob corrected. "Not perfectly so, but close enough."

"But how would the apprentice even have known?" Maggie asked.

"There had to be a description already out there. After all, the master went to look at another column that was already carved from this. Oh, and by the way, notice that it also models DNA, the basic knowledge/life column of our own existence, as well. How did they know that, except by a description from someone else who'd been here to see it."

"That couple from Provence," Maggie said thoughtfully. "The ones the twelve told us about that might have been us. They must have brought the knowledge back with them."

"And think about it – what other knowledge they must have brought back! From that visit we see two traditions blossoming in that same area of France. For mystical Judaism it was Blind Isaac and the teachings of the Kabbalah. For the Christians it was the Gnosticism of the Cathars, the Templars, and everything that has come down through the secret societies to the twelve themselves. Both of those movements developed in the area of Provence over the two centuries after the pilgrim's return. If there was ever a source for Judeo-Christian mysticisms, those two pilgrims were it."

"Look," Maggie said suddenly, "Doesn't it look like there's a face in that tree? A big face formed out of the branches themselves, looking down at us?"

"Adam Kadmon," Jacob whispered.

"Adam who?" Maggie asked.

"Adam Kadmon, the first Adam," Jacob said. "You know, the Kabbalah says there were four Adams – the archetypal model, the Genesis Adam of creation; the Adam of the Garden; and finally, the Adam of the expulsion. Because Adam Kadmon was the model for everything, the Kabbalah claims his face appears in the tree itself, just as the tree reflects the shape and power spots of the garden, and the spiritual powers that command the created universe.

"And it's not just Kabbalah – the notion of primordial man is found in many other traditions, from the Hindu

162

Upanishads to Iraqi Mandean theology. The concept runs through ancient texts from Mesopotamia, India, Syria, eastern Turkey, and Egypt. In Kabbalah it involves the letters of the name of God, and some multi-dimensional, light-energy projection having to do with man being made in God's image. It also deals with the embodiment of the world. The concept is complex, and I don't remember the details. If I did, I might have a road map to this tree, and to the garden itself. We'd know just where to go."

"It reminds me of the Green Man faces we saw in Rosslyn Chapel," Maggie said.

They stood together, holding hands and staring up at the amazing, tree-borne image. Then, suddenly, they were startled by a voice close behind them.

"Forget the tree. I'll show you where to go," the voice said. Jacob and Maggie turned in surprise. At the entrance to their cave sat a large, coiled serpent, wearing the face and features of a man.

Chapter 52

"Don't be afraid," said the snake, and then, with a smile, added, "Of course, all angels begin their conversations that way. It's amazing how those words, spoken with a tone of sincerity, will calm human beings. It's as good as hypnosis."

"Who are you?" Maggie asked, trying not to show the horror she felt. "Where did you come from?"

"As to who I am, I think we all know the answer to that question. As to where I came from, do you mean originally, or just now? The answers are quite different, after all."

"Just now," Maggie stammered. "Where did you come from?"

"From under the tree, my dear," said the snake. "I notice the two of you slept there last night without asking permission."

"We didn't see you in there," said Jacob, as curiosity began overriding his fear. "If we had, you can be sure we wouldn't have stayed."

"Do I appear repulsive to you then?" the snake said with a smile. "I imagine it's the combination of face and hands with serpentine body. To be honest, it bothered me at first, too, but over the millennia I've grown used to it. In any event, you didn't see me because I was in my hole. I have rather a spacious dwelling-place down there, which I share with many friends. Perhaps you'd care to visit?"

"No, thank you," Maggie said firmly, taking a step back. "I'd feel quite claustrophobic, going down that hole."

"I understand completely," said the snake. "As an angel, the cosmos wasn't large enough, and now look at what seems spacious to me. But I was younger, more ambitious then than I am now." The snake sighed deeply, and Jacob wondered if it could possibly be expecting sympathy.

"I don't expect you to waste tears on me," the snake said sharply. It could read minds with ease, Jacob noted. "I tried that years ago, when I asked Enoch to plead with the Old Man for our forgiveness. He made it clear we don't get a second chance, though I hardly think it fair. After all, angels are as susceptible as humans to temptation. I had a discussion with Jesus on that very subject. He was not particularly sympathetic either, so I don't know why I shouldn't be allowed some pleasure in his particularly painful execution."

"Do you plan to hurt us?" Maggie asked.

The snake smiled. "That's a difficult question for me to answer, my dear," said the snake. "If you mean physically injure you here and now, the answer is no. You are in the garden, after all, and the garden is a protected place."

"You hurt Eve in the garden," Maggie responded.

"No, I merely opened her eyes to the possibilities," said the snake. "She made the decision." And picking up on a passing thought of Jacob's, he went on, "I was never so crass as the angel in the story of Zeus, taking the form of a swan to rape Leda. That sort of thing happens beyond these walls, but not in the garden. Here, seduction takes another form."

"Did you seduce her?" Maggie asked.

"Isn't it interesting," said the snake. "Once every thousand years another human or two are allowed into the garden. You'd think there would be something new to talk about, but no – I keep getting the same questions, over and over and over again. I don't ask you about your sex life, do I? Why don't we talk about that, instead?"

Maggie blushed. The way he said it, she couldn't help but think of last night – even though she knew the snake could read her mind. "Stop that!" she said angrily.

"Now you know how I feel," the snake said smoothly. "Why should you expect me to reveal what pleasure I had with Eve? Some have surmised Cain's behavior reflected his parentage, but my methods work just as well, it seems, in *loco parentis.* Still, it would only be fair: If the Old Man could have Mary, I deserved Eve. It was, after all, my finest hour."

"It ruined their chances," Jacob said. "Your business with Eve pushed them into a world full of cruelty, greed, and death. You alienated us all from God, and put every soul in fear of damnation. That's a lot more than a one night stand, I'd say."

"Who can predict the consequences of any one night stand, as you call it? What is it that brings forth a Caesar, a Napoleon or a Hitler? It was an encounter with a dove that gave Mary a Jesus – according to medieval art. And it was a desire to mate with human women that brought down angels. So then, don't tell me Eve's seduction was anything worse than business as usual."

"But are you saying sex is a cardinal sin?" Jacob asked.

"Not at all," said the snake. "Of course, I'm not the one who makes that decision, but I think I can speak with some authority on the subject. No, the thing that really annoys the Old Man is the desire to break the rules of existence. That is, existence as the OM made it."

"What do you mean?" Jacob asked. He could feel himself drawn in by this being who knew the answers to his questions. "Sex certainly has to be a part of God's plan."

"And it is," said the snake. "But it's never enough, is it? That's why man and the angels have this bizarre impulse to improve on things. Angels slept with human women and produced demigods, giants with the capability to build vast cities and tinker with the building blocks of nature. When God destroyed them with the flood, mankind took over the same damn pursuits. They were doing crude breeding experiments in Sodom and Gomorrah when it was destroyed; in the Middle Ages it was alchemy, the impulse to change lead to gold – to change matter itself. For the Jews it was making a golem, the desire to make a man from mud like God did Adam. In your age it's become rampant – splitting the atom, transplanting pigs' hearts into human bodies, building pretty sex robots who can manage a Turing-test conversation. I love it! Modern scientists with minds like Hieronymus Bosch. Next, they'll be building the supermen Hitler aspired to – the heroes, the giants we angels had bred for earth thousands of years ago now will be made by genetic manipulation. But before that happens, it will all be over."

"What do you mean by 'over'?" Maggie asked.

"You humans are so very predictable," said the snake. "Every time, the questions start with Eve and end with wanting to know the future – even when the truth is staring you in the face. Happily, I can tell *you* what didn't mean anything to the last visitors. What's done is done and can't be changed. This is the end of the sixth day, when it all winds down again."

Chapter 53

"Why should we believe a word you say?" Jacob asked.

"Don't you know?" the serpent smiled. "People have always come to me for knowledge. It's my stock in trade."

"What do you mean?"

"Who was the hero in the story of Prometheus? We enabled the fire from heaven, and a lot of other stuff, too. Why, you'd still be hiding in caves if it weren't for my angels' enormous contribution to your so-called human civilization."

"Legend has it, the gods punished Prometheus," Jacob said.

"Bound him to a rock, where birds peck out his eyes for all eternity. It's so unfair! I do you a favor, and that's the thanks I get. Don't you see how ironic it is? I get in trouble for doing you a favor, and then you praise God instead of me. Where's the justice in that?

"Or look at me right now. Half angel, half snake. It's degrading, don't you think? This is my aspect when I'm here – it's one reason I don't spend much time in the garden anymore. You should have seen me when I was younger, before I became trapped, like you, in time. That's one of the reasons we have so much in common, the watchers and you."

Maggie glanced over her shoulder. "You mean, there are more of you here?"

"Not *right* here," said the snake. "After all, they must be about their father's business."

"Well, you must be busy," Jacob remarked. "Why are you hanging around here?"

"To visit with you, of course, and to answer any questions you might have. It only happens once in a millennium, or so. I wouldn't miss it for the world. After all," the snake added, "Why are *you* here?"

"We were sent," Jacob said defensively.

"And why do you think that happened?"

"I'm not really sure," Jacob admitted. "I hope to do God's work."

"Nonsense," said the snake. "You are here because I arranged it."

"That's not true!" Maggie said angrily. "We're here because the twelve said they needed people of faith to come through the door. They told us they couldn't come here themselves."

"And they were right. Consider all those dead, learned pilgrims blowing about in the entryway. All they wanted was information about Paul, but they got me, instead. You, on the other hand, are with me now precisely because you are a part of the truth of Genesis. I wouldn't waste this visit on anyone less."

"You won't shake our faith," Maggie said quietly. "If anything, you confirm it."

"Yes, that's right, more knowledge of the way things are! You're on the right track now, children. So, fire away – ask me anything you like. I'll tell you the truth, but you won't believe me. It really doesn't matter to me, of course, whether you do or not. It all turns out the same in the end. So, don't believe me if you don't want to. Most of my pilgrims reject what I tell them. It's too farfetched, they say. Do you realize the ignorance of the Middle Ages could have been avoided, the so-called Enlightenment could have arrived centuries sooner, if my last visitors here had only had better communication skills? Instead, they wasted years in a monastery, and we saw knowledge hanging on by a fingernail, kept alive in China and India and by a few crazy Irish monks. Of course, *my* people know what's what. They know how to seed ideas. But it can't happen too suddenly. Then it's called the work of the devil, and we have to start over again."

"Wait a minute," Jacob interrupted. "When you say 'my people', do you mean the other fallen angels?"

"Please, call them watchers. 'Fallen angels' sounds so melodramatic. I have humans on the payroll, too, of course. For instance, the committee that sent you...."

"I don't believe you," Jacob interrupted.

"You see – what did I tell you? But trust me, I have no secrets. What have I got to lose? Those people with their secret ceremonies range from the sublime to the ridiculous. I've humored them along for years, for centuries, in fact, and what has it gotten me? If we'd put the whole story on television by the eleventh century, you people would have recolonized Mars or cloned yourselves to bits by now."

Maggie was still fretting about the committee. "If the secret societies have slowed you down by keeping secrets to themselves, then aren't they really on God's side, and not on yours?"

"There you go again." It was said in perfect imitation of Ronald Reagan – even to the smile. The snake added, "I'll bet you didn't know I've authored some of the most successful presidential slogans, did you? 'Lock her up!' was one of mine."

"I often suspected," Jacob responded, under his breath.

"It's not just the secret societies," the snake continued. "Look at the way the church kept outside scholars from studying the Dead Sea scrolls. They have a tradition of sitting on information they don't understand, or which doesn't serve their best interests. Hell, the Vatican Library is full of materials like that! You think the library at Alexandria was a loss by fire, but what about the loss by lock on Vatican materials that *came* from Alexandria, or before that, from Atlantis? Look how long you had to wait to decipher Linear B or Egyptian hieroglyphics or Sumerian cuneiform – even Indian Sanskrit! Don't you think those languages were translated into Greek long before Vatican secrecy took charge? It's been there all along, sitting in stuffy Roman vaults. Even some writings of the watchers are there and translated. Just think, if that writing had been available to anyone with a library card in Roswell, New Mexico in 1947, there'd have been no lies about weather balloons."

The snake paused for a moment, then turned directly toward Jacob. "So, what did you think? That someday you, sitting in the Bangor Library stacks, were going to crack a new level of Bible code and copyright the work of some lost author of four thousand years ago?"

Jacob turned red. It was something he'd fantasized about.

"You see," the devil said with a sly grin, "theologians, too, can cite scripture for their purpose. In fact, they may be guiltiest of all.

"But never mind that – it goes without saying. No, it annoys me no end that some of my best works have been deeded over to those sanctimonious assholes. For example, nothing divides religion like the patriarchal/matriarchal battles that go on. With the right documentation, I'd have had goddess worship back in full swing within a hundred years of the crucifixion. As it was, we made do with Maryology until the Inanna/Isis materials were back on the shelf. My only comfort in all that has been what a great embarrassment it's been to Mary herself."

The snake smiled at his own remark. "That's what we call in the trade an 'inside joke'. It doesn't buy the groceries. But I digress – ask me a question!"

"Why are you taking out your distress on mankind?" Maggie asked softly.

"Because your behavior is stupid, selfish, and habitually dishonest. You call me the father of lies, then you lie to each other 'til you no longer comprehend truth when it's staring you in the face. Your newspapers tally the political lies, and then the body counts that follow. All that, and yet you still assume you'll be forgiven! And you wonder why I'm angry?

"Or simply consider the fact serpents were here, on 'your' earth, eons before you stumbled into possession of it. Then we, the watchers, were here with our *own* creation. We made giants, heroes, demigods. Your miserable science is just now realizing how easy it is to clone, diddle DNA, and mix species. Interesting, isn't it? I gave away those secrets a thousand years ago, and the idiots garbled the truth. And what did we get for our trouble? Five hundred years of bad alchemy, and the Jewish golem. What a joke on me, eh? Did you bring a recorder?"

"No," Jacob replied.

"Well, try to get it right this time, or you'll only make us both look like fools."

"Was the man you saw two thousand years ago really Jesus?" Maggie asked.

"He was the worst of all. I knew him from before and recognized his potential – I offered him everything in my possession. Did I get any thanks for my trouble? He went storming out of here, and three years later he was history. What can I say?"

"You mentioned the watchers bred with human women and produced giants," Jacob said. "Is that true?"

"Oh, yes. We have our little desires too, you know. There was a race we were playing with – genetically, I mean – trying to make them smarter, more attractive. In short, more like us. And we succeeded beyond our own expectations. They seemed lovely to us – half animal, half angel, the best of both worlds. Of course we bred with them, and of course our offspring were magnificent. Mortal and immortal in one being: All the Sumerian, Egyptian, Greek and Roman hero stories, the Mahabharata tales, the Nordic legends – all of them the giants of a world lost, except to your mythology, and my hell."

"What happened to them?" Maggie asked.

"Even you know the answer to that one. Most of them were swept away in massive earthquakes, tidal waves – the flood of the Noah story, more or less. Well, so be it. They were in decline anyway. They built vast civilizations – Mu, Atlantis – but they lost track of their angelic side. Wars, nuclear wars, lasers, missiles – everything I couldn't explain to my visitors a thousand years ago. But I know *you* can understand."

Maggie shifted uncomfortably. "Tell us, please, about the creation of Adam and Eve," she said. "Weren't there other humans on earth already?"

"Late arrivals, inferior products. Very late in the game the OM got interested in our experiments, and tried to improve on it. Not very clever, his Adam and Eve, but they didn't have to be, skipping around in here all day, protected from the outside world. We knew the Garden was here, of course, and our children tried to get in. A lot of hero-quest stories came from those adventures. Finally, we realized the only way to get in was to get them out. I pulled a 'Job' on the Old Man. You know, 'How can you be certain Adam and Eve *really* love you unless you test them? Just a little test, nothing too tricky. Just one little thou-shalt-not in a garden full of pleasure. Where's the harm in that?' So, he let me in here to do a little tempting. It was what you call a piece of cake."

"And where are the animals?" Maggie asked, noting Eli had worked his way closer to her as the conversation went on. "I thought Eden contained at least two of all the animals God created."

"I ate them," said the snake, looking wistfully at the goat. "Not all at once, of course," he added. "But whenever I'm here I manage to wipe out a few more species. I've tried keeping pace with the earth's record of destruction – though I must say I've gained a few extra pounds in the last hundred years or so, just keeping up. Anyway, the few animals left have developed a kind of sixth sense. They know when I'm in town, and lay low."

Maggie thought she noticed a distressed look cross Eli's eyes, and decided to change the subject. "Didn't Jesus' death change you, your existence in the world?" she asked.

"You are joking? No, I see you think that's a serious question. You know, it's up to the OM, of course, but to my way of thinking, there's none of you deserves to be saved. Anytime I get to spend five minutes on anyone's case, they corrupt as quickly as Eve. You people haven't changed in six thousand years. Christ or no, you're all Adams and Eves and worse. You are all murderers, thieves, liars and lechers, if what Jesus said about sinning in your hearts is true. And the Old Man knows your hearts – believe me there. Jesus may have died for you, but you haven't done squat for him. So why should OM care more for you than he did for Adam and Eve? He was quite fond of them, you know, until I poisoned it." The devil smiled.

"Well, we may not be perfect, but we're making some progress," Maggie said defensively. "We've avoided nuclear war, fought a plague, and we're working to feed and house the poor."

The serpent laughed out loud. "Don't proclaim your good works to me! You humans have made a science of organized greed – call it capitalism or Darwinism, but kill-or-be-killed it is. You steal from the poor and give to the rich – it's been that way as long as there have been humans. As for war, there's never an end to it. And now you're *really* getting into sins that annoy the Old Man."

"What are those?' Jacob asked, as if he didn't already know.

"As I told you, fooling with the essence of creation – splitting atoms, corrupting DNA, splicing genes, combining unlike species. It's what got the watchers kicked out of grace, and what triggered the last worldwide destruction. It eats away at the essence of what the Old Man called 'good,' and he just won't abide it – crucifixion or no. It's the unforgivable sin."

"Do you consider this your best work, then, to lead men and women down this road to ruin?" Jacob asked.

"Not at all," the snake said, smiling once again. "My greatest trick is convincing the world I don't exist, when in fact I'm running it all. Is there a more common image in the world than mine? Angels, fallen angels, demons and devils – we're in your movies, your advertising and art museums, on paint cans and candy, in comic books and classics. Your children tattoo us to their bodies. We are ubiquitous. We are so common that no one but the ignorant, the unsophisticated, the superstitious – and a few Kabbalist rabbis – take our existence seriously. If I'd tried to vanish into the secret doctrine, I'd have believers galore. By broadcasting Satan, Satan becomes invisible. It's a trick particularly well-suited to the mass media. Consider that old 'Church Chat' routine, or John Lovett in the red devil costume on Saturday Night Live. The show was never so amusing after that."

"Are you telling me Satan watches television?" Maggie said with disgust.

"Watch it? I invented it! It's so much easier, you know. Why bother motivating people to sin when they'd just as soon waste their lives instead? After all, the results are exactly the same."

"Anything else you're particularly proud of?" Jacob asked with irony.

"Oh yes," said the serpent. "Call me a romantic, but I think Santa Claus tops the list. If anyone ever said that Santa Claus was an invention of the devil, they'd be – dare I say it? – crucified. It would be Scrooge versus Tiny Tim all over again.

"But think about it! In those first seven years of a child's life, Santa *is* Jesus. Santa is the man who brings goodies from the sky for good little boys and girls. He even arrives near the pagan date, just after winter solstice time, for Christ's birthday.

"The beauty part is that Santa is a lie, a fraud, a fake. He's too good to be true, and as soon as children reach the age of reason, it hits them right between the eyes. If they haven't heard the news before they start school, then it's a double blow – their parents have been lying to them on this key issue of their young faith. Learning the truth makes the little believers feel like fools.

"'You *still* believe in Santa Claus?' some older brat says to the kindergartener. 'Grow up! *There is no Santa Claus. Your parents lied to you!*'

"And there's no denying the truth. 'Your friend is right,' shamed parents confess, 'we only did it for fun.' Bingo! That way, we get the kid conditioned to convey spiritual lies and disappointments to the next generation of suckers. And, of course, loss of faith in Jesus comes next.

"But say, you two are in the seminary! You must see the echoes here in the cynical rantings of embittered theologians – the old Jesus Seminar groupies, for example, who sat there in smug condescension, like that brat in grade school talking down to the Santa believer: 'Oh come on! You *still* believe Jesus rose from the dead, that he brought you grace and salvation? Grow up!'

"Once burned twice shy, the old saying goes. Burn the little darlings once on Santa, and you create a basis of doubt for the rest of their lives. It's the gift that keeps on giving, and it comes right out of the Old Man's sack.

"But enough about me," said the serpent, and suddenly his bizarre appearance became something more menacing. "You'll never learn anything this way, and I've got a scapegoat to eat." And with one smooth, lightning-fast motion, the serpent pythoned around Elijah's waist and slithered almost effortlessly upward, disappearing with the terrified, bleating goat into the gnarled branches of the enormous, ancient tree.

Chapter 54

It happened so quickly, Maggie never even gasped. "Oh, no," she said softly, but the words cut through Jacob like a scream.

"We'll catch him," Jacob reassured her. "You climb that side, I'll climb over here!" He looked hard at her and thought, "Stay in touch with me." She nodded yes to him, and he disappeared into the tree.

Maggie had no idea how she would stop the beast, but she was willing to try. In grade school she'd been the only girl to climb the rope all the way to the gym ceiling – but that was a long time ago. Still, she felt surprisingly light as she pulled herself onto the first branch. "I wonder which tree I'm climbing?" she thought. From the ground the two trees looked completely intertwined, but once she was into it, the other tree seemed to disappear in the sort of mist they'd walked through when they entered the garden. She concentrated on each branch as it came to hand, and tried not to think.

As soon as his feet left the ground, Jacob became distracted by random memories. He remembered a treadmill he used to use. The treadmill had a digital clock that started at 00:00 when he turned it on to start his twenty-minute run. This clock was a problem for him – specifically, he couldn't help reading the numbers as years in Israel. At 00:30 he'd see Jesus' ministry; at 00:35, Paul's vision of the risen Christ; at 01:35, Rome destroying the remnants of Jewish Jerusalem, followed by a variety of occupiers and invaders on the clock: 6:14 the Sassanid Persians; 6:35 the Umayyad Caliphate; 7:50 the Abbasid Caliphate; 9:09 the Fatimid Caliphate; 15:17 the Ottoman Sultanate;18:44 the Tanzimat Ottoman Empire; 19:17 the British Mandate; 19:48 Israel.

At first it was just a flash of date-memories, without a vision attached to it. But as he exercised day after day, the visions grew until time seemed to slow to an impossible crawl. Now he was hearing Jesus crying out to his father, "Why have you forsaken me?" At last he had to give up the treadmill. It seemed to take him a lifetime every morning, just to get in a twenty-minute run. Headphones, even tape masking the clock couldn't shut out the sequence of numbers, the tumble of dates, the cruelty of mankind's history that ran its course as he ran in position. The habit was firmly fixed in his brain. "I'm not getting anywhere with this," he thought one day, and never used the machine again.

Where the treadmill memory ended, another began – until he realized what was happening, and shook himself free. "This is a mind game, a serpent's trap to slow you down," he told himself. He felt his mind clear a little, and looked around. Instead of a twisted tangle of branches, there seemed to be a symmetrical, luminous quality to the limbs as they curved upward, with offshoots like rungs on a circular stair. Jacob thought about his namesake, Jacob son of Isaac, and his vision at Bethel. As he climbed, he recited the passage from Genesis 28:

Jacob left Beer-sheba, and went toward Haran. And he came to a certain place, and stayed there that night, because the sun had set. Taking one of the stones of the place, he put it under his head and lay down in that place to sleep. And he dreamed that there was a ladder set up on the earth, and the top of it reached to heaven; and behold, the angels of God were ascending and descending on it!

"Jacob is finally going up that ladder," he thought. "This must be what I was meant to do, but none of this seems possible. Coincidence? Reincarnation? Even if that were true, it hardly makes sense. Not that any of this makes sense. I'm chasing Satan up a tree to save a goat! Even the first Jacob was smarter than that."

Jacob felt his momentary exhilaration drain away, and he paused to sit on a particularly thick branch. "Who am I kidding," he thought. "I'm no hero. All I want to do is get this goat back for Maggie and get out of the tree, out of the garden. I guess I'm not even a real theologian, seeing as how truth is staring me in the face and I just don't feel like staring back. I'm not a particularly good person – fact is, I'm selfish, lazy, irreverent, I shouldn't even be here." Jacob felt himself near despair. He looked down at his right hand where it rested on the branch, and saw the iridescent bark twist in his hand. Jacob suddenly realized he was sitting on the snake.

The great head of the beast swung back through the foliage until his face was practically touching Jacob's nose. "You'll never find the goat this way," hissed the snake. "Here you are, feeling sorry for yourself, while I've shown the most admirable restraint in not ripping that tasty scapegoat limb from limb. There's nothing I like better, you know, than goat kid spiced with the sins of Israel."

Determined not to show his terror, Jacob jumped to an adjacent branch. "Where is Eli?" he shouted. "What have you done with him? He was sent to the demon Azazel, not to you! You have no right..." Jacob ran out of indignation as his pounding heart began to slow.

"Azazel and I are closer than you think," the serpent said with a slight lift of his head. "Azazel works for me, hangs out in the desert at Yom Kippur, waits to deliver me the goat. You, on the other hand, have no claim whatsoever. Just because your girlfriend thinks it's cute, and you give it a name, does not change its fate to be my lunch. Of course, it *is* mine to do with what I want – including making a deal, if you'd like."

"I'm not giving you my soul," Jacob said in a level voice.

"Oh, nothing so tawdry as that," the serpent said with a smile. "Nothing of the sort. We could simply play a little game, something you're knowledgeable in. A question of theology, perhaps? I know! I'll ask you three questions, and if you even come close to getting them right, I'll give you back the goat. What do you say?"

"Is this a trick?" Jacob asked.

"Me? Trick someone?" Satan said with mock innocence. "How can you *think* such a thing! Anyway," the snake said with sudden directness, "what choice do you have?"

Jacob realized the snake was right. "All right," Jacob said. "Ask your questions."

"What is the nature of creation?" the serpent asked.

"You mean physically?" Jacob asked.

"That's a question, not an answer," the serpent said. "I ask the question, you answer it. Is that so hard for you to understand?"

177

"Okay, okay," Jacob said. "It's just a very big question, that's all, and I've never tried to answer it in a sentence or two. In fact, I've never tried to answer it at all – except by chipping away at the edges. The Bible tells us that God spoke the worlds into being. My understanding of speech is that it creates a vibration, and that happens to be the way physicists envision the nature of matter, as well. At the heart of everything is a vibrating something – some scientists describe it as a looped string – that's the ultimate building block for subatomic particles, atoms, molecules, all the way up to stars and galaxies. Differentiation comes with size, but everything is built upon that common, fundamental vibration." Jacob paused for a reaction.

"Is that it?" asked the snake. "You're right as far as you've gone, but you forgot the best part!"

"What's that?" Jacob asked suspiciously.

"Why, duality of course!" said the serpent. "You can't have vibration without here and there! You can't have positive without negative, hot without cold, yes without no. The Old Man gets all the credit for creation, but without opposites, nothing would exist. Even your scientists realize that the sum total of all creation is zero! Bring all the negative and positive matter together, and what do you get? Complete annihilation! It's such a tasty proposition, I can hardly wait!"

"If that's the case – if all creation adds up to a big zero – then what are we doing here?" Jacob asked. "Why hasn't everything eliminated itself?"

"I'm glad you asked me that question," the serpent said with enthusiasm.

"It's the little deal that no one likes to talk about. The deal that got run out of scripture by the church fathers. Augustine knew it as Manicheanism, but gave it up for political reasons. You don't get named a saint and father of the church by pushing duality, that's for sure.

"But consider the nature of creation for a minute. It's constructed of opposites, and yet it doesn't self-destruct! It's what I like to call God's deal with the devil. He's in charge up there and I'm in charge down here. We allow each other room to exist, and that way, everything keeps going along just fine."

"I wouldn't call it so fine," Jacob corrected. "Evil in the world means millions starve; there's sickness and death and cruelty and catastrophe. And anyway, you're a created being, just like me. What gives you the idea you're on an equal footing with God?"

"Did I say that?" asked the serpent, in an innocent tone. "I certainly wouldn't want to leave you with a wrong impression! It's true that I'm created, but I'm intrinsic to the nature of existence. If I hadn't fallen from heaven, the Old Man would have thrown me out anyway. After all, I *am* one of those Elohim the Bible credits with the creation. That's *Elohim*, plural for gods, not singular. But nobody else wants to give me the credit I deserve. Anyway, since I'm sure you'll let people know, I'll give you a pass on that first question."

"Thanks a lot," Jacob said with undisguised irony.

"Question two," said the serpent quickly, "What is the nature of time?"

"This is another physics question," Jacob complained. "Hardly my area of expertise."

"If you don't know that time has everything to do with theology, then you are dumber than I thought," said the snake. "Get on with it."

"Okay, okay," Jacob replied. He suddenly remembered something one of his high school teachers had said to him many years ago: "You are smarter than you pretend to be, Mr. Alexandre, but not as smart as you think you are."

"Time," Jacob said, "is another dimension, like up and down. But not one we created creatures can escape. Time began with creation, the Big Bang, and it will end when all the other dimensions end. That's what they mean by 'the end of time,' and why God, who exists outside of creation, can move freely without regard to time. But if we can't escape time, we can manipulate it to some extent. Einstein showed that when we increase our speed, our time slows down relative to those people who *didn't* speed up. It's not much, but it does prove that time is merely another dimension interrelated to the rest of the physical universe."

"What?" asked the serpent with feigned surprise. "Nothing theological? I'm afraid I'll flunk you on this one. You haven't learned a thing since Calvin came up with the notion of predestination. Time as a dimension is riddled through like Swiss cheese, and created things stumble back and forth all the time. Your scientists call them wormholes, and a wormhole through folded space will get you there before you left! Even your lamest science fiction writers know that, so why don't the theologians? How do you suppose your friend Jesus made such an impact throughout creation? He appeared as a created being, and changed the very fabric of reality from beginning to end. That shouldn't be so hard to understand. How can you claim Jesus as a covering for your sins today, if not by a fracture in time? And what about prophecy? I swear, the conditions I've been given to work under would drive a less dedicated devil crazy! Anyway, you get one more chance to win the goat. What is the nature of this tree?"

Jacob paused to think. It occurred to him there was something ironic in the fact that when he searched for the deepest truths, his faith went to physics and not theology. His first answer was based on physics, and he got it partly correct. The second answer was based on Einstein, and he failed miserably. If he stuck with physics, not his field, he would most likely be wrong, and wronging his faith, as well. He took a far-out chance.

"The Kabbalah describes the tree as Adam Kadmon, a prototype for Adam made in the image and likeness of both God and man," Jacob blurted out.

"Wrong, wrong, wrong!" the serpent fairly screamed with delight. "And I get a goat sandwich for lunch!"

"Wait, just wait a minute!" Jacob said in alarm. "Look, I just got here. How am I supposed to know the nature of this tree if I haven't even had time to look around? Give me a chance to explore a bit, and let me answer your question then. I promise I won't take much time."

The serpent considered the offer. "Oh, very well," he agreed, after a pause. "I'd be interested to hear a more informed response from you, and I can wait for lunch. After all, we have all the time in the world. Just whisper my name when you're ready. I'll be there." And with that, the snake was gone.

Chapter 55

Maggie had climbed and climbed, but without finding a thing. Finally, she stopped to rest a moment and listen for something, "Anything," she thought, "beyond this rustle of leaves and my own heavy breathing."

As soon as she stopped, she felt re-energized. "This tree is amazing," she thought. "It's like Jacob described New York City before the pandemic – so electric with other peoples' energy that you never get tired." Remembering Jacob made her worry, and she closed her eyes. "We should have climbed together," she thought. "I feel so alone."

"You're not alone," she heard a little voice say.

Maggie looked up. Not a foot above her head, on a narrow limb, sat a small yellow bird.

"You can talk!" Maggie said, with surprise and delight.

"Can't everything?" asked the bird.

Chapter 56

Jacob did a double-take, the snake left so quickly. Now he had a goal, however, and he felt better for it.

"The nature of the tree, the nature of the tree," he mused. "So far, it's only limbs and leaves, as much as I've climbed. Maybe if I went out along one of these branches, I'd be able to get some perspective on where I am and what this tree is all about."

He stood up, brushed himself off, and wiped his hands on some leaves, trying to rid himself of the feel and thought of snakeskin. Turning away from the trunk of the tree, he started out along the straight limb he was standing on.

After several minutes, Jacob began to wonder. "The tree never seemed this big from the ground," he thought. "I've been walking a long time, and the branch seems scarcely any thinner. Maybe it's a trick of perspective, or maybe I'm not moving at all." He didn't believe it, though; he was moving, and the branch *was* getting thinner.

He pushed a clump of leaves out of his face, and suddenly had a clear view. He looked down and saw a white-clapboard cottage by a small lake. It was on a little island, actually, with a wooden footbridge to the shore. It was a beautiful high-summer day, and sunlight glinted off the calm surface of the lake. A wooden rowboat, pulled close to shore, lay secured by a rope to a small birch tree. Jacob could almost touch grandpa's 48-star flag that hung from the flagpole. He knew there were only 48, since he'd counted them many, many times. Several trees reached up to where he was standing, trees that he had climbed. They offered an easy way to the ground.

Jacob heard a scream. It was a young boy, he could see, just off shore and struggling in the water. Just then the cottage door slammed open, and a pretty woman in a red dress rushed down the steps.

"My God," Jacob thought numbly, I know this place! The boy, the boy is drowning! I've got to help save him!" And then a split second later, as the terror of personal memory seized him, he thought, "That woman down there is my mother – and the drowning boy – it's me!"

Chapter 57

"Little bird," Maggie asked, "Can you tell me if you've seen a goat named Elijah in this tree? He was taken by the snake, and I'm worried the snake may eat him!"

"The snake may," said the bird, "but not right away. Your friend has made an agreement with him, so the goat is safe for now. Your friend, however, is in great danger."

"Jacob?" asked Maggie, suddenly afraid. "Oh please, can you help him?"

"I've already sent help, and I hope they'll be in time."

"Is Jacob far away?" Maggie asked.

"Right now he's very far, but we can travel toward him, if you like. It's not very far to where he was a moment ago," the bird added cryptically. But Maggie didn't pretend to understand, or even care.

"Oh please, birdie, take me to him!" was all she said.

They set out sideways along the limb, the bird flitting from branch to branch while Maggie followed behind. There were many leaves to push through, and Maggie kept saying, "I'm sorry, I'm sorry," to the bird, for being so slow. The bird flew ahead and back, not saying a word, but keeping a close eye on Maggie. Eventually they came to the massive, entwined trunks of the tree. It seemed to her that she'd reached a huge wooden wall, but the bird showed Maggie how easily she could move from branch to branch to circle the trunks halfway.

"We're almost there," said the bird encouragingly, as they started out along another limb. The bird did not tell Maggie they were on the limb where Jacob had made his deal with the devil.

Chapter 58

Jacob had extended his leg almost to the nearest birch tree, when an iron hand grasped his shoulder. "Stop! Don't move," Jacob heard a voice say, and yet he struggled to break free of the thing that was holding him.

"Let go of me, I have to help save him," was all Jacob could think, even while he felt the authority of the hand that held him back.

He glanced back over his shoulder. It was a tall man dressed in white, with piercing blue eyes and a strength Jacob could no longer resist.

"Come back with me, quickly," the angel said. "You are in great danger here. And don't look back!" Jacob didn't have to look back to know his mother had already found the boy and was pulling him into shore. Despite his weight, she would manage to carry him to dry ground, lay him face down over a log, and press on his back to pump the lake water from his lungs.

"I only wanted to help," Jacob said lamely, after they had followed the limb back into the leaves, well away from his view of the lake.

"I know," the angel said sympathetically, "but if you had interfered with that time in any way, you'd have been stuck there forever. You'd have been like a ghost, worse than a ghost, really, since you would never be able to move onto something else. You'd become part of an alternate time-loop, isolated from history so as not to change the way things are."

"But it would be good to change a lot of history," Jacob argued. "What about all the atrocities, the meaningless wars, the holocaust? If we can access history, why not change it?"

"Because that's not the point of creation. The point of creation is to try each individual in the circumstances they are in. What else is judgment based upon? If we change the circumstances, we change the ultimate consequences of man's fate. Saints could be made into sinners by their enemies, Hitlers could be made into heroes by their friends, and free will would become meaningless to heaven and hell.

Anyone with access to the past could fine-tune their environment to manipulate the fate of their soul.

"So, when somebody does break through to change the past, we isolate that bit of revised history in a closed pocket – a different dimension, if you will. The people involved become shadow images, but the soul of the invading being is encapsulated in that pocket forever. In effect it becomes their own private hell."

"But some of those situations wouldn't be so bad, actually," Jacob mused. "After all, you could pick the best time in your life to relive again and again. What would be wrong with that?"

The angel stopped and turned to face Jacob. "The problem is, the person who revisits the past knows too much to be comfortable with it. You can experience the hope and joy of your first love, for example, but you know the ultimate outcome of the affair – the lies, the cruelty, the disappointments, the pain that inevitably followed. And you can't change that, because the pocket isn't that big. It's like being condemned to hearing the same song over and over again. It may once have been your favorite song, but ultimately it becomes a nightmare if that's all you will ever hear, all there will ever be."

Jacob suddenly understood what the angel was saying. "How did I happen to come on that part of my own history," Jacob asked at last. "The odds of that happening are almost impossible."

"Not at all," said the angel. "It's the nature of the tree that as you go out on a limb, it reads your individual story, your karmic code, the details of your history. Most people can't pick the part of their life they walk in on, but they can observe until they come to a memory they can't resist reliving, and then intrude at that point."

"You make it sound like this happens all the time," Jacob interrupted. "I thought only a few people ever came to the garden."

"There are more paths to the past than you can imagine," the angel replied.

Jacob was about to ask the angel who he was and how he knew these things, when a small, yellow bird landed on Jacob's shoulder, and Maggie's face appeared through the foliage. Jacob ran to hug her, not even noticing that the little bird, and the angel who stood between them, had disappeared.

"Maggie, thank God! I am so glad to see you! Are you all right? How did you find me?" Jacob gave her no time to even think an answer to his questions.

"Whoa, slow down," Maggie said. "A little bird told me where to find you – and said you were in danger! Are you okay?"

"Fine, I'm fine," Jacob answered, "but I guess I was in trouble until this angel came along." Jacob looked around, suddenly realizing the angel had gone. "Did you see him?" Jacob asked Maggie. "He was right here a second ago, a tall man in white? I knew he was an angel – a guardian angel as it turns out, who pulled me back from a big mistake."

"No, but I felt a voice as we came through the trees," Maggie said. "I guess that must have been him. What did he tell you?"

"Not enough to answer the serpent, I'm afraid," Jacob said. "Maggie, I ran into him again. He told me if I can tell him about the true nature of this tree, we can get Eli back. Otherwise...."

"There won't be an otherwise," Maggie said softly. "We'll figure it out. Let's sit down and review what we know."

They sat down on the branch where they'd been standing, leaning on one another and holding hands. It felt good just being together, and they sat like this for several minutes, thinking about nothing in particular until Maggie suddenly sat upright.

Do you hear that?" Maggie whispered.

Jacob listened, not noticing anything but the wind rustling the leaves. "Jacob, there *is* no wind – that's what I mean," Maggie said, looking around. For an instant she thought she saw something out of the corner of her eye.

"What's that?" she asked, and then after a minute said, "Oh my gosh!" Jacob looked where she was staring.

"What are you looking at?" Jacob asked. "I don't see a thing."

"Everything! Everybody! The place is packed like the New York subway at rush hour!" Maggie jumped to her feet.

"I never realized, I never knew..." she said, her voice trailing off in amazement.

"What are you talking about?" Jacob asked again, standing up next to her. He looked all around and saw nothing but leaves.

Maggie caught her breath. "Jacob, stop staring and start looking." She said it softly, as if they were being overheard. "Use your intuition, your third eye, whatever. Don't look directly, just catch a glimpse, look *through* the leaves."

Jacob drew a blank. "Oh, for heaven's sake," Maggie finally said in desperation, "just read my mind! See what I'm seeing all around us!"

Jacob cleared his vision and his mind, and waited. What he saw next simply astounded him. He and Maggie were not alone on this tree limb. In fact, they were packed together cheek to jowl with dozens – no, hundreds of beings, walking up and down, *riding* up and down, as if they were in the middle of a bank of escalators going in different directions, overlapping, moving up and down all around them.

"What the hell?" Jacob said, not knowing what to make of it.

"Not hell, really – quite the opposite." It was Jacob's angel, coming out of the crowd, speaking directly into their minds. "This is the reality you don't have to see, another aspect of free will. If you knew you were always on public view, you'd never be yourselves."

"You mean it's not just here in the tree that this goes on?" Jacob asked in amazement. "Are you saying it's this crowded wherever I go?"

"Well, perhaps not *this* crowded," the angel said, smiling. "This is really the heart of creation, and a lot goes on here all the time. All these angels are on assignment, going where they're needed. But it's true, you're never out of sight of at least a few angels, demons, ghosts, elementals, whatever. The space you feel is just an illusion, to keep mankind from going crazy." The angel, sensing their disorientation, added sympathetically, "It doesn't bother us, but you can tune this out any time you start feeling claustrophobic."

"Thanks a lot," Jacob said, and then wondered if it was a sin to be sarcastic to an angel. "Is there anything else going on all around us all the time that you're not telling us about?"

"Universes," said the angel, "But you don't have to worry about those." And with that, he disappeared into the crowd.

"It gives new meaning to that old song, 'I Never See Maggie Alone,' doesn't it?" Jacob said.

"I wonder if they move aside for the snake," Maggie said, as beings brushed past them on all sides. These creatures didn't need limbs to stand on, and they were courteous enough not to push the humans, who were still somewhat subject to the law of gravity. Still, Maggie was feeling off balance.

"Let's sit down and put this out of our minds," Jacob said. "We'll never get Eli back if we have to witness all this confusion." Maggie agreed, and in a second the crowds disappeared from view. They felt completely alone again, sitting together in the branches of the enormous, silent tree.

Chapter 59

"Let's review what we know," Maggie said. "That's what we were about to do when all hell broke loose, and it's what we've got to concentrate on now, the nature of the tree, if we want to get Elijah back."

"We know the tree is at the heart of creation," Jacob said, "because that's what the angel just told us. It also seems to be control central for spiritual events, since the beings we saw are just doing their jobs, and there are plenty of them doing what they do. Either they are incredibly inefficient, or there's a lot to do around here. We also know the tree is accommodating to fools who go out on a limb, like me. That means it's attentive to individual vibrations. It reaches out in time as well as space, and there's a hole at its base that seems to be a wormhole to hell."

"Do you suppose," Maggie said slowly, "that if hell is below us, heaven and God are at the top of this tree?" Jacob and Maggie stared at one another.

"The descriptions of heaven I've come across bear no relation to tree houses," Jacob said with a smile. "They're more along the lines of crystal palaces, like the visions of Teresa of Avila. Of course, that could be an analogy for seeing through multiple dimensions – especially for Teresa, someone who'd never encountered anything more trippy than, say, the rose window at Chartres Cathedral. But I'm not sure that's what the serpent wants to know about the tree. I suspect he's more interested in the role *he* plays – that is, how evil figures into the equation. He seems convinced that without him, all creation would fall apart. Frankly, I think he's crazy on that score – knowledgeable but crazy, so he's badly misreading the information that's available to him. This may not be just a game for him, as he pretends. He may really not know the whole nature of the tree."

"If that's the case, then we may have to tell him a lie to get our goat back," Maggie said. "He may not believe the truth, or it may make him so angry that he'll kill Eli out of spite."

"I wouldn't put it past him," Jacob agreed. "But if we lie, what jeopardy does that put *us* in? I don't know the consequences of bad behavior in the tree of life – even if it is for a good cause."

Maybe if we climb higher, we'll get smarter," Maggie said. "Perhaps we could catch a ride on one of those up escalators."

"That means we'd have to see the crowds around us again," Jacob said reluctantly.

"Maybe we'll get to like it – like you like New York," Maggie said brightly. "Anyway, concentrate. It should be easier this time."

They were both surprised at how easy it was to rejoin this spiritual dimension. Hitching a ride, though, proved more daunting. "It's as if we're there and not there," Jacob said. "I see what they're doing, but my hand passes through what they're riding on. I guess we'll have to climb."

"Try the trunks," said a voice in Maggie's ear. It was the yellow bird, perched on her shoulder.

"Where did you go?" Maggie asked. "I wanted to thank you for leading me to Jacob, but you just disappeared."

"I'll stay with you for a while, if you'd like," said the bird. "I know your goat, and I'd like to help you save him from the snake. If you go to where the trunks intertwine, you'll find a more substantial ladder. It has a powerful influence, though, so you should be prepared. After all, it's the double helix of creation, and the energy, the complexity, can be disconcerting. Don't try to understand it – just relax and watch, and you'll be alright."

They walked along the limb till they reached the trunks of the intertwined trees. This time, however, they saw the trunks weren't solid, but related, vastly complex structures, translucent, and bound to one another by moving, spiraling staircases in between. "Step on," said the bird.

Chapter 60

As their feet touched the ladder, the world changed. At first it seemed everything suddenly paused long enough for them to see in extraordinary detail. Jacob focused on one green leaf, a leaf that moments ago would have looked like any other. Now this leaf became the leaf of leaves, the penultimate leaf, the master pattern for all the leaves in the universe. The colors were extraordinary – green became every color of the rainbow, and more – colors Jacob had never seen or dreamed of seeing. Stunned by the beauty, Jacob looked closer. Hundreds of veins, lines, cells fit together in the most intricate of puzzles, the most phenomenal of artwork, the most poetic of patterns. Life pulsed through the leaf with a power, an energy Jacob had never imagined possible. Jacob's eyes became microscopes: the life of microorganisms within this life of leaf pulsed together, aiding, threatening, consuming, healing, until his mind could no longer sort out the order from the chaos. Within those organisms, smaller organisms fought simpler but no less fascinating battles, while everything that was Leaf surged and flowed and reacted to everything around them.

"My God," was all Jacob could murmur, while Maggie said nothing at all. She had looked at her own right hand, the hand she'd lived with all her life, a hand she never knew existed. First the color of her skin, radiant, translucent, red and blue and white and purple, every color, pulsing with lifelines, stories, character, mystery, wisdom, danger, truth, friendship, power – part of her yet apart from her, the hand of all hands – and yet *her* hand. How could such a miracle be possible?

Wherever they turned their attention, another miracle appeared. Maggie looked at what she'd called the "little yellow bird." "Little" wasn't it at all. When she looked, it filled her whole vision, it was enormous in every sense of the word – hugely beautiful, hugely wise, hugely powerful – an all-seeing creature that could overwhelm a dinosaur, should the need arise. And yellow? How could she have described its intrinsic beauty so flatly? The bird radiated iridescence, as if the most shimmering of peacocks had perched on her shoulder, instead of a modest canary.

"Is this how the world is?" Maggie whispered to the bird. Why didn't I know this before?"

"You don't normally have time," the bird replied. "If you looked at every young face in your classroom – *really* looked at them, as you're seeing right now – you'd never have the time or inclination to teach them anything. You'd be too busy learning from *them* – about God."

Jacob realized he was crying, for perhaps the first time in years. "To think what I have missed," he said softly. Memories of his mother's eyes, his boyhood dog, his best friend in fourth grade, his first love in high school. His memory of each face was perfect, each was close enough to touch, and each smiled with love when he did. Jacob was completely overcome with love. He turned and held Maggie in his arms as if she were his only hope for returning all the love he had been given in his life. They clung together, eyes wide open, while the ladder spiraled upward through the trees of life and knowing.

Chapter 61

"This is our stop," the bird said suddenly, and following his direction, Jacob and Maggie stepped onto the nearest branch. Neither had any idea how long they'd been riding upward or how far they had come. As soon as they stepped off their escalator, however, their ordinary view of things returned.

Jacob looked around with care, but all he saw was the thick, green foliage of the tree. The branch where they stood was just as thick as before, and Jacob wondered if they'd moved at all, or whether it had been just an incredible hallucination.

Maggie picked up on his thought, but dismissed it. "No, we *have* come quite a way, Jacob," she interrupted. "Look, for one thing there aren't any angels traveling every which way around us up here. And for another, I would trust this bird with my very life. This bird would not – could not – lie to us. If you doubt anything about that ride, ask my friend."

"I'm honored by your trust," said the bird, "but Jacob's right, in a way. Movement here is a matter of conjecture, and the perception of going from place to place may not actually be real, in a larger sense. But as far as *we* are concerned, we've moved – and come a long way, at that. Follow me along this branch," the bird said, and fluttered through the leaves.

"Wait!" Jacob called. "What about the danger at the end of the branch -- of getting lost in our past?"

"We're above all that here," the bird called back faintly. "Come on, now!" Maggie and Jacob looked at each other, shrugged, and followed cautiously along the limb. It wasn't long until they caught up with the bird, who was perched at the end of the narrowed branch. Their view was still obscured by foliage, and Jacob waited for the bird's instructions.

"This is your present time up here," the bird said. "I thought you might like to look at the state of things. When we push past the leaves, just relax, look out, and listen to my voice. I can tune things for you to some extent, if you'll let me."

Holding Maggie's hand, Jacob sidled up to the last bough of leaves and pushed them aside. It felt as if they looked out over the whole world, and it reminded Jacob of the passage from Matthew 4:

Again, the devil took him to a very high mountain, and showed him all the kingdoms of the world and the glory of them; and he said to him, "All these will I give you, if you will fall down and worship me."

"It does look glorious from up here, doesn't it," the bird said. "But look at why it was easy for Jesus to reject the offer."

As they watched, the bird brought their view closer, until they could see the true condition of things. Drought, fire and famine, floods and falling water tables, polluted rivers, oceans and air, dying rain forests, political wars and the greed of the wealthy, diseases of blood and organ and skin, madness and the abuse of children, pesticides and radioactive waste, strip-mining and the deaths of whole species filled their sight, as the bird took them on lightening tours of Africa, Asia, Europe, the Americas, and even the Arctic poles. All was on its way to ruin, a waste and a desolation, as the failed stewardship of mankind revealed itself to them.

"This is what you've done with the creation that was given to you," the bird said softly. Jacob let the branch swing back, obscuring the view from his eyes, but not the view from his heart.

"Now," said the bird after a minute, "we must climb higher."

"I don't think I can stand a clearer view than the one we just saw," Jacob said, with a grieving heart. "Whatever could there possibly be left to see that we haven't already seen?"

"The future – what you would call prophecy," said the bird. "At this late date, of course, it takes very little imagination to see the outcome of earthly things. But foolish humankind has the most amazing ability to ignore what it doesn't want to see – even when it's staring you in the face."

They reached a place where lateral branches grew with particular thickness. "Here's a shortcut to the future," said the bird. "You can climb here."

They scrambled up several limbs. "Not too far, now," cautioned the bird. "You don't have to go very far from where we were to come to the end of days. Let's walk out on this branch and see where we've come."

They walked to the end of the branch and parted the leaves. The air was black with natural and unnatural catastrophe. A huge meteor fell into the ocean, causing earthquakes, volcanic eruptions and tidal waves. The sky was blackened by these upheavals, and by fire and nuclear war. "It's the golden censer and the wrath of the first four angels," Jacob said, and recited out loud the passages from Revelation:

Then the angel took the censer and filled it with fire from the altar and threw it on the earth; and there were peals of thunder, voices, flashes of lightning, and an earthquake....

The first angel blew his trumpet, and there followed hail and fire, mixed with blood, which fell on the earth; and a third of the earth was burnt up, and a third of the trees were burnt up, and all green grass was burnt up.

The second angel blew his trumpet, and something like a great mountain, burning with fire, was thrown into the sea; and a third of the sea became blood, a third of the living creatures in the sea died, and a third of the ships were destroyed.

The third angel blew his trumpet, and a great star fell from heaven, blazing like a torch, and it fell on a third of the rivers and on the fountains of water. The name of the star is Wormwood. A third of the waters became wormwood, and many men died of the water, because it was made bitter.

The fourth angel blew his trumpet, and a third of the sun was struck, and a third of the moon, and a third of the stars, so that a third of their light was darkened; a third of the day was kept from shining, and likewise, a third of the night.

"A good description of nuclear winter," Maggie said. "I always wondered how John could have envisioned such a thing, but it's no great feat with a view like this. Did you know that Chernobyl in their language *means* wormwood? With the damage done by facilities like that, and Fukushima still melting down in Japan, it could pollute a third of the waters."

"And the meteor that wiped out the dinosaurs 65 million years ago," Jacob said, "made the earth burn and then freeze, as the dirt thrown up blackened the skies and blocked out the sun. Another one even half that size – or more likely, a nuclear war – and there goes a third of the light, at least."

"You're looking at it," said the bird. "Welcome to the future."

Chapter 62

"Now we go just a branch or two higher," said the bird, "to see what your friend the snake will soon be up to. This will be his heyday, and you have to understand it if you want to understand him. He can't or won't see beyond the monumental chaos this time will soon represent – the stubbornness of mankind against repentance makes him a happy snake indeed."

They stood on the higher branch, looking out on a scene similar to the one below. "It looks the same to me," said Maggie. "Where is the difference?"

"It's a spiritual difference," said the bird. "It's the spiritual consequences of releasing pure evil into what's left of the earth. You remember that God bound many of the fallen angels in the pit? Now those furies get released."

Jacob continued his quote from Revelation:

Then I looked, and I heard an eagle crying with a loud voice, as it flew in midheaven, "Woe, woe, woe to those who dwell on the earth, at the blasts of the other trumpets which the three angels are about to blow!"

And the fifth angel blew his trumpet, and I saw a star fallen from heaven to earth, and he was given the key of the shaft of the bottomless pit; he opened the shaft of the bottomless pit, and from the shaft rose smoke like the smoke of a great furnace, and the sun and the air were darkened with the smoke from the shaft. Then from the smoke came locusts on the earth, and they were given power like the power of scorpions of the earth; they were told not to harm the grass of the earth or any green growth or any tree, but only those of mankind who have not the seal of God upon their foreheads; they were allowed to torture them for five months, but not to kill them, and their torture was like the torture of a scorpion, when it stings a man. And in those days, men will seek death and will not find it; they will long to die, and death will fly from them.

In appearance the locusts were like horses arrayed for battle; on their heads were what looked like crowns of gold; their faces were like human faces, their hair like women's hair, and their teeth like lions' teeth; they had scales like iron breastplates, and the noise of their wings was like the noise of many chariots with horses rushing into battle. They have tails like scorpions, and stings, and their power of hurting men for five months lies in their tails. They have as king over them the angel of the bottomless pit; his name in Hebrew is Abaddon, and in Greek he is called Apollyon, destroyer.

"It sounds like an air attack before the troops move in," Maggie said. "Drones look something like locusts, and they carry their 'sting' in the undercarriage. But why would spiritual beings use military tactics to conquer mankind?"

"Because they are created beings like you – and fallen, just like you," said the bird. They will rely on physical equipment and military tactics because that's all they have left to them. After all, for years they've been visiting the earth, testing your technology against theirs. You call them flying saucers, UFOs, but in reality they are the same fallen angels who came down to earth and then bred with the daughters of men. They've relied on technology since the fall, and have taught man how to use it, as well. Surely this doesn't come as any surprise?"

"No, not really," Jacob said. "For years there have been writers and mystics who saw UFOs as evidence of spiritual beings, fallen angels. It's just strange to think that scripture describes them in all-out war with us. But you're right about the similar tactics, since Revelation tells us that a ground invasion follows the air attacks:

Then the sixth angel blew his trumpet, and I heard a voice from the four horns of the golden altar before God, saying to the sixth angel who had the trumpet, 'Release the four angels who are bound at the great river Euphrates.' So the four angels were released, who had been held ready for the hour, the day, the month, and the year, to kill a third of mankind. The number of the troops of cavalry was twice ten thousand times ten thousand; I heard their number. And this was how I saw the horses in my vision: the riders wore breastplates the color of fire and of sapphire and of sulfur, and the heads of the horses were like lions' heads, and fire and smoke and sulfur issued from their mouths. By these three plagues a third of mankind was killed, by the fire and smoke and sulfur issuing from their mouths. For the power of the horses is in their mouths and in their tails; their tails are like serpents, with heads, and by means of them they wound."

"A third of mankind would be more than two and a half billion people," Maggie said dully, and then to obscure that thought, added, "Those horses – the fire from their mouths sounds more like tanks than horses."

"Well, what did John know of tanks?" Jacob asked. "He could only describe things in terms he knew, and he does say, 'And this was how I saw the horses.' He was describing a vision as best he could, and I think he did a pretty good job, considering. And the number of troops – 200 million – just happens to be the size of the Chinese army. I doubt there were that many people in the whole world when Revelation was written. I wonder how good we'll be, describing some of the things we've seen since we got here. Do you suppose anyone will believe us?"

"I doubt it," Maggie said. "I don't think *I* would. And why should they? Take UFOs. Tens of thousands of people have seen them, and thousands have filed eye-witness reports. Good photos and videos exist, and ex-military men have even reported working on reverse-engineering alien technology. Yet everyone thinks it's a joke, and the press won't give it the time of day."

"If you think that's bad," Jacob said, "try telling main line Protestants about the fallen angels. Just describing our encounter with the snake will be a big hit, I'm sure."

"I hope you're done feeling sorry for yourself," said the bird. "There's more to do if you want to get Eli back."

That got Maggie's attention. "How *can* we get Eli back?" she asked. "A creature so evil he would destroy the whole world – why would he spare a goat? Out of the goodness of his heart?"

"The serpent wants something from the two of you, some insight he can't get on his own. I don't know what it is, and I don't think I'm the one to figure it out. I think it will take another fallen creature to read his motivation – and that means you."

Chapter 63

The bird had left them on the end of the branch, where they could go on watching Satan marshaling his troops. It was not a continuum of future time, Jacob realized, but an excerpt. He could watch from beginning to end and then it would begin again, a tape loop in time. A different branch would tell another part of the story.

"You know," Jacob said after a while, "it may be that the serpent knows very well what's in store for him, and yet he's dragged forward inexorably – not because he's being forced into a showdown, but because he can't wait to indulge his full wrath in the scene we're watching below. It's like a gambler who can't resist the losing bet, the addict who shoots the tainted heroin he knows will kill him. The great tempter is himself tempted by an act of evil great enough to contain his own destruction. His self-loathing must be immense, because he sees himself as eternally unforgivable. Now what would such a creature think he could learn from us?"

"That he hasn't made an error in understanding God's judgment?" Maggie asked. "What if he's not really sure of his fate? I know it's hard to imagine, but I think that almost everything we've seen here is more comprehensible than the nature of evil, and how judgment may be tempered with mercy. After all, that's the final battle of good and evil, isn't it? Eternal torment is evil meted out to evildoers, but it's still evil. I think Satan wants to know for sure that he's condemned without any possibility of parole. He wants to know that it doesn't matter *what* he does – that the outcome for him is inevitable. That his case is hopeless."

"You may be right," Jacob said. "He confirmed that passage in the Book of Enoch, telling how the fallen angels ask Enoch to intercede for them – to beg God for mercy for their sins. God tells Enoch, in effect, that it's none of his business. I guess the implication is that angels have their role and we have ours."

"And yet angels are always interfering with *our* fate," Maggie countered, "for good or evil. An angel pulled you back from the brink just a little while ago, and Satan has sure been leading us around.   So, if they can play with our fate, why aren't we allowed to intercede in theirs?"

"What I don't know," Jacob said, and then added, "What I *really* don't know, is the nature of evil – at least clearly enough to articulate what it is. I guess I've always treated it like that Supreme Court justice who said he couldn't define pornography, but knew it when he saw it. A truly evil act is one without any redeeming value, which is why the bad guys in movies get portrayed as remarkably bad. When they exhibit any humor or kindness, even to their victims, the audience gets confused and the plot gets diluted."

"Perhaps if we went higher, we could see the outcome," Maggie said.

"I suspect there are limits to what we can see," Jacob said. "Anyway, I'm sure Satan has read as much as John reported in Revelation, and if we are right, he still refuses to accept the judgment as final and irrevocable. The father of lies lies to himself, as well. We already know he believes there's an equal weight to good and evil, so obviously Satan is no authority on the nature of evil, either. Does anyone around here fully understand the nature of evil?"

The bird emerged through the foliage and perched on Maggie's shoulder. "There is someone here who does," said the bird.

Chapter 64

"You mean God, don't you," Maggie said. It was a statement, not a question. Jacob had understood the bird, as well. "I don't think we're prepared to meet God, birdy! I know I'd be terrified."

"And yet you met Satan, didn't you?" asked the bird. "That's when you should have been afraid. God knows people, walks and talks with them. He did with Adam and Eve and Enoch and Moses, and it didn't hurt them. It just made them glow."

"But we're not worthy," Jacob began.

"No one is," said the bird. "That goes without saying. But you are part of his creation, and he's always interested in that. He may not want to see you, of course, but he must have had a reason for admitting you to the garden. If he does want to see you, I wouldn't pass up the opportunity."

"If we were going to visit – and I'm not saying that we will – then where would we go to find him?" Jacob asked. He had never been good at asking directions, but this was a unique situation.

"You can go up or down," said the bird. "It really makes no difference. If it were my visit, I guess I'd return to the garden. It's less disorienting for creatures, being on the earth. Up above, you don't know what you're looking at, you're out of your body, and the whole situation is so bizarre you'll miss half the conversation. If you were in it for the awe, then I'd say go up, for sure. For some people, the awe *is* the message. But I think you have some serious issues to deal with, and to be rendered speechless is not the best mode for communication with God. Anyway, the Lord hasn't walked in Eden for far too long. That's why it's looking so shabby. Getting him down there will make a world of difference to the place."

"And what about the snake, and more importantly, our little goat?" Maggie asked. "Don't we need to be up here to rescue Eli?"

"Not really," said the bird. "When you are ready, the snake will find you. Long story short, that's the tragedy of the world."

"You know, I think I'm ready to put my feet on solid ground again," Maggie said to Jacob. "This has been more than interesting, but people weren't meant to live in trees."

"Actually, you haven't been entirely living, as you understand it," corrected the bird. "Haven't you noticed that for all the time you've been up here, you haven't felt the need to eat or sleep or pee? You'll feel considerably heavier when you leave the trees, because that's when your physical body fully rejoins the etheric."

"But... I *look* like me," Maggie said, thinking about the vision of her hand.

"Oh, you're you, alright," said the bird. "More you than when your physical body gets old and lame and tired. That's when you'll remember *this* body, and cherish it all the more." Then, before leaving them, the bird whispered something else in Maggie's ear.

Jacob and Maggie opted to climb down to the garden. At first Maggie thought they must be miles above the earth, but the bird had assured them the distances they'd experienced were not as great as they'd imagined. The bird was apparently correct on this, for after climbing down a dozen branches or so, their feet hit the ground.

"I don't believe it," Maggie said, looking back up the branches from where they'd come. "I can see both trees entirely, and it doesn't seem so big from here. Oh, it's big alright, but not the miles and miles it feels like when you're standing up there."

"It looks to be about the height and shape of a huge oak I used to play in as a child," Jacob said, feeling more weighty, more authoritative than he had in a while. He thought it must be the gravity of his own body speaking.

"You know, from here it suddenly reminds me of my hundred-year-old apple tree in the back yard where I grew up," Maggie said. "My dad built a little platform for me on some lower branches, and I'd sit up there for hours. Jacob, I just realized – I didn't see any fruit growing up there on either side, on either tree!"

"I think those options are lost to us now," Jacob said, somewhat wistfully. The thought moved him to take Maggie's hand in his, and wander down the hill to the orchard to find them something to eat.

The orchard smelled wonderful, and every kind of fruit was within easy reach. "Oh, if only we'd been able to get Eli back," Maggie thought. She felt guilty at how heavenly a particular pear tasted to her.

When they'd eaten their fill, Jacob said, "I wonder if we should pray to God to ask him to come down. He must know we're here and that we'd like to talk with him, but perhaps it's proper to put in a request."

"Well, first we should figure out what it is we want to ask him," Maggie said. "After all, we don't really want a dissertation on the nature of evil so much as to find out what it is we have to tell the devil to free Elijah. And then there's the whole question of free will, and whether we'd be asking too much. In a way, we'll be asking God to do our work for us."

"It wouldn't be the first time," Jacob said. "People do that all the time – pray for a miracle when it's already in their power to do what is needed. I'd really rather be thanking God than asking for yet another favor. But I guess that won't be possible."

"So, while we're waiting, let's try to figure things out on our own," Maggie said cheerily. "After all, isn't that what life's all about? Anyway, here's the situation: One, Satan got our goat, and won't give him back until we tell him something he wants to know about the tree; Two, we don't know what it is he wants to learn from us, but we suspect it has to do with God's future judgment of him; Three, we think it's a lost cause for Satan, but we don't want to upset him – at least, not 'til we get Eli back. Did I miss anything?"

"No, I think you got all the basics," Jacob replied. "That's the immediate situation. But if we actually get the chance to talk with God, what else should we ask him? I mean, what about all those tough theological quandaries we've wrestled with over the years? This will be our big opportunity to learn the truth. Aren't there some key issues to think about, as well?"

"Somehow, all the theoretical stuff seems far less important than getting Eli back," Maggie said. "Anyway, if we had all the answers, we'd be out of a job. Who needs theology schools when God has revealed the unvarnished truth?"

"He already has, and yet there's no end to picking it apart," Jacob said. "After the 'vision' comes the 'revision'. Who knows? We might wind up being responsible for a boom in seminary attendance, not to mention the careers of dozens of authors redacting what we learn from the mouth of God."

"Well, first things first," Maggie said. "We have to get Elijah back. What are we going to tell Satan about the nature of the tree?"

"That it links heaven and hell through space and time," Jacob answered. "That it is central to creation, and as such, it's the spiritual prototype, a model of the double helix structure of DNA. Unfortunately, however, the serpent already knows all this, and it won't be enough to convince him."

"What about the relationship of the tree of life to the tree of knowledge?" Maggie asked. "They have certainly become inseparable, they're so entwined. Yet the first was considered all good, while the desire for the other brought mankind to ruin. Does that mean Satan's right about the interdependence of good and evil – that creation is hung on duality?"

"You could read it that way, and yet that doesn't obviate judgment," Jacob replied. "You remember Jesus' parable about letting the wheat and the tares grow up together, so the harvest is not uprooted by weeding out the bad? I don't see how anything could uproot the tree of knowledge now without uprooting the tree of life, as well. But all that will happen, almost of its own accord, at the end of time.

"Think about that scene of horror we were witness to, as Satan massed his armies for destruction. If anything would make people repent, you'd think it would be that. And yet Revelation 9 tells us:

The rest of mankind, who were not killed by these plagues, did not repent of the works of their hands nor give up worshiping demons and idols of gold and silver and bronze and stone and wood, which cannot either see or hear or walk; nor did they repent of their murders or their sorceries or their immorality or their thefts."

"Doesn't John's language there strike you as somewhat archaic?" Maggie asked in response to Jacob's quote. "That talk of worshiping idols sounds too primitive to be real."

Jacob laughed. "Just look at the way people worship their smartphones! Those are idols built of gold and silver contacts, and silicon chips for stone. They house the new religion, and people spend their days and nights staring at them; they do everything worshipful but pray to them, and some even pray when their phone gets wet. Don't forget – the internet's www prefix translates in Hebrew to *vav, vav, vav* – which you know equals 666. Caught in the worldwide web we are. Could anyone ask for a clearer sign than that?"

By the time they had finished eating it was almost dark. They had left their gear where they'd dropped it under the trees, and now it was too dark to try to retrieve it. Instead, they made a simple bedding of fir boughs on the grassy ground beneath the trees of the orchard, and soon enough fell into a deep, peaceful sleep.

Chapter 65

The sun was well up when they awoke, but it wasn't the light that roused them. It was the crackling fire, the smell of coffee, and the sound of someone singing what sounded like an old Irish shanty.

Jacob and Maggie sat up and stared. A tiny, gray-haired woman in an old gray dress was squatting before the fire, cooking breakfast.

"It's about time you two were up," she said. "How do blueberry pancakes sound to you?"

"Who are you?" Jacob asked in quiet amazement. "And where did you find coffee? I haven't smelled anything that good since I left Bangor."

"Oh, I have my sources," said the old woman. "I had a hunch this would taste good, though it's not common fare in Eden."

"You have maple syrup!" Maggie said, equally amazed. She'd been sitting there in silent wonder, but the syrup was just too much.

"Well, I don't get much chance to cook here in the garden," the old lady said. "Actually, you folks remind me of the last couple who visited here. And awhile back I fed a traveler named Gilgamesh, a nice enough fellow. He was looking for immortality, but he didn't get it. Came close, though, until the snake cheated him out of it. Anyway, I told him this immortality business isn't all it's cracked up to be. He didn't believe me, of course. Hardly anyone does."

She jerked the skillet upward in a graceful motion that demonstrated the complete confidence of the cook. Maggie and Jacob watched in awe as twelve pancakes turned in the air and fell perfectly back into place.

"There have been other people in the garden, as well," the old lady went on, "but nobody has the time to sit down and share a meal. Everybody's so busy, nowadays. So, with you two, I decided to just not bother asking. There you were, sound asleep, so I said to myself, Siduri, if you don't want your cooking skills to go right down the tubes, you'd better whip up a tasty breakfast for that young couple over there."

"This is very kind of you, Siduri," Maggie said. "I would have said so sooner, but the surprise of seeing you here cooking pancakes rather took my breath away."

"Yes, how do you happen to be here?" Jacob asked. "We didn't think there was anyone else in the garden besides ourselves, a few animals, and the snake. Everyone else seems to be in the tree."

"It's really far too crowded up there," the old lady said. "I don't know how they stand it, all that pushing and shoving and bustling about. It's certainly not my idea of any way to live. Even the snake hangs out up there when he can – though he's shunned, of course. Nobody will speak to him, and nothing empties a branch faster than his arrival. Nevertheless, he still chooses not to get it." She shook her head.

"The snake stole Eli from us," Maggie said. "At least *I* feel he did. It was this year's scapegoat from Israel, so I suppose he has a claim on him. But Eli is a living creature, a beautiful, silky goat kid who doesn't deserve to die just to satisfy some antique ceremony that was made meaningless by Jesus' sacrifice on the cross!"

"Not meaningless to orthodox Jews, my dear," the old lady said. "You know, they have *always* liked doing things the hardest way possible."

"Oh, I'm sorry," Maggie said, suddenly embarrassed. "You could very well be Jewish yourself, and I never even thought before I opened my mouth."

"Not to worry. If you're going to attribute a religion to me, I guess you'd have to call it messianic monotheism." Siduri laughed at her own private joke.

"Now, my children, these pancakes are ready when you are." She served them on white china dishes, pancakes beautiful to look at, with just the right amount of syrup. Maggie was startled by the knife and fork – it was just like her mother's best silverware, the set she reserved for special occasions. "I knew you would notice," Siduri said, smiling.

They ate their surprise pancakes in silence, completely absorbed in the richness of the flavors. Afterwards, sipping the best cup of coffee he'd ever tasted, Jacob thought over what Siduri had said.

"You advised Gilgamesh, didn't you?" Jacob finally asked. "It was more than just knocking immortality. As I remember it now…. I remember the translation of the speech from the Babylonian version of the story. I believe you said:

Gilgamesh, where do you roam?
You will not find the eternal life you seek.
When the gods created mankind
They appointed death for mankind,
Kept eternal life in their own hands.
So, Gilgamesh, let your stomach be full,
Day and night enjoy yourself in every way,
Every day arrange for pleasures,
Day and night, dance and play,
Wear fresh clothes.
Keep your head washed, bathe in water,
Appreciate the child who holds your hand,
Let your wife enjoy herself in your lap.
This is the work of mankind.

"Did I say all that?" the old lady asked. "I was quite a poet, if I do say so myself. I'm impressed my words have been remembered all these years – that *you* remember them. I can't say what good they did. As I told you, Gilgamesh held immortality in his hands, and was cheated out of it by the snake. He should have savored his human side, for that's where his hope was."

"The snake wants us to trust him," Maggie said, "but there's no way, we just can't. He claims to be co-creator of the world, yet he doesn't seem to understand his own desperate future. How can anyone trust a creature that's so filled with self-deception?"

"You can't, my dear," said Siduri. "And as to that co-creation business, all the fallen angels claim a hand in it. Some of them worked on it, sure, just as angels continue with it today. But so do all created creatures, for good or evil. Even you two are working on creation – but not as co-equals with the Word. The Word does not require the duality claimed by Satan and his demons. They will lie about that until the end – and then evil will disappear, and the true nature of things will be revealed. Even they will understand, in the end. Before that, they will go on lying to themselves and to you."

"Will the snake ever return Eli to us?" Maggie asked, hopefully.

"Were pigs given wings?" responded Siduri. "The fact the goat means so much to you has sealed its fate in Satan's eyes. No matter what you do for him, no matter what he's promised, if you leave it up to him it won't turn out well for the goat – or for you."

"What *can* we do then?" Maggie asked desperately. "How will we find Elijah? The snake is the only one who knows where he is."

"I know where the goat is," said the old lady, "but you won't like hearing what I tell you."

"Oh please," said Maggie, practically in tears. "Please tell us where we can find him!"

The old lady settled back on her haunches. "I will tell you on condition that you follow my instructions *exactly*. If you do not, then your fate will be worse than the goat's. Do you understand?"

"Oh yes, thank you," Maggie said gratefully.

"Don't thank me yet," Siduri said. "Wait until I tell you what you have to do. You'll recall the wormhole in the cave of roots under the tree? Your goat is down there – quite a way down there. The only way you can rescue him is to go after him yourselves."

Jacob felt a chill run the length of his spine. "No," he said softly, "not down there."

"I'm afraid so," said the old lady. "I said you wouldn't like it. Shall we forget it, then?"

"No!" Maggie said. "I'll go myself if I have to, but I'm not leaving the garden without Eli!"

"Brave girl," Siduri said, looking at Jacob. Jacob felt his face redden.

"I didn't say I *wouldn't* go," Jacob said. "It's just that I'm claustrophobic. I hate tight places, and that's one of the tightest I've seen."

"It's even tighter than that – tighter than you can imagine," Siduri replied. "It's so tight, in fact, that most creatures in there plead to come out again. Never mind, though. Once you get in there it widens out in a physical sense. Just be sure to follow my instructions."

"Have you traveled there yourself?" Maggie asked.

"Not for two thousand years," Siduri responded. "I haven't felt the inclination to return. Self-inflicted suffering is hard to watch, but they do grow out of it in time."

The sun was high in the sky by now, and breakfast was over. Maggie suddenly felt restless to get started, and stood up. "Will you give us our instructions now?" she asked Siduri.

"Of course," she said. "First, be sure to take your gear. You won't find any grassy orchards to camp in, and you may need your medical supplies. The going can be rough. Once you're down to the bottom of the hole, you'll find yourself on a smoky plain overlooking a river of fire."

"Sounds like the history of Cleveland," Jacob interjected. Maggie jabbed him in the ribs.

"Walk to the shore and look for the boatman. When you find him, say to him: 'We are not yet dead, we are not yet judged.' He will expect a fee for transporting you across. Give him half of this." The old lady picked up a pancake left over from breakfast, and broke it in half. As she handed it to Maggie, the two halves turned to gold.

"Tell him to take you to Satan's fortress. It looks like a mountain range against the sky, but it gets smaller as you get closer. Tell the boatman to wait on the shore for you, and you will pay him the other half when he returns you to the other side. He will laugh at the suggestion you'll be leaving, but he will wait – for a while, at least. Do you have a thermos?"

The question took Jacob by surprise. "Um, yes. It's up with the rest of our gear," he said.

"Go get your thermos and bring it down here," Siduri said. "Maggie will wait here with me."

While Jacob walked back up the hill to the tree, Siduri motioned Maggie to sit next to her.

Maggie came around from the other side of the fire and sat by Siduri's feet. "Good, good," said the old lady. "Now, I want to tell you a story about what you call 'reality.' It's from the Indian text called the Mahabharata, about an old man named Markandeya.

"It seems this Markandeya was the only person left alive at the end of the world. All other life had perished, and he wandered through the dead, gray world alone. He walked and walked, but there was no place to rest his head. Exhausted, in dark despair, he took one last turn around, and there he saw an amazing sight. Behind him, to his great surprise, stood a fig tree, and beneath it sat a beautiful, smiling child.

"'I can see you need to rest awhile,' said the child to Markandeya, and the child opened his mouth. A sudden wind came up, and old Markandeya was swept into the child's mouth and dropped into the child's belly. There he found rivers, trees, herds of cattle and sheep. Men cut grain, women carried water, villages prospered in the shining sun. Yes, the entire earth lay before him, and Markandeya walked the continents from ocean to ocean for a hundred years, yet never reached the end of this world. Finally, the wind arose again, and Markandeya was lifted out of the child's body, out of the mouth. There was the child, still sitting under the fig tree. The child smiled up at him and said, 'I hope your rest was good.'"

Jacob returned just as the story ended. "Perfect timing," Siduri said. "Now, empty out that thermos and fill it with what's left of the coffee. Remember, *this is not for you to drink*! You must give it to the gatekeeper at the fortress, and he will let you in. Somewhere inside, he will tell you where, you will find your goat. That part is up to you. When you find him, return the way you came – and don't look back! Looking back would bring delay, perhaps a fatal one. I can't stress that enough. Don't look back! Have you got it?"

"Don't look back," Maggie and Jacob said in unison. "Got it."

"Good luck!" said Siduri, and ambled off into the forest.

Maggie suddenly jumped to her feet. "Wait!" she cried. "You didn't tell me the meaning of that story!" But Siduri was already gone.

"What story?" Jacob asked.

"Let's get going," Maggie said. "I'll tell you on the way."

Chapter 66

They headed up hill toward the root cave, to where they'd stashed their gear. They walked single file, Jacob in the lead, while Maggie repeated Siduri's story to him.

"She certainly *seemed* like the character in the old story," Jacob said. "She's known as the 'alewife' in the Epic of Gilgamesh, and she's the only sensible voice in that litany of vain hope, loss, and tragedy. She didn't say anything about Gilgamesh's parentage, though. There were two stories about his father – one, that he was a king, the other, that he was a demon. Of course, they could have been one in the same. The hero legends were all about the half-breed angels, as far as I'm concerned. All those hero tales from the Indian, Greek and Roman mythologies were based on ancient stories about the Nephilim, and so was the story of Gilgamesh. And yet she spoke about him with affection. Do you suppose God, at the end of duality, would forgive even the fallen angels?"

"But what of the story she told about Markandeya?" Maggie wanted to know. "She must have been trying to tell us something."

"We'll know soon enough," Jacob said. By now they had entered the cave, and were standing by the hole. Jacob shone his flashlight into the black depths, but could see nothing. "It will be a tight fit, but that should help keep us from falling," Jacob observed, trying to sound positive. He was already feeling slightly nauseated, and figured he'd better move now, before it got worse. "I'll go first," he said, and slid into the hole.

Once they started down, Jacob was relieved to find there were handholds and footholds for them to use. He hadn't mentioned it to Maggie, but he'd had no idea how they would climb back up a smooth hole – especially with a goat in tow. Maggie kept her eyes closed tight, and felt her way down. She tried not to dislodge dirt and rocks, since she knew they were falling on Jacob, but it was impossible not to knock some loose. Below her feet she could hear the clatter of gravel, and Jacob's occasional swearing. She kept repeating, "I'm sorry," but she knew he understood.

It seemed like she'd been descending forever when she suddenly heard Jacob yell. His feet had hit ground, and he realized he'd landed in the back end of a small cave. He crouched down to look around, and saw a red glow lighting the stone walls ahead.

Maggie dropped down behind him. "What's that light?" she whispered. "It looks like there's a fire burning there."

"Let's go see," Jacob said. They made their way to the mouth of the cave, and peered out.

The opening lay halfway up the side of a small hill, and they gazed onto a scene of fire and desolation. The rough, blasted landscape offered not one green thing. Instead, boulders and deep clefts in rock stripped of soil tumbled downward to a river that bubbled with flame, as methane rising from below the water would ignite and bloom and die again. Across the river they could see what looked like a small mountain range, with spiked peaks of black, barren rock set against a polluted, yellow sky. The smell of smoke and sulfur fumes was terrible, overwhelming, and they both reached for their airline virus masks to cover their noses and mouths.

"I didn't think it was possible, but this is worse than the battle we witnessed at Armageddon," Maggie told Jacob.

"It's been here longer," Jacob said. "They've had time to perfect it. We'd better head for the shore. I hope the air is clearer down below us." They stumbled down the rocky hillside and walked along a rough path to the water. Jacob looked up and down the shoreline, but saw no boat or boatman.

"Perhaps he's on the other side," Maggie said, "and we have to wait 'til he gets back." A large bubble of sulfurous gas exploded into flame right in front of them. Choking and gagging, they stumbled backwards from the shore's edge.

"We should have been burned," Maggie sputtered. "But that huge flame felt almost cold. Do you suppose Dante's description of icy flame is true?"

"Maybe," said Jacob, "or maybe it's just part of our expectation of what hell is supposed to be like. Or maybe we're somehow protected from the flames because we're alive. I don't know and I don't much care – so long as we're not fried to a crisp. Now, where's that damned boatman?"

214

"I assume you mean me," a cracked voice said from behind them. A crippled old man with singed hair and a scraggly beard stepped out from behind a boulder. He was so bent over he'd been hidden from their sight by a rock not more than five feet tall. His antique, threadbare clothes were topped by a black slicker and hat to ward off the peculiar waters he traveled.

"Yes, I guess I do," Jacob said sheepishly. "Sorry, but we've had a rough time getting this far."

"Most people do," said the boatman.

"So, where *is* your boat?" Maggie inquired, trying to change the subject. The boatman gestured toward the water, where a large, squarish metal barge sat pulled up on the shore. Maggie was sure it hadn't been there a second ago, but didn't ask any questions. She was beginning to think it was better not to ask questions down here.

"We are not yet dead, we are not yet judged," Jacob said, "but we need you to ferry us to the fortress and wait for us until we return."

"So, you think you'll return from the fortress?" The boatman laughed, just as Siduri had predicted.

Maggie ignored the humor. "Here is half your fee," she said, and handed the boatman one piece of the golden pancake. "We'll give you the rest when we are back here again."

"You pay well," said the boatman. "I will take you and wait for you on the other shore – but not forever. I have other passengers to ferry across, though theirs is a one-way trip. Come with me." He led them to a door in the high-sided boat. When they were on board, he closed the door and locked it.

"Why are the sides of the boat so high?" Jacob asked.

"You'll see soon enough," said the boatman. Without visible power, without motor or pole or sail, the boat moved out into the water. Immediately a groan went up, as if the river itself were a creature being cut in two by the boat.

"What's that horrible noise!" Jacob asked, fearing the answer.

"The giants in the river," the boatman said. "For various reasons, their souls are condemned to the fire and ice. They can't go ashore, they can't drown, and they see this boat as their only hope. They claw and grasp at the hull as she passes, but they can't lay hold or climb on board. They know it's hopeless, but they try each time we pass by." He stopped talking, and they heard it clearly now, the scraping and the pleas.

It seemed like forever, but they came at last to the other shore. "The fortress is that way," said the boatman. "It looks like a distant mountain, but looks are deceiving. Stay on the path and you'll be there shortly. Just beware of voices that call to you from here and there, asking you to leave the path, asking you for help. You cannot help them, but they can hurt you." The boatman seemed almost friendly, and Jacob thanked him for his advice.

They set out along a path strewn with lava, and hard-going. It was dark, as well, but Maggie had the impression it was always like this, a closed, controlled environment. It reminded her of Disney World, where she'd seen some elaborate outdoor scenes recreated on a set. The sulfurous yellow sky was just as ugly, just as poisonous as before, but they'd almost become used to the acrid smell. "I've smelled papermills in Maine worse than this," Jacob said to Maggie as they walked along.

A half hour later they were at the fortress gate. "It looks more like a cave than a fortress," Maggie remarked, and Jacob had to agree. The front of the castle was carved into the rough rock face like the facades carved into the red stone cliffs at Petra. Unlike Petra, however, there was no elegance or beauty to the work. The front of the building was dark, foreboding, with blackened stone and slits for windows. Meanwhile, the jagged mountaintop above made the setting so ominous that anyone approaching the gate would expect the master of the house to be neither man nor angel, but some horrible, dragon-like creature, enormous in size and power.

"What an architectural ego trip," Jacob said, looking up at the structure.

"It's not much, but he calls it home," Maggie joined in. "Early overblown Romanesque, wouldn't you say?" They laughed nervously, and she added, "Shall we see if Dracula's at home?"

They walked up to the massive iron door. They saw no bell-pull or knocker, so Jacob picked up a stone and pounded on the door. A moment later, a red-faced demon in formal dress opened the door and looked out.

"Yes, what is it?" he asked.

"We would like to come in," Maggie said, "and if you'll let us, we have a present for you."

"And what present could you give that would make me break my trust with the lord of this realm?" the demon asked.

"This," Maggie said, presenting the thermos.

The demon took it from her hand and unscrewed the lid. Tears welled in his eyes. "You don't know how happy you have made me," he said at last. "Please, come in. Stay as long as you wish."

They entered a great stone hall, with Persian carpets covering the flagstone floor. A roaring fire in the enormous stone fireplace actually heated the room. Maggie looked around anxiously, and then turned to the demon. "Sir," she said deferentially, "could you possibly tell us where we might find a little goat named Eli? We've come all the way here to take him home."

"I take it you don't understand what you've given me," the demon said, still clutching the thermos.

"I'm sure it tasted better when it was fresh brewed," Jacob said.

"The liquid in this container means my release," the demon said reverently. "It's the gift from heaven that every creature in hell prays for every moment of every tortured day. I will do everything I can to repay you, and I will travel with you back to the tree – if you'll allow me to join you on the journey." He said this, and then drank it down.

"This is amazing!" Jacob said. "Who would have thought we'd find an ally in hell?"

"Of course you can join us," said Maggie. "You're right – we didn't realize the significance of what it was we carried here to give to you. But it was intended for you, so there must be a reason for it. Anyway, we need your help in rescuing Eli. Have you seen him here?"

"Yes, yes indeed," the demon said. "We hear his mournful cries throughout the fortress. They give Satan particular delight, and whet his appetite for the goat's destruction. He finds something particularly tasty in destroying the innocent – and we rarely find innocence down here. Your goat has intensified our lives here, but in very different ways. For Satan it's been appetite. For me it's been treason. Day and night I've been thinking about how *I* might save the kid."

"You know," Maggie said to the demon, "it may have been those very thoughts that singled you out for salvation. And if that's the case, then Eli has helped save your soul, or whatever it is demons have. That should mean penance for Elijah – enough to lift the sins of Israel off his shoulders forever. Now, let's go get him!"

"No, not yet," the demon said. "First we have to make sure Satan doesn't return too soon. You see, he's now so paranoid he's become rather psychic. I'm afraid if we just grab the goat and run, he'll return before we get even as far as the river. You're not in the garden anymore, and he'll feel no constraints of civility. This is his domain, and if he catches you here he'll punish us with whatever horror strikes his fancy." The demon shuttered at the thought.

"But if he's psychic, how can we rescue Eli?" Maggie asked.

"We need to involve him in something more important," said the demon, "something so important to him he won't even notice that his prize snack is getting away. And I think I know what that might be.

"You see, he meets on a regular basis with a group of humans he calls the twelve. They are a secret society that acts as a go-between for Satan and the principalities and powers of the world."

"You mean *our* twelve?" Jacob asked. "They were the ones who sent us to the garden in the first place!"

"That would make sense," said the demon. "They would want a report on any conversations between the spiritual world and theirs, and if they heard the garden was opening again, they'd be the ones to send a representative. They have a huge vested interest in keeping control of things – and Satan has a vested interest in making them think they are in control."

"And are they in control?" Maggie asked.

"They serve Satan," said the demon, "and those who live by the sword die by the sword. Oh, I'm sure Satan has promised they'll live like royalty in the afterlife, and they are egotistical enough to believe him."

"Who would be that foolish?" Maggie asked. "They seemed like smart people."

"Oh, they're smart, alright," said the demon. "That's the hook Satan uses – the hook he has always used. He trades them knowledge, especially technology, for their loyalty. What you call alien technology – from laser weapons to flying saucers – has all come from the knowledge of the fallen angels. Right now, they are working on quantum combined with something called space-time crystals – units that generate energy and coherence without end. With that they hope to replicate the abilities of the spiritual world over time and distance with their breakthrough powers of human technology. If and when they succeed in engineering these plans, they believe their access to knowledge will be unstoppable and limitless. They think they'll be gods, but they're in for a surprise."

"How close are they?" Jacob asked.

"Very close, now," the demon said. "After all, they've been working on it since 1947 – when they got the Roswell delivery. They gained a lot from that so-called accident. They've reverse engineered computer chips, fiber optics, night vision, composite metals, stealth technology, and working models of anti-gravity flying machines – just from that one delivery. Give them quantum control over space-time, and the package is complete. The twelve will have virtually every technological marvel the fallen angels have created."

"So, you're saying a meeting of the twelve would be enough to distract Satan from what we're doing here?" Jacob asked.

"Yes, I'm sure it would," the demon said.

"That's all very well," Maggie interjected, "but how, from the depths of this pit, do we arrange a meeting of the twelve? Email? Is the fortress set up for Zoom?"

"What's Zoom?" the demon asked.

"You live in hell and you haven't heard of Zoom?" Jacob said. "What's the netherworld coming to?"

"Jacob, please," Maggie winced. "We're trying to be serious here. How can we get the twelve to distract Satan?" she asked the demon. "Is there a way?"

"I think there is," he replied. "One of the twelve is possessed by a demon friend of mine. My friend is the one who keeps me posted on what the twelve are up to. A member can't call a meeting without good reason, but I think we can give him a reason ourselves – a crucial reason that would require Satan's attendance."

"What reason is that?" Jacob asked.

"That you are in hell, in the fortress, learning what the twelve are up to," said the demon. "If they knew that, they would want to do everything in their power to destroy you – before you could return to the world and destroy them. That's a very good reason for them to call a meeting. The drawback, of course, is that you will be placed in immediate, terrible danger. You will be hunted by every corrupt power, human and spiritual, on the face of the earth."

"Is that the best you can come up with?" Maggie asked. "What good is saving Eli if we all wind up dying some horrible death? Why can't they meet to exchange early Christmas presents, or something like that?"

"There has to be a powerful reason – and it has to be true," said the demon. "My friend won't jeopardize his member's position by lying to help save a goat. But this bit of knowledge will raise his prestige in the others' eyes. Knowledge is power, after all, and he'll be telling them something they didn't know. A lot of prestige is attached to that."

"But how do we avoid the wrath to come?" Jacob asked. "I suppose we could seek protection in the tree, but I was actually looking forward to returning to Bangor, to teaching a course or two again. I didn't expect to be checking under the bed for monsters every night."

"I may be able to help you there," said the demon. "I will if I can. But now you have to make your decision. We have to call that meeting if you want to save the goat. It's up to you."

Chapter 67

The decision was made: Jacob, Maggie and the demon were of one mind.

"Now, how do we arrange this meeting of the twelve?" Jacob asked. "Can you speak with the possessing demon somehow, let him know it has to happen right away?" Jacob was remembering the boatman's warning that he had other things to do besides wait for them. "If we get stuck on this side of the river with Eli in tow, we could be caught facing a very angry Satan."

"It's not 'could,' it's 'will be,'" the demon said. "Demons can communicate directly, but it's not that easy. It seems we're so lost in our own problems, we don't hear one another very well. So, I *think* the message to my friend. He 'senses' a generalized anxiety on my part, relating to you and the goat. He then thinks, 'Something is happening at the fortress that only I am aware of. This will advance me among the twelve. I must call a meeting right away.'

"Now, I happen to know that Satan is in Europe right now, attending a meeting of the World Trade Organization. He heads a subcommittee on the World Wide Web, which he finds amusing."

"Just a minute," Maggie said. "Even members of the WTO would surely notice that one of their subcommittee chairmen was a snake. How does he disguise himself?"

"Oh, he only looks like himself in the garden," the demon replied. "That's where God cursed him. He works in the world in a variety of roles. In the WTO he is Mr. Satino, a delegate from Rome. Mr. Satino also meets on a regular basis with the men who run the Vatican, and especially the Vatican Bank. It seems they have a lot in common with each other, and they're always plotting new ways to manipulate the pope. This pope is pretty shrewd himself, though. He knows what they're up to, and has done his best to frustrate them. But he's getting old.

"Anyway, it will take my friend an hour, I think, to get the twelve together for the meeting. Fortunately, they only meet in person. The technologies of meeting by conference call or satellite are their own invention, and they don't trust them – with good reason. They know how thoroughly electronic communications are examined – after all, they have access to the computer banks where phone and electronic communications are monitored and stored for the NSA. They themselves are listening to the whole world, all the time."

"Well, I guess you should tell your friend to call the meeting," Jacob said. "We don't have much time."

"I already have," the demon said. "I did it the moment we were of one mind."

"Let's get Eli, then," Maggie said. "We really *don't* have much time!"

Torches in hand, they walked through room after room of the fortress. The light reflected off treasures the world had not seen for millennia.

"It's an amazing collection," Jacob said, marveling at the oil paintings and statues that gleamed golden in the torchlight – replicas of forgotten gods and heroes, the powerful and rich.

"He's a collector," said the demon. "He especially likes statues of those people who are now damned souls, and the wealth of fallen temples and churches. He's an avid supporter of the world's great museums, you know. He believes the next generation should have the opportunity to develop a taste for the dissipations of the past. He believes in education. He often says, 'Those who know history are condemned to repeat it.'"

They came to the end of the hall and a large, blackened oak door, which the demon swung open. "Your goat's being quiet," the demon said. "He knows you are here." It was a small room, empty of furniture except for a large, gilded box with some kind of carved top. In the flickering light, Jacob suddenly realized with a shock what it was.

"That box – it can't be," Jacob stammered, "I thought it was back in Israel, in the underground temple. That can't really be the Ark of the Covenant!"

"You're right – it can't be," the demon said with a grin. "In fact, it's the replica Solomon had made – the one he intended to send to Ethiopia, until the Queen of Sheba and their son stole the real one and left this behind in the Holy of Holies. A nasty trick, one worthy of Satan. His reward was several souls and this box, which he desecrates when he's got nothing better to do. Your scapegoat's inside."

Maggie and Jacob rushed to the box and together pushed back the heavy lid set with two golden cherubim. Jacob noticed the carved angels' faces appeared demonic. As they slid back the lid, Eli's head popped out. "You certainly took your time," he thought to Maggie, who hauled him out single-handedly and hugged him with all her strength.

"And now we have to leave," the demon said. "The twelve will be in conference very soon now, and we haven't much time."

"Just a minute," Jacob said. "I have something to do." A massive brass candlestick, some four feet tall, stood beside Solomon's fake ark. Grabbing the candlestick, Jacob swung it like a baseball bat, smashing the replica ark again and again. At first swing, the angel/demons broke from the cover and crashed to the floor, their wings and heads bouncing and breaking on the stone slabs. The ancient wood splintered easily under the blows, and the box was quickly reduced to splinters.

"You certainly know how to get his attention," the demon said in a subdued tone. They made their way back to the grand hall, where the demon swung open the massive outer door. "Ignore any voices you may hear, voices that call out to you, calling for help," the demon cautioned.

"The boatman gave us the same warning," Jacob said, "but we heard nothing as we walked along."

"That's because you were coming into hell," the demon said. "You will be amazed at the reaction from souls who think you are leaving. Just ignore what you hear and ignore what you see, and you'll be alright." With goat in hand, they raced out the door and down the path toward the fiery shore.

Chapter 68

Most of the twelve were not in a good mood as, one by one, they assembled at their closest meeting location, the roundtable in Turin. They were all busy people, people of weight, of purpose, and they did not take well to unplanned meetings on short notice. They had a traditional agreement that any one of them could call such a meeting, but it was with the clear understanding that it had better be damned important. The member foolish enough to call a meeting frivolously could expect to lose any opportunity to repeat the mistake.

For this reason, the member possessed by the demon was sweating uncontrollably. He had been informed by his demon about the problem in hell, but had no conscious idea how he would have acquired such knowledge. To begin with, he had no understanding that he was, in actual fact, possessed. That he heard voices at night, crazy voices that made no sense, made him doubt his own sanity from time to time, but never had he doubted his own control.

Satan, of course, knew the demon was there. He'd assigned him to keep track of things when he couldn't be there himself. Satan was a very busy player in the created world, and couldn't waste all his time on the politics and finance of tyranny. Those corruptions were already well established. He had to spend at least some time corrupting wealthy charities, evangelical churches, and various other self-righteous do-gooders. That's where the real fun lay.

"Now what is this all about, Harold?" the chairman asked, when they had at last all taken their seats around the table. They couldn't help but notice Harold's extreme agitation.

"Yes, well I can't tell you how I know this," Harold said at last, hoping that his introduction would preempt any questions. "It seems that couple we sent off to Eden – they have made their way down the hole to hell, and are even now in the process of rescuing the goat."

There was a kind of explosion in the chair occupied by Mr. Satino. At least some of the members thought they saw a flash of fire, as well, but it passed quickly, and Mr. Satino, for the sake of propriety, remained in his place. None of the twelve understood Mr. Satino's true nature, although they suspected the source of his power. No, it would not do to scare the manipulators in control of the created world out of their rational, conniving minds. At least, not yet.

"Well, gentlemen, if you'll excuse me," Mr. Satino said. "It seems there are concerns I must attend to."

Chapter 69

"What's that?" Maggie asked, as they raced along. "At first it sounded like a single voice, but it's getting far too loud for that."

A collective moan had risen all around them, from crags in the rocks and holes in the ground. Where they had seen only rough terrain before, there now appeared faces twisted with the pain of spiritual separation from the light. Maggie realized with a start that what she'd seen as gray stones were the roughened images of leathered, graying people. A few of the barren souls clung desperately to one another, but with nothing in them to share, there was nothing to gain in return. Now all of them were suddenly motivated by a single hope – that they could somehow join those who were attempting to get back to the garden.

Before Maggie could cry out, though, the scene changed completely. Gone were the sulfurous sky, the heaps of souls, the river in flame. Suddenly they were walking through a forest of ancient oaks into a most delightful country valley. On either side of the hedged lane, men and women scythed ripened wheat into sheaves, while their young children played round the golden heaps of stacked wheat, shouting and tossing a red ball into the clear blue sky. Ahead, the curving road led to a village of thatched-roof cottages set beside a meandering river. Above the thatching stretched the graceful white steeple of a village church. Directly ahead of them, an old man slowly led a large flock of sheep up the road toward them, blocking their way.

"Welcome to our village, strangers," the old man said with a smile. "I hope you'll stay the night. We have an excellent inn in the village, with the best ale in the county. If you don't believe me, try a taste. I know you'll agree, if you only take a taste." The old man uncorked an earthen jug he took from his shoulder, and passed it to Maggie.

"Don't drink that," said the demon in a sharp tone. "That is poison, and this is a trap. Satan knows you're here, and he's on his way."

Instantly, the scene was the fire and desolation of before. The old man was a wizened devil, while the sheep were corpses, living dead, walking slowly toward them. The demon waved his hand, and the roadblock disappeared in a burst of flame.

"My God," said Maggie. "*That's* the reason for Siduri's story! She was warning us against our senses – that what we think we see may not be what's really there."

"Come on!" the demon urged. "He could get here any minute! If he reaches us before we leave here, we will never, ever escape." They ran down the road, while Eli scampered along behind. He could have outrun all of them, but preferred to bounce instead. It felt so good to be out of that box.

To their great relief, they could see the boatman waiting for them as they neared the shore. "I'm glad you're here," the boatman said. "I have been ignoring what seems like a message from Satan not to let you pass. The sooner our agreement is completed, the better fate it will be for me."

As soon as they were aboard, the boat fairly flew across the fiery water. The flames, now burning hot, seemed particularly high and fierce, with great tongues curling down as if the fire itself thought to reach them where they crouched around Eli in the center of the boat. Even when they reached the other shore, the flames seemed to stretch beyond the banks in order to keep the refugees from leaving the shelter of the hull.

"Come on!" cried the demon. "I will protect you!" The demon spread his great leathery wings around them, moving them forward onto the shore, while the flames turned his wings a translucent red. Maggie looked back at the demon, and saw the great pain in his face.

"Are you all right?" she cried.

"This is only a sample of what is to come," the demon said. "Don't worry about me – just keep moving. He's very close now, and his power over these elements grows enormous."

Lightening flashed all around them, striking the ground with deafening explosions. They scrambled up the cliff face, and ducked into the cave.

"Thank God!" Jacob said, as they worked their way toward the back of the cave, scrambling away from bolts of lightning that struck continuously at the mouth of the cave and licked toward them along the floor.

"We're not there yet!" shouted the demon above the noise. "We have to climb that hole as fast as we can. Watch out for cave-ins – there could be devils hurling rocks down on us, slowing our way until he arrives. I will go first – I can adjust my size as a shield, and help haul you up, but I won't be behind you if you fall, so be careful. I will carry Eli." Maggie was relieved to hear the last remark.

"What if we meet Satan coming down the hole as we're going up?" Jacob asked.

"Don't even think it," the demon said. "Everything below the opening is within his domain, so as long as we are here we're at his mercy. Our only hope is to get out."

They set to climbing with grim determination. The demon went first, with Eli curled on his head like a fur hat. Maggie came next, scrambling from handhold to handhold, and mindful that all the gravel she loosened was falling on Jacob below. She was glad he was there, though, like a safety blanket in case she should slip. For his part, Jacob tried to find handholds that would secure the two of them, should Maggie lose her footing. He was not at all confident he could stop the two of them from falling all the way back to the bottom.

Chapter 70

"It feels like I've been climbing up this damned hole almost forever," Maggie was thinking, when she suddenly heard Eli bleat in terror.

"What, Eli! What is it!" she thought, and then saw the scene above through Eli's eyes. It seems Satan had arrived at the hole just as Eli, riding on the demon's head, emerged from the hole.

"Here's my snack now!" Satan screamed furiously, and snatched Eli up with a coil of his tail. The distraction gave the demon enough time to fully emerge from the hole and force Satan back toward the opening to the garden. Satan sensed he'd made a tactical mistake.

"Traitor!" he screamed at the demon. "Who gave you permission to betray my fortress, to leave my service, to come up here? You will suffer torments greater than any yet inflicted! You and your friends, for all eternity, will curse the day you ever saw this goat, or thought to steal from me."

Maggie peered over the edge of the hole to see if it was safe to come out. She knew that Jacob was not aware of the confrontation going on, and the danger they were in. Still, she felt the best thing possible for them was to get free of the hole and into the garden. She could see the serpent outlined in the opening, blocking their way. She could also see Eli, held in Satan's powerful grip.

"I am released from your service, viper," said the demon, "by a force greater than yours. I have been given the gift to become your sworn enemy."

"That... is not possible," Satan said without conviction. "I never heard of such a thing. From the beginning of time we fell together, without looking back, without the hope of forgiveness. We are of one mind, one fate. Now you tell me the rules have changed?"

"Is it not something we all have hungered for?" the demon said scornfully. "Should I not believe you would negotiate away all your dominions, your allies, your fellow demons, for the barest chance of personal salvation? You would stab us in the back if you thought it would help. Why

I was blessed like this, I can't explain. It is unmerited grace, and I cling to it with every bit of my being."

"Enjoy it while you may – for now I'm going to destroy you," Satan said, and letting go of Eli, he spun around and seized the demon in his coils. The demon let out a dreadful groan. The serpent's grip was powerful, but the tangled tree roots left no room for him to loop round the demon again. Maggie guessed the serpent would need a better hold to truly destroy the demon – and to get a better hold, he would need more room. Satan recognized the problem as well, and started dragging the demon toward the garden, out from under the tree.

Maggie saw her chance, and slipped out of the hole. She reached back down and tugged on Jacob. "He's got the demon in his grip," she whispered, "but he needs more room to inflict real damage. We should get Eli and get out of here. I'd like to help, but I don't think there's anything we can do. We'd just be in the way."

"We can't just leave him," Jacob protested. "He's faced everything for us at the risk of incredible torture– we can't run away now!"

"What else *can* we do?" Maggie cried. "After the demon, he'll come for us and destroy Eli. Then all this will have been wasted."

"Maybe if we could distract him," Jacob said. They crouched behind a clump of roots, watching Satan drag their demon to what looked like certain doom. Suddenly Eli pushed between them.

"Don't give up yet," Eli thought to them. "Our demon may have a surprise in store for Satan – and for himself too, I think. It's the gift he's been given, the restoration of his full moral authority. We'll know in a minute if I'm right." The three of them huddled together behind the root ball, watching the scene before them.

As soon as the demon was touched by the light of day, his form began to change. His twisted face began to smooth, and the horns on his head separated into flowing, golden hair. As his hunched, reddened body turned to light, he was suddenly clothed in the white garment of an angel, with large white wings replacing his scorched leather devil wings.

In amazement, Satan let loose his grip, and the angel rose over him. "So, we *can* be forgiven," Satan whispered, staring at his former demon.

Jacob, Maggie, and Eli emerged from the cave to stand by the angel. Satan looked at the angel and then at Jacob, assessing the situation. Stuck in his serpent's body, he was at a decided disadvantage.

After a minute, Satan turned to Jacob and smiled. "So, this is the way you answer my question! Well, I've always been partial to drama, so I'll give you an A, teacher. Take the goat – we'll call it even." They stood aside as Satan slithered into the cave and down the hole.

"But we won't be safe in Bangor, either, if Satan comes after us," Maggie protested. "What will we do to protect ourselves?"

"No one is ever completely safe," said the angel, "if by that you mean finding a place where he can't go. He'll come after you like he comes after everyone, but you know where your defense lies. Stay true to your faith, and he won't be able to harm you in any meaningful way. And as for the other, I'll be around to keep an eye on things. You won't see me, but I'll be there. I owe you my salvation, and I won't let him interfere with yours. Now come, I'll walk with you to the garden gate.

"He's going home to check the damage," the angel added with a smile. "When he discovers the smashed ark he will not be happy with you. I suspect it's time for you to go home, too."

Chapter 71

They were back in the hallway again. Peter stopped when they reached the door, and considered the writing on the wall. His flashlight revealed that four or five ancient languages repeated the same phrase, "Creation ends in revelation." Taking a sharpie from his pack, he added the same words in English.

The door swung open of its own accord. Standing outside, waiting for them in the gathering twilight, Peter held his finger to his lips. "We're being closely watched," he whispered. "Follow me – quickly."

He led them to one of the large, abandoned tents that stood by the mound. "Grab that side," he said to Jacob, "and pull it back." Working together, they uncovered a sand-colored Land Rover and climbed in, Peter at the wheel, while Maggie, in the back seat, once again held Eli on her lap. They took off at high speed, bouncing across what looked to Jacob like undifferentiated sand. They drove in silence for awhile, until they could begin to see the traces of a dirt track. Once they were on road, Peter began to relax.

"After all the excitement with the twelve, I figured you'd be coming through that door any minute," Peter said. "I don't know what you were doing, but it was driving them crazy. They insisted on being here when you guys came out, but I don't trust them anymore. In fact, they're watching us right now, by satellite. The thing is, they had an emergency meeting called they had to stay home for, so they didn't have enough time to get here before you came out. We just have to make sure they don't intercept us. You must know something pretty important, to get them as worked up as this."

"We know something about them," Jacob responded through clenched teeth. "They've sold out the world for a power trip, and it's going to lead to the whole apocalypse scenario in Revelation before they're through. There won't be anything left worth saving in the world, by the time they're through dealing with Satan."

"Satan, you say?" Peter asked. "Maybe you should tell me what you saw behind that door."

"It's a long story, and we've been to hell and back today," Jacob said. "I will tell you about the twelve, though. They may think they're running the world, but they're only tools for Satino."

"I've had dealings with Satino!" Peter said angrily. "He lied to me about something really critical to our national security, and I trusted him. I swore if I ever got him alone again, I would do the world a favor and make it his last day on earth."

"I've got news for you," Jacob replied. "You can't kill him – nobody can. Satino *is* Satan, and just off the top of my head, I'd guess he lied to you about some piece of alien technology."

Peter hit the brakes, and the Land Rover screeched to a halt. "You guys know about the alien technology?" he fairly yelled. "That's all above top secret. Even the NSA hasn't been debriefed on that."

"Not only do we know about it, we know who the aliens are. They're Satan's agents, the fallen angels, and they use technology like the white man used glass beads to rob the Indians – to get what's really valuable from us in exchange for their cheap electronic toys. Satan and the rest of the twelve are the brokers in this exchange, and their fate is to bring the world to ruin. We saw the future behind that door, and it involves an apocalypse complete with drones and nukes and laser weapons."

"It doesn't surprise me," Peter said. "I've fit the pieces together from what my sources tell me, and the picture I get says that's where we're headed. The problem is, I can't convince anyone else. I asked for authorization to take out Satino, after what he did to us. Even the guys who know how badly he hurt us – even them – they wouldn't let me touch him." Peter put the Land Rover in gear again, and set off down the dirt track.

"I tell you, you can't kill him," Jacob said loudly, above the roar. "Oh, you may be able to damage Satino's body, but it's just a disguise. He'd be back in 24 hours, as Satino or someone else, to pick up where he left off. And by the way, at least one of the twelve is possessed. That demon reports to Satan – and that demon was how we kept track of Satan's whereabouts."

"Are you saying the rest of the twelve can't be killed, either?" Peter asked.

"No, they're human – possessed or not," Jacob replied. "The world would be better off without them, that's for sure. The more destructive technology they spread around, the more death, destruction and disease *we'll* have to face. They've already killed too many in the name of progress."

"Do you think they could be flipped?" Maggie asked, thinking about the pancakes in the garden.

Jacob picked up her thought. "Only by God," he replied.

Peter drove along in silence for several miles as he worked on a plan. "Ja," he said at last, "Don't you or Maggie say anything about the twelve – not even when you're back in school. When you're rested you can tell me all about the story of your trip, but don't tell anyone else. It's a matter of national security. And especially don't mention Rosslyn, or the meeting there. Okay?"

"Sure, Peter, whatever you say," Jacob said. "Frankly, I don't know how we'd be able to tell any part of this story. Not if we want to keep our friends – not to mention our jobs. Who would believe any of this?"

"You'd be surprised," Peter said. They came to a patch of paved road, not smooth, but smooth enough, and Jacob and Maggie soon fell into a sound sleep.

Several hours later, Peter shook them awake. "Come on, guys," Peter said, "your plane's waiting."

They climbed out of the car and looked around in the bright morning light. A small, metal utility building and a substantial runway were the only manmade landmarks in an otherwise vast expanse of desert. "Usually this is covered with sand," Peter said. "They swept the place just for you." A sleek military jet with U.S. markings stood by with open door. Maggie took Eli and climbed the steps. As Jacob started after her, Peter called to him.

"I'm not going back," Peter said. "There's something I have to do. If it happens that we don't see each other again for a while – I just want to thank you now, just in case." He gave Jacob a hug.

Somehow Jacob knew what Peter had in mind. "Do you need any help?" he offered, knowing already what the answer would be.

"No, I have to do this alone," Peter said. "You'll hear what's happening soon, one way or another. If you're contacted by the twelve, if they want you to come give them a report or anything like that, don't do it. Put them off as long as possible. I'll be in touch." They hugged once again; then Jacob climbed on board, and sat down next to Maggie and the goat.

Epilogue

They'd been back to teaching for almost two weeks when Jacob had a call from Peter. "What's it like, being *the* authority on good and evil?" Peter said cheerily.

"To tell you the truth, nothing has changed," Jacob said. "Seriously, Maggie and I talked about it on the flight back to Bangor, and realized there was very little we could tell anyone. I mean, what could we say that anyone would believe? Almost all of the faculty have already discounted the truth of Genesis – they think they know all about myth, and its 'sacred' role in faith. If we talked literal truth to them, they'd go crazy. They have so allied a literal reading of the Bible with mindless fundamentalism that they'd rather die than admit the possibility. To go a step further and tell people that Eden *still* exists, that the tree of life and the tree of knowledge have twisted around each other to link heaven and hell – *and that we climbed it* – would do nothing for our tenure track, believe me.

"So, Maggie and I talked it over and decided not to say anything at all. We thought instead we might write a novel about it – nothing with our names on it, of course. Or we'll find someone else to write it, and see what happens."

They talked for a while about this and that, including Maggie's landlord's reaction to the goat in her apartment. "Looks like we're going to buy a little house down on the coast," Jacob said. "I think we can afford it if we pool our resources."

Suddenly, Peter asked, "Hey, do you guys ever get the *London Times* up there?"

"Hardly ever," Jacob said with a laugh. "Why?"

"Just a clipping I thought would interest you," Peter said. "I'll send you a copy for your scrapbook."

Three days later, Jacob received the following article, headlined, "Scotland: Gas Explosion Damages Rosslyn Chapel." It read in part:

An apparent build-up and explosion of methane gas in the crypt beneath the historic Rosslyn Chapel has damaged some support columns and a carved stone coffin lid from the

17th century, though no major structural damage was done, Roslin police reported yesterday. A part of the privately-owned Sinclair estate, the chapel is known for its elaborate stone carvings, with ties to Templar symbolism and the history of Freemasonry. Police report that no one was injured in the explosion, the cause of which is still under investigation.

Peter had circled the words, "no one was injured," with a smiley face and wrote in the margin, "Don't believe everything you read in the funny papers – see you guys soon. Love....

A week after that, the seminary president asked Jacob and Maggie to meet with her after classes. "As you probably know by now, the government and this institution have had a long-standing agreement to cooperate on many matters pertaining to our country's relations with the Middle East. I had a call from Peter this morning, and he authorized both of you to discuss what you learned about your encounter with Eden."

Maggie and Jacob nearly jumped out of their seats. "Peter swore us to secrecy!" Jacob said at last. "All of this was meant to be kept quiet – a matter of national security, and all that! And he told *you* about it?"

"Not *much* about it," she smiled, "but enough to intrigue me, I must admit. We have provided faculty for a number of overseas assignments in the past, but never have we been told to encourage a discussion. Would one of you be open to relate some of your adventure at next Sunday's chapel service? And then we can let it evolve from there."

Jacob and Maggie talked it over, and decided Maggie should do the honors. It was the first time in more than 150 years of worship that a goat took part in the seminary's Sunday chapel service.*

A week later, Maggie found a small piece of root in her jacket pocket. She suddenly remembered something.

"Jacob!" she called, "You remember my yellow bird, the bird that helped me find you in the tree?"

"Of course, silly," Jacob replied.

---

*Maggie's sermon appears in Appendix B.

"The bird whispered to me, just before we left the tree. Its last words to me were, 'Take what you took from here, and plant it in the well that came from a tree. It's the place where the birds sing the song of creation.' I had no idea what the bird was talking about, but look – this is what I took from Eden." She held the piece of root out for him to see.

Jacob looked thoughtfully at the root in her hand. "I know a well that fits the description," he said at last. "These days it's called Montezuma's Well, and it's located in Rimrock, Arizona. The Yavapai people believe the well came from a tree that grew on the spot where this amazing desert well now sits. Even now the well produces more than a million gallons daily to water the Verde Valley. The Yavapai people believe their ancestors were born from that well."

"Do the Yavapai also sing like birds?" Maggie asked, laughing at the thought.

"Actually, they do," Jacob replied with a smile. "The Yavapai do bird singing and dancing they learned from the Mojave. The birdsong tells the story of the Yuman creation. It takes the singers from sundown to sunrise to tell the whole cycle. The bird songs are accompanied by playing gourds made from cottonwood – wood from the same kind of giant trees that grow by the outflow from the well. Back in the day, those Native Americans hand-dug narrow trenches, some for miles, to channel the water from the well to their gardens. So, the well that birthed the people fed them, too. The little grove that shelters that outflow is beautiful, a favorite place of mine."

"Jacob, that has to be the place this root must go."

A month later, Jacob, Maggie, Peter and Eli traveled to Rimrock and walked the narrow, dirt path down to the edge of Montezuma's Well. A few ancient cliff dwellings still clung to the rocks above. "It's so big," Maggie said, looking over the still surface. "It looks more like a pond than a well."

Peter said, "If I were doing my job, I'd confiscate that root for analysis. There could be some power inherent in that thing."

"You've got a different job to do today," Maggie said, as she tossed the root into the well.

"But how do you know that root came from the right tree?" Peter asked.

"Sometimes you just have to take a chance," Jacob replied.

Fifteen minutes later they had walked down to the outflow grove, beneath the cliffs and cottonwoods. That's where Peter performed the wedding ceremony – with a goat and an angel as witnesses.

Appendix A

"Exegeting Exegesis,"
an address by Dr. Margaret Colburn

I could speak to you this morning about the joys of reading the Bible in Hebrew, Greek and Aramaic. Instead, I feel I should speak out about the box we place ourselves in when we limit our study of scripture to narrow forms of exegesis. For the sake of the new students, let me explain that 'exegesis,' in the broadest sense, means bringing scholarship and imagination to bear on the study of scripture. Unfortunately, this comprehensive approach has too often been reduced to literary criticism – studying the text by deconstructing it. Hence my first pun: Exit Jesus.

Ironically, this approach worked when everyone believed that God, through Moses, wrote the Torah. When we knew the author through faith, we could compare passage to passage to find the meaning. Today, scholars claim *at least* four writers – the Jahwist, Elohist, Priestly, and Deuteronomist – commonly called J,E,P, and D, an acronym which gives us our second pun: I pronounce that acronym 'gipped.' Who these writers were and what they were driving at is anybody's educated guess, and that's what scholars have been doing for years – educated guessing in the name of scholarship. And in the pursuit of these vapors, our seminary students have indeed been gipped.

Here's the problem: when we limit our study to a text we no longer consider inspired, or even consistent, then we're handcuffed to a far more limiting belief. For example, if we believe we're only reading what some unknown, disgruntled priest might have contributed to text redacted in the time of King David, or what some unknown woman writer may have contributed to the introduction of some passage construed to be "feminine," then we have created a vacuum into which we insert *ourselves* as author. In other words, as we deconstruct to find the author, we wind up rearranging text – in our minds, at least – to fit our own prejudices. Every scholar of this mindset has become his or her own Bible redactor, and another brick in religion's new Tower of Babel.

Some of this problem comes as the result of scholars' investing too much of their imaginations in one direction, scholars who don't remain open to the other roads that exegesis should lead us to explore. A prime example of such narrow-mindedness shows up in the following observation. This passage comes from *Understanding Genesis,* a book by an influential scholar, Dr. Nahum Sarna:

It should be obvious that by the nature of things, none of these stories can possibly be the product of human memory, nor in any modern sense of the word scientific accounts of the origin and nature of the physical world. Biblical man, despite his undoubted intellectual and spiritual endowments, did not base his views of the universe and its laws on the critical use of empirical data. He had not, as yet, discovered the principles and methods of disciplined inquiry, critical observation or analytical experimentation. Rather, his thinking was imaginative and his expressions of thought were concrete, pictorial, emotional, and poetic. Hence, it is a naive and futile exercise to attempt to reconcile the biblical accounts of creation with the findings of modern science.

Granted, Prof. Sarna's book was published decades ago. Nevertheless, this is a valid example of the narrow view that still prevails at scholar-dominated seminaries – despite the fact that scientists themselves admit more and more parallels between science and, for example, the creation story in Genesis. Still, we hear our Torah teachers proclaiming, "Use your imagination – but don't go there... or there... or there!" "Imagine the life situation of the writer," say these teachers. "Imagine social and political situations of their day. Just don't imagine that God could actually have spoken to the writer, or had a hand in what they wrote, or inspired actual prophesy. No, no, no, don't go there!"

The result is that we've created a truly schizophrenic setting for our students. Study the Bible every which way but God's way, we tell them. Assume that all prophecy must have been written after the fact. And for heaven's sake, don't imagine that Paul's approach to exegeting the

Hebrew Bible as prophecy for the coming of Christ could possibly be true.

But if anything we are doing here is to have any ultimate meaning, then exegesis must not be reduced to simply deconstructing scripture, like peeling an onion. As with the onion, you'll quickly find the parts are less than the whole, and when you're done, you're left with a core of nothing – nothing at all – staring back. Deconstructing scripture is also like the story of the goose that laid golden eggs. The impatient king ordered the cook to dismember the goose, and bring him all the golden eggs inside. But when they cut the goose open, there were no eggs inside – no eggs at all.

Of course, we want to know who wrote the Bible, this profoundly important document that purports to tell us the truth about God's creation and God's will for his people. But in that scholarly search, we must not dismiss out of hand the possibility that it was God, after all, who was the author – or *somehow* the inspiration behind the authors. We must expand our scholarly imaginations to include the possibility of authors who felt moved to write writings inspired by more than just the social or political milieu of their day – who felt moved to write because God wanted them to – and who, through sacred inspiration or actual knowledge, knew more about actual history and actual science than we in all our wisdom have decreed they could.

In the beginning, we studied the Bible for its instruction, its *Torah*. Jews and Christians examined every word for its meaning, and they held every word to be sacred. According to Matthew's gospel, Jesus himself reminds us of the precision and importance of scripture when he said:

Don't think that I have come to abolish the Torah or the Prophets; I have come not to abolish but to complete. Yes indeed! I tell you that until heaven and earth pass away, not so much as a yud [letter] or a stroke will pass from the Torah – not until everything that must happen has happened. So whoever disobeys the least of these mitzvot and teaches others to do so will be called the least in the Kingdom of Heaven. But whoever obeys them and so teaches will be called great in the Kingdom of Heaven. For I tell you that unless your righteousness is far greater than that of the Torah-teachers and P'rushim, *you will certainly not enter the Kingdom of Heaven! (Matthew 5:17-20)*

It seems we Torah-teachers might be in deep trouble, based on Jesus' warning. After all, the scribes, the Torah-teachers of Jesus' day, were teaching the law as law. According to them, the first five books of the Hebrew Bible were dictated to Moses by God sometime around 1220 B.C.E., shortly after the Exodus from Egypt. Today, we Torah-teachers teach that the first five books of the Bible were pieced together by writers and editors who cut and pasted scripture to meet the socio-political needs of their communities. And we base it all on text analysis that's thinner than thin ice. If anything were needed to further dissuade the faithful, the message from today's Torah-teachers – you and me – is perfectly designed to fit the bill. It's no wonder one of my fundamentalist friends can say with a straight face, "This century doesn't need Satan. The job's been filled by seminary teachers."

It's not as if any of us intend to undermine students' faith, but we all know that it happens. There is an old Apache tradition that you don't tell the ancient stories during the summer, because the serpent might hear them and carry them back to the underworld, where they will be corrupted. No, we teachers don't intend to do wrong – but we have been telling the ancient stories in terms that reach the serpent's hearing, and the results of our teaching are coming home to roost.

Prof. Richard Hays of Duke Divinity School described the effect on his own undergraduate career. In an article about his experiences as a student at Yale Divinity, he said:

The first thing that struck me was the way in which biblical scholars would end up fragmenting the text. Having been an English major at Yale, I had been very much shaped by the perspectives of the New Criticism. All of my instincts as a reader were to trace and savor and appreciate internal tensions and ambiguities in texts as essential to their overall literary sense. Whereas the tendency for biblical critics, particularly coming out of Germany, was to assume any time there was a tension in the text it must be a seam that showed it had come from some other source. I *was genuinely mystified and baffled by what I saw biblical scholars doing to texts – failing to read them whole.... It had to do with a kind of tone deafness to metaphor and to literary effects of all sorts. But it also had to do with presuppositions that were* a priori *skeptical and hostile toward the claims of the text – about the possibility of God's action in history, about the possibility that spiritual powers might actually operate in historical events.*

I could have closed with that quote about Satan from my evangelical friend, but I have a happier alternative. It comes from something the noted bible scholar N.T. Wright wrote in an issue of *Christianity Today*:

At the moment, a great many devout Christians do not believe that anything good can come out of serious, academic, historical study. They just don't believe it. Their seminary gave them plenty of evidence that these guys have got their heads in the clouds, or their heads in the sand, or both, and that the real world is different. I struggle to show again and again that when you really do business with the Bible at the fullest historical and theological level, then it is passionately and dramatically relevant, life changing, and community changing. And I suppose *I would like to kick-start a biblical renewal within the church – not simply a renewal of private piety, though God knows, if you got the sort of renewal I am talking about, it would drive people to their knees, it would fill their hearts with joy, it would challenge them at every possible level.*

Today I challenge you with all the passion voiced by N.T. Wright: study the Bible as if it matters, because it does – it matters far more than the sum of its parts. But when you find yourselves feeling comfortable with what you've learned, remember Paul's words in First Corinthians:
Where is the wise man? Where is the scribe? Where is the debater of this age? Has not God made foolish the wisdom of this world?

Appendix B

"Healing the Scapegoat,"
a sermon by Dr. Margaret Colburn

If I told you Dr. Alexandre and I just returned from a sabbatical in the Garden of Eden, you probably wouldn't believe me. If I told you the trees of knowledge and life are in an unrelenting embrace, you probably wouldn't believe me. If I told you grace is embodied in twelve perfectly flipped pancakes, you probably wouldn't believe me. But perhaps you'll believe me when I tell you, as an integral part of creation, that our spiritual fate is linked with the physical fate of the earth, and the outcome is in our hands. With time running short, our fate depends on our healing the sins we have heaped on the back of our innocent scapegoat, the earth.

Why do I think this is true? At a Yom Kippur service within the Temple Mount, Dr. Alexandre and I were entrusted with the sin-bearing scapegoat of Israel. It was our duty to deliver him to the wilderness devil, Azazel, who would eat the goat and, in the process, remove Israel's sins, as well.

But we fell in love with this goat kid, sins and all; the goat was no longer a mere vehicle for others' salvation, but the embodiment of salvation itself. Its rescue motivated God to even forgive a helpful demon – the first time ever, perhaps. And there could be room for more, where and whenever love might take seed and flourish. Even in hell, perhaps, since even Satan harbors a surprising hope for forgiveness in his conniving heart.

Eden is billed as the place where perfection resides, and that's why it was hedged off from the rest of earth. But Eden bears some of the burden when the earth is growing sicker. Everything in heaven and on earth is connected, is interrelated as completely as those two trees I mentioned. But humanity is making the earth our scapegoat, in the mistaken belief that sacrificing it will transport our souls to a better place. As a result, earth is struggling and dying under the weight of our sins. Our earthly garden is on its way to becoming an uninhabitable hell – a hell of our making from which, some think, we'll be raptured away. Yet we cannot separate ourselves, because, essence-wise, we are God's love breathed into the dust of mother earth.

That old expression, "The grass is always greener in the other fellow's yard," denotes our view of heaven as the greener place we're looking forward to. But the assignment was to tend our earthly garden, to plant and prune and water and love this jewel of creation. We've been neglecting our duties, but we may yet be able to save ourselves by saving the scapegoat. We can do this by loving the earth more than our own comforts. Just as Jacob and I crept into hell to save a scapegoat, all of us now must liberate our sin-bearer by providing for earth's relief. We must declare a time of healing from the exploitations, the resulting pollutions, and the ongoing extinctions – our own included – that we have been laying on the body of this sacred garden we call home.

God is our father, earth our mother – but more than that, earth is our beloved school, our *alma mater*, the mother who nurses us. The earth was not created to be anything other than the school where we come to learn. This world was created for us, just as heaven was intended for the angels. Too many of us claim the answer to our problems is to cede earth to the devil, while we take the fallen angels' place above. But we've got that wrong! We have to learn that our place in the hierarchy of creation is here, at least for now. Even though we visit the other side on occasions such as death and near-death experiences, the earth is where we reincarnate until we learn the lessons of forgiveness, and of love.

Our first impulse is to ask God's forgiveness to flow in our direction, but then we learn, forgiveness comes as we forgive. It derives out of love, and that love must come from all directions – but it must come from us especially, and the sooner we learn that, the sooner healing starts.

Some people have asked me where Eden is hiding. Dimensionally, Eden stands behind a two-way mirror, watchers feeling sadness for us as things deteriorate. When we try looking back, all we see is ourselves in the reflection. We must train our eyes to see through our reflected self, to see the pain they are feeling that we are inflicting. Until we learn that, we won't be able to fully acknowledge the pain we are inflicting on ourselves. Until we learn that, they will remain the watchers and we will remain the egos. Ego is the dark mirror that keeps us from seeing the connections, from studying the good, and from understanding that our lack of love can infect everything else, as well.

Another few degrees of global warming, and the earth will be close-gripped by the jaws of heat. Our plants, soils, oceans and fresh water, air, animals, birds and insects, all born from the word and breath of God, are about to be extinguished. They are food for the Azazel of our imagining, the sin eater drooling over our scapegoat earth. Still, we go on polluting everything we touch with greed, ego, self-righteousness, and murderous disapproval of one another. We dump our pollution on the earth with the intention of making it our scapegoat pass into heaven.

But that is not an act of salvation. When we martyr our mother, we martyr ourselves. To put it simply, we are totally connected. If crucifying Jesus was meant to teach us anything, it was meant to teach us that.

The essence, the totality of God is love, we say. But how does love, God's love, manifest to us? How do we understand it? We think of it in terms of the creation! Think of friends and family, a beloved pet, a view that amazes, music and stories that touch our hearts. We delight in and embrace relationships of total acceptance and love. We understand love, even God's love, in terms of this world. If it weren't for the green of trees, the blue of ocean and sky, the red of sunsets, the physical, emotion-filled hugs from one another – we just wouldn't have a clue. Our capacity to understand love is measured in terms of the creation, because we ourselves are the ladders connecting heaven and earth.

How do we know this? Well, for one thing we know it through the visions of near-death experiencers. When we go through the tunnel and into the light, where do we wind up? Often in a beautiful field with supernal flowers and trees, with loving family to greet us and to make us feel at home. Paul called it the third heaven, the Garden of Eden.

247

Its physical parallel is the earth, which God called good. Eden is what earth was and could be again.

But think for a minute. Why would God welcome us into the perfect garden of heaven next door, when our track record has been to pollute and destroy the garden we came from, our garden at home? This is our practice run, our trial run for heaven, and we're not passing the test.

Here's another thought for you. If you are a believer in reincarnation, what kind of earth do you want to return to when you get birthed again? One with poisoned soil, undrinkable water, unbreathable air? One with cities so polluted you have to carry oxygen to breathe? Country-sides where trees and flowers are dead, the streams gone dry, a dustbowl on its way to becoming a desert?

We want God to love us, to take us to his home when we die, but it may be conditional on what we have done to the home we've left behind. Earth is in her dying throes, and because all is connected, God's love and forgiveness may flow best to those willing to help restore his creation here. We have gained enough technology from the tree of knowledge to heal the planet; the question is, do we have enough love through our mother, the tree of life, to do the necessary work, as well? Will we continue to feed our scapegoat earth to the devil, or will we act with the restorative love of our hands and hearts to heal the world?

As long as I've known Dr. Alexandre, he has pondered over the question of evil. Well, I'm pleased to give you the simple answer we discovered. It's contained, by the way, in Jesus' parable of the wheat and weeds. *(Matthew 13:24-30)* In this story, creation is the garden, love is the harvest, and God is Love with a capital L. Thus cast, our story goes:

Love created a garden, in which Love planted love. But an enemy sowed weeds, and as the love grew, so too did the weeds. Love did not pull the weeds as the garden grew, so love would stay rooted. And when the harvest came, Love harvested the love to be a part of Love itself. It's said the weeds get burned, but even ash aspires to reincarnation.

The moral? We are chosen for growing as love. Either we grow in love, ultimately to merge with Love itself, or we grow as weeds – until the end. In the end, duality vanishes, and only Love survives. Are we ready for this to end?